Pack Gamble Part One

An Omegaverse Romance

The Rockview Omegaverse

Hannah Haze

Foreword

I've wanted to write a 'we've woken up married' story for a while and what fun it has been! I love these characters!

This book is a sweeter 'why choose' (reverse harem) omegaverse with one female omega character and five alpha males, plenty of steamy scenes, lots of humour and some angst. This book is a duet and the happy ending won't be coming until book two. Mentions of a previous assault will be featured in book two. For more detailed content warnings, please visit my website.

If you do spot any typos in this book, please drop me a line so I can make it right: hannahhazewrites@gmail.com (Or just drop me an email anyway. I love to chat!).

You can find a guide to my omegaverse at the end of this book. If you're new to omegaverse, you may want to take a look.

Chapter One

Ow!

Ow ow ow ow!

My head!

My head hurts so darn badly. Like someone has a hold of my temple in a vise and is crushing my skull. The worst possible pain you could ever imagine.

What the hell did I drink last night? How *much* did I drink last night?

I need water. Lots and lots and lots of water. And every painkiller ever known to man.

If I can stand.

I doubt that's going to be possible without vomiting. Maybe I can roll or crawl or drag myself across the floor.

I pry open one eyelid, groaning involuntarily with the effort.

Maybe Isla will fetch me water and painkillers. Although she's also going to give me one hell of a lecture.

The light – despite being dull and gray – hurts my eye so badly, I groan a second time and slam it shut.

Maybe if I just go back to sleep, all the pain and nausea will be over when I wake up again in an hour or two.

Then again, my mouth and throat are drier than the Sahara Desert, even though I somehow also need to pee real badly. Urgh, biology. It sucks.

I try again, dragging my eyes open with more determination this time.

It takes a minute for the room to stop spinning and come into view.

Hotel room.

It takes me another minute. But, yep, hotel room is correct. We're in Las Vegas for our cousin's bachelorette party.

I'm sharing a room with my big sister and my best friend (who probably had to put me to bed last night).

That lecture coming my way is going to be a truly big stonking one.

Only I don't remember the hotel room being quite this big. In fact, this hotel room is gigantic. The size of a small apartment. It's going to take me all day to crawl across the plush-looking carpet and find the bathroom.

Did we get an upgrade? It must have been a darn good upgrade; this room is a palace, and it smells ... it smells divine. All woody and dark and masculine.

Masculine?

Wait ...

What the fuck?

I'm an omega. I'm sharing a room with an omega.

Unless they're pumping pheromones through the AC, it shouldn't smell masculine, should it?

I have a bad feeling about this. A very bad feeling.

Closing my eyes, I roll over, in what I now realize is one gigantic, very soft, very plush bed. A bed our Vegas budget can most definitely not afford.

Please let me be wrong. Please let me be wrong.

No more screw ups. Isla is going to kill me.

I take a deep inhale – more of that scent floods my sinuses.

Oh shit.

Be brave, Avery.

I count to three in my head, then snap open my eyes, muffling a little screech, when I find myself face to face with a sleeping giant.

A sleeping *alpha* giant.

Holy crap, how the hell did that happen?

For a minute, I'm too mesmerized by his face to move. He has a square jaw, defined cheekbones, dark, thick eyelashes and a mop of dark, thick hair.

How on earth did I end up in bed with a man like this?

I peek under the covers. I'm naked. I peek to the side. So is he and, holy crap, the man is an Adonis. I don't think I've seen a man with that many muscles in real life before. Definitely not without his clothes and in my bed.

Or his bed.

Or some random bed.

Shit, where the hell am I?

Focus, Avery.

Clothes!

Carefully, so as not to disturb the sleeping Adonis, I raise my head – sending pain spiraling through my temples

– and peer more closely around the room in search of my lucky dress and the panties I was wearing last night.

There's something slung over a chair by a dressing table.

I peek at the man again, ensuring he is definitely still sleeping, and then I slip out from under the covers and creep towards the chair.

Standing is not fun. Not fun at all. My body and my head are in agreement that vertical is a mistake. I should remain horizontal.

I crouch over my knees, breathing through a wave of nausea, and hanging onto the bed to stop myself tumbling to the floor. When it passes, I tiptoe on unsteady feet to that chair. I'm a pace away when I freeze.

The garment hanging over the chair is no little black dress.

Nope. It's white. And it isn't little. It's a big dress.

A big, fat dress.

A big, fat *wedding* dress!

What the hell!

I spin around the room!

There's a discarded bottle of champagne and two glasses on the floor, a trail of confetti across the carpet, and a 'Just Married' banner hanging off the end of the bed.

Just married?!

Just married?!

Oh shit!

Shit shit shit shit *shit*!

My head and my stomach swoop together and my lungs stop working.

I can't breathe and I can't think.

I'm going to be sick!

I spy a door standing ajar across this giant room and I

sprint towards it, slamming the door behind me, flicking the lock and sinking onto the cool tiled floor.

Oh God! Oh God! Oh God!

Married! Married?!

I can't be married?!

I hug my legs and bury my face in my knees.

Isla is going to kill me.

Followed by my mom. Who will kill me and then take to her bed to weep about it for days, months and years. And my dad? Oh my God, my dad?

I am in so much trouble.

I am such an idiot.

I have ruined my life for ever and ever and—

What the hell?!

I scream and leap about a foot off the ground.

What was that? A voice in my head. A really loud, very gruff, very sexy-sounding voice in my head.

This has to be a dream, right? A nightmare? If I just pinch my leg hard enough, like so, then I'm going to—

Wake up.

I pinch my thigh as hard as I can, scowling at the pain. I wait. Nothing. I'm still here on the bathroom floor with the worst hangover of my life.

You're in the bathroom?

Shit, that voice again. In my head. I jump to my feet, wobbling madly and nearly toppling over. I grip my hands to my forehead.

What is happening? I've never been so hungover that I've hallucinated and started to hear voices before. But maybe, if I drank a swimming pool-load of vodka, it could be possible.

Could you just keep quiet for one second?

Oh my goodness and trust my luck that the voice I

imagine in my head is not only sexy sounding but really darn bossy and grumpy as well.

Please, please, just ... shush.

Me shush? You're the one in my head – a head that is really, really darn sore. You be quiet.

You're the one in my *head.*

"Nope," I say out loud, finding my reflection in the mirror. "I most definitely exist. You're imaginary."

My reflection is not a very pretty one. My hair is a tangle around my head, my eyes are ringed with mascara, and is that a massive hickey on my neck? I squint at the mirror. At least I remembered to take my contact lenses out last night.

"Hello?" that voice says again, only much louder now, almost as if it's floating right outside the bathroom door and no longer in my head. "I *am* outside the bathroom door," it says, and as if to confirm it, the doorknob rattles violently.

I scream a second time, slip on what looks like a pair of boxers on the floor behind me, and tumble to the ground.

With a thud, I land on my ass, which now hurts as much as my head.

"Are you okay?" the voice says. And I remember the man from the bed.

And the wedding dress.

And the confetti. And the 'Just Married' banner.

"What the hell?!" the voice says.

I stumble up to my knees and crawl to the wall-length mirror, getting right up and personal with my hideous reflection. I examine the hickey on my neck.

It isn't a hickey at all. It's a wound. A bite mark. Right at the bottom of my throat.

My vision swims and swoops and my lungs stop working completely.

"Oh God," I gasp, "oh God, oh God, oh God."

I can't breathe. I can't breathe.

This can't be happening.

I can't breathe.

Black spots dance across my vision, the bathroom spins, my cheeks burn so hot –

"Omega!" That voice again. "Don't panic!"

Don't panic? Don't panic?! Is he serious?

Because, unless this is a very vivid, very real nightmare, or my mind has been completely warped by the alcohol, that bite on my neck is a claiming mark. Which means … which means …

I'm going to pass out. My throat burns. So do my lungs. All screaming for oxygen.

"It's okay, Omega. It's going to be okay."

It's not. It's not going to be okay, because me and the alpha standing on the other side of the door – the one who was sleeping in the bed, the one talking in my head – are bonded.

Chapter Two

Avery

The alpha rattles the door more violently.

"Open the door," he says, "open the door right now."

But I can't. I'm too busy struggling to breathe.

"Shit," I hear him mutter and then something heavy slams against the door once, twice, three times, before the lock gives way on the fourth and the very naked alpha comes crashing through.

If I had any oxygen in my lungs, I'd scream for a third time. Instead, I'm writhing on the ground, my hands scrabbling at my throat, those dark spots on my vision growing larger and larger and larger–

"Omega!" I open my eyes and stare right into his, his irises a deep shade of blue like the sky right after sunset. "Good girl, good girl. Can you breathe for me?"

I shake my head wildly, although my gaze doesn't leave his – those eyes of his are far too magnetic.

"Breathe," he says again, more gently this time, his hands hovering above my shoulders for a fraction of a second, before he leans in closer and draws them down my arms.

It doesn't help. I still can't breathe. I've still fucked up my life. I will still be in so much trouble with everyone I love and—

The alpha purrs. A deep rumbling sound that reverberates around his wide, muscular chest. The noise does something to my nervous system, something I can't control, and I can't explain. It's like a sedative, a deeply soothing, incredibly sexy sedative, that has me feeling like I'm floating. My body relaxes, my lungs start functioning and even the pain in my head seems to dissipate.

He keeps purring like this for several minutes and, frankly, I don't want him to stop. Partly because it's so ... nice. And partly because when he stops, we're going to have to start talking and what exactly are we going to say to each other?

"How about we start with names?" he says.

"Huh?"

"I think we should start with names."

Right, names.

"Avery," I say.

"Avery," he says, blue eyes flickering over my face.

"And yours is?" He cocks an eyebrow. "Look, you didn't know mine, so why you think I'd know—"

"Cruise."

"Cruise? Is that a first name or a—"

He leans a little closer, pinching my chin and tilting it to one side. He examines the bite mark at the base of my throat.

"I did that?" he asks uncertainly.

"As I can hear your voice in my head and you seem to be able to hear mine?" he nods, "then I'm guessing so."

"How?" he asks, fingers still cradling my chin in a way that feels far too ... nice. "How did this happen?"

"I was hoping *you* might be able to tell *me*."

To my disappointment, he releases my chin and rocks backwards. The man is stupidly good looking, but now under the bright lights of the bathroom, I see he isn't looking so good himself. Dark shadows ring his eyes.

"You think I'm good looking?" he says, rubbing his head with his knuckles.

"I assume that is probably why I let you do the thing," I say, waving my hand in the direction of the bite mark.

"I don't remember doing it," he says, almost with a little disappointment. "I don't remember any wedding. All I do remember was sitting at the roulette table–"

"Me too!" I say, raising up on my knees. "I was at the roulette table, and I was starting to do really well. I remember I just had this feeling, you know, this feeling that the night was going to be my lucky one." The memory comes flooding back like a movie in my head. "So, I put all my money on my lucky number (nine). And it turns out I was right, because I won a ton load of money, I mean a ton load. So much money, and ..." I frown. "Wait, is that why you married me? For my money?"

The alpha snorts and clambers up to his feet. "We're not married."

"Erm, I think we might be." I bury my face in my hands. "The whole shebang. Married and bonded. Shit, shit, shit, shit, shit."

The alpha begins pacing, walking across the length of the ridiculously large bathroom and then back again.

Which reminds me ...

"Where are we?" Did we blow all my winnings on a honeymoon suite?

"My hotel room."

"Your hotel room. You always stay in honeymoon suites when you come to Vegas? Wait!" I jump to my feet. "Please don't tell me you're already married. Please don't tell me you're staying here with your partner and–"

"No, I am single, or at least I was. I don't know what the fuck I am now." He halts his pacing. "This isn't a honeymoon suite. It's just a regular suite."

I laugh. "A regular suite? I don't know what they told you when you booked this place, but you were swindled, dude. This isn't a regular suite. It's a palace." I narrow my eyes. "Where exactly is my money?"

He scowls back at me. "I've no interest in your money."

"Sure," I say flatly.

He scowls harder. "Are you sure you didn't marry *me* for *my* money?"

"Do you have any?"

He doesn't answer, simply stares at me.

"Well, Mr. Cruise, this was ..." I say, climbing gingerly to my feet. My head may be better, but I still feel like I might vomit any minute. "But I'd better go find my sister before she starts calling the cops and hammering down the doors of every hotel room on the Strip."

I hook my panties out of the sink and shimmy them up my legs, then trot out of the bathroom, eyes flicking around the room in search of my dress, or something else I can wear that isn't a wedding gown.

"You can't leave," the alpha says, as I open a wardrobe

door and discover several pressed suits and crisp shirts hanging in a row.

"I can," I say, yanking a blue shirt off a hanger and sliding my arms into the sleeves. If I roll them up, I'm sure I can pull it off as a shirt dress, sort of. Better than a wedding dress, anyway. I do up the buttons and, spying my phone on a table, head for the door.

"We're married!" he says.

"Can't we annul it? Isn't that what celebs do all the time?"

I don't have shoes, but I bet I could pinch some flip-flops from the spa – hotels like this one always have a spa.

"I think we ought to sit down and consider this, consider the implications and our options, decide what we should do next."

"Nope," I say, hand on the doorknob.

"I at least need your damned surname if I'm going to get this thing annulled!"

"Loren, Avery Loren."

I swing open the door and peek outside. Seeing the coast is clear and nobody is going to witness my walk of shame, I take a step outside, then another and another and–

"Urgh!" I yell as something forceful and painful in the pit of my gut yanks me backwards.

That will be the bond, the alpha says flatly in my mind.

"What the ..." I mumble, turning around to find him leaning against the doorframe, thankfully in a pair of boxers now.

"The bond. You know the connection between us. Freshly made and all brand new."

I frown and take a decided step backwards, away from him, but the pain in my gut is so searing I almost vomit.

"Oh jeez, that really, really hurts."

The alpha huffs, then steps out into the hallway and grabs my elbow. Immediately, his proximity lessens the pain, and he hauls me back inside the room.

"I don't understand," I say with a pout as he lowers me into an armchair, taking a seat in one opposite.

"It's the bond. It's too new. It makes it too painful to be apart."

"You're kidding, right? That isn't a thing."

"It is."

"Then why have I never heard about it? Plus, I know plenty of mated omegas and alphas. And they are not doubled over in pain every time they separate."

"Usually newly bonded mates are too busy fucking, too busy locked to each other's ... sides, to feel it."

"Hmmm."

"It only lasts a set amount of time. While the bond is fresh and new."

I eye him. "So, what exactly are you saying here? We're stuck together? I can't leave your side?"

"You can."

"But it will hurt."

"Yes."

"Just me, or the both of us?"

"Both of us."

"But if I took a load of painkillers ..."

He shakes his head. "It was agony just now and you only took a few steps away from me. Imagine how bad that pain will be if the distance is increased. The bond doesn't work that way. It wants us together while it's new."

"Right." I'm not good with pain.

"I noticed."

"And I suppose you, as the big burly alpha, are very good with pain."

He stares at me. Then drags his hand down his face. "You really don't know who I am, do you?"

I shrug my shoulder, like, duh.

"Cruise Hamilton. From Pack Hamilton."

I blink. Is that meant to mean something?

"I need a drink," he mutters, dragging the room's telephone towards him.

And I really need to call my sister. I wasn't joking about that search party. I stare down at the phone in my hand. It's out of battery.

"Do you have a charger?" I ask. He points to the desk in the corner, covered in papers, and a laptop. I guess this really is his room.

I plug a cable into my phone and within a couple of seconds, the cell chirps to life, my screen crowding with a hell of a lot of missed calls.

"Crap!"

"What?" he says, sounding alarmed as he hangs up the phone. "It's not social media, is it?"

Jeez, I didn't even think of that. I am a notoriously bad drunk poster. I scroll quickly through my various apps, relieved to find no wedding photos announcing our recent nuptials to the world.

"Not on mine," I say.

He walks over to stand next to me by the desk – the man still has very few clothes on, it's hard to know where to look. He reaches for his cell. "Mine neither," he says, "but …"

He twists the screen my way and there's a photo of the two of us filling the phone. I'm dressed in that white gown, he's in a tux and we're draped all over each other in a very intimate manner.

"Delete it!" I order.

"No," he says, snatching his phone away. "My lawyer might want it."

"Lawyer?" I say, but before I can quiz him, my phone blasts out 'Maneater' in my hand.

The man gives me an unamused stare.

"It's a joke," I tell him, glancing at the screen.

Isla.

There is no point in avoiding this.

"Hey sis!" I say in my most cheerful voice.

"Avery? Is that you? Oh, thank God. Where are you? Where have you been? We've been looking–"

"I'm at the spa," I lie.

"The spa?" she says, sounding not one bit convinced. "But you said you were going back to the room last night and then you weren't there, and you didn't come in last night and we've—"

"Nope, I changed my mind and went for a little gamble—"

"On your own! Avery! That's really dangerous! Are you sure you're okay?"

"I won some money, Isla! And had one or two too many drinks–"

"Are you crazy?"

"Anyway, I have one hell of a hangover, so the spa seemed like—"

"Which spa?"

"Cuuuurrrrr coooor ... what's that, Isla? ... cuuuuurrrrrrr ... you're breaking up ... I'll call you later."

I hang up, my shoulders sagging in relief. The cell starts ringing again immediately in my hand, but I send it straight to voicemail. She knows I'm safe, that's the main thing, and I need some head space to sort this mess out before she starts with all the lecturing.

I let out a huff of air and find the alpha staring at me with one raised eyebrow.

"That was your sister?" he asks.

"Yes."

"You didn't tell her what is going on."

"She'll have an actual fit. You thought my panic attack was bad back there in the bathroom? Nothing, trust me, compared to how Isla is going to take this news."

"Why?"

"Why?" I say to him in disbelief. "Bonded! Married! To a complete stranger, an alpha I know absolutely zero about."

"You know my name."

"And that is all. I don't know your age—"

"33."

"Your job—"

"Tech."

"Or even if you are a dog or a cat man."

"Dog."

"Wrong, the correct answer is both."

"I hate cats. They're mean."

"Only to assholes." I look him up and down, trying not to notice how many muscles this man has. "Are you an asshole?"

He considers this question. "Sometimes."

"Great," I mutter, that panicky feeling in my stomach threatening to take hold of me again.

The alpha takes a concerned step towards me. "But only to people who deserve to be treated that way."

I manage a nod.

"Look, Avery," he says, and God, my name in his mouth, in that deep husky voice, sounds ... nice. "We'll sort this out. I'll get my best people on it."

People? He has people?

"But even if there is a solution, even if there is a way to reverse this," I say, waving my hand towards that bite mark, a bite mark which feels warm and rather satisfying, "we're still stuck together for the foreseeable future, aren't we?"

He considers this for a few seconds more. I can hear his thoughts murmuring in my mind, but they're too quick for me to follow. "Yes, I think we are. I'm sorry."

I chew on my bottom lip. This is why omegas stick together and look out for one another. This is why rich omegas have bodyguards protecting them. This is why omegas shouldn't sneak off from the group and head out on their own. To avoid this exact situation. Bonded and mated to some dickhead alpha because your hormones got the better of you.

"Why did you sneak off from your friends? Your sister is right, that's dangerous."

"Bachelorette parties aren't really my thing."

"Because?"

My gaze falls to the carpet, and he doesn't push me for an answer.

He doesn't seem like a dickhead – please, please God, don't let him be a dickhead. And maybe I'm being naïve and foolish, but he seems as genuinely confused and bewildered about this situation as I am. I don't think he targeted a drunk omega and took advantage of her. In fact, he looked as drunk as I did in that wedding snap.

"It doesn't excuse my behavior," he says, looking suitably ashamed. "I don't know what the fuck happened. I've never done anything like this before. I've never even had a one-night stand before."

"You haven't?"

"You have?" he says, frowning.

I wag my finger at him. "This isn't exactly a time to get all judgie with me."

"No, no, I'm sorry." He scrubs his hand through his hair. "Shit, it must be the bond ... the idea of you with another man just ... I'm not usually the jealous type."

Yeah, the idea of him with another woman ...

"This bond-thing is a headfuck," I mutter.

He smiles – an expression which brightens those blue eyes of his and has my stomach flipping somersaults. "It is." He shakes his head. "My pack will–"

"Pack?" I say, my mouth dropping so far open he must see my tonsils. "You have a pack."

Chapter Three

Cruise

Is this girl for real?

I can't sense any hint of duplicity through the bond. She seems one hundred percent, completely genuinely clueless.

Is that a good thing or bad?

"Yes, I have a pack."

"How many of you are there?"

"Five."

"Five!" she says, her eyebrows leaping up her forehead. I guess it's unusual for a pack to be as big as ours. "All alphas or do you have an om–"

"All alphas," I say firmly.

"Are any of your packmates bonded?"

"I told you, we don't have an omega."

"Why?"

"Do you have an alpha?"

"Well ... no."

We stand in silence, both considering that for a moment.

"Most packs have an omega," she says.

"Most omegas have a pack."

We stare at each other.

"So, we're stuck together," she says at last. "For the time being, anyway."

I'm not sure I see that as a downside in this situation. In fact, I could see quite a few upsides, although the reaction of my packmates won't be one of them. Especially when I bring her home with me. Then again ... She smells like sweet sticky honey, and her dark eyes are frankly seductive, and then there are those thighs.

Shit!

"You can come stay at our place in LA until we get this sorted," I tell her, warming to the idea incredibly quickly.

She stares at me. "I can't just move in with a stranger."

"We have a pool house. You can stay there. All yours." Frankly, it seems like a perfect situation. A sweet-smelling little omega in the pool house. I like the idea of that a lot. "It would be all yours."

"Or you could come stay with me," she says, crossing her arms over her chest.

"Not possible. We have our company and—"

"So what?"

"You have room for five alphas?" I say skeptically. "Five large alphas. There's not one of us shorter than six feet."

She swallows.

"No, but I do have a job."

"What do you do?"

She hesitates, which seems strange. Is she embarrassed of her job? Oh fuck, please don't let her be one of those cam-girls. She's pretty enough to be one and she certainly has the body.

I study her face. "Drug dealer?"

She shakes her head.

"Mortician?"

"Eww, no."

"Stripper?" I say with a frown. I'm being a jerk, but I don't like the idea of other guys seeing her naked.

"No." She fidgets on her chair, chewing her bottom lip in a way I want to mimic. "Well ... I'm waiting tables."

Waiting tables? Is that all? "At Hooters?" I ask, the frown still hovering on my brow. The idea of other men looking at her tits really, really pisses me off.

"No, just a diner back home in Cardval."

"Ask for time off."

"Ha! I can't afford that."

"This bond-situation will last a week. Ten days max."

"I still can't afford to miss out on my pay."

"Why? You won't need to pay any rent while you're staying with us."

"Right! But I'll still need to eat. I'll still need money for toiletries and books and—"

"I'll cover your lost wages."

"Sure you will," she says with a massive helping of sarcasm.

"You really don't know who I am, do you?"

She rests her hand on her hip in a way that emphasizes the curve of her waist and rolls her eyes. She is wearing one of my shirts and the hem grazes her mid-thigh in a way that is damn, damn, damn sexy. The woman is stunning. Dark tousled hair, dark eyes and my bite mark on her throat. Shit, all I want to do is lick my tongue over that bite mark, suck on it hard.

I swallow down the urge, trying to think of the most unerotic thoughts I can, because otherwise I'm going to be harder than a steel rod and, in only my briefs, she won't be able to miss it.

"You keep saying that in some stupidly cryptic fashion. Am I meant to know who you are, Cruise ... Cruise ...?"

"Hamilton."

"Hamilton."

"As in Pack Hamilton."

She stares at me blankly.

"As in Hamilton Enterprises," I say.

Realization slowly dawns across her face. I don't think this is a scam. Whatever happened between the two of us last night to land us both in this fucked-up situation, I don't believe there was any intention or duplicity on her side.

I may struggle to get my pack to believe that. Like I said, I'm not known for my spur-of-the-moment, throw-caution-to-the-wind kind of actions.

"Hamilton Enterprises," she repeats, glancing down at her phone. A Hamilton cell. Model $Z_{7.0}$. "As in *the* Hamilton Enterprises?"

"Yes."

"As in the firm that made this phone?"

"Yes."

"And my laptop?"

"Probably."

"But you're ... you're ..."

I frown. "I'm what?"

"I don't know," she says, gaping at me. But her amazement doesn't last long; soon it's replaced with suspicion. "You're messing with me. Anyone could claim–"

I march over to my laptop and bring up a photo of me

and my pack under our company logo. I lift the device into my arms and show her the screen.

"Anyone could–"

I huff and bring up the wiki page for our company next, showing her the part where it lists the founding partners. Before she can claim that's a fake too, I find our company webpage and show her the list of CEOs, my photo – admittedly a few years old – plastered next to my name.

"Oh jeez," she says, stumbling towards the armchair and dropping down into its embrace. "Oh jeez."

Not exactly the reaction I was expecting. Then again, I'm not sure what reaction I was expecting. Some enthusiasm maybe. My pride is a little wounded. Okay, this situation is a screw-up, but I'm not a bad catch, am I?

I mean, I glance down at my body, I work out. I'm a billionaire. My face isn't half bad–

"Your face is not a problem," she mutters. "Trust me. I just can't see this working out. Or how we're going to keep this quiet."

"From whom?"

"The world!" she says, waving her hands around. "I mean, it seems we're damn lucky there isn't anything on social media this morning."

"Yeah," I say sinking back into the armchair opposite her, trying not to gape at those long, bare legs of hers, and the golden skin of her thighs. Shit, the woman smells like candy. Good enough to eat.

And it's been a long, long time since I ate out an omega.

Where the hell is that drink?

"So, what are we going to do, Mr. Cruise Hamilton, CEO of Hamilton Enterprises?" she asks.

"Like I said, I'll get my best people on this. In the meantime, you can come and stay in our pool house until the effects of the newly formed bond have worn off."

We stare at each other again and then my eyes slip to the wound on her neck. I've been dreaming my whole life of claiming and bonding an omega. Of sinking my teeth into her neck and making her mine. And now I have, and I can't remember a damn thing about it.

"Me neither," she says, and is it my imagination or does she sound about as disappointed as I feel?

I've no time to contemplate this, though, because there's a loud hammering on the door.

"Room service," I say. Thank God. I've never needed the hair of the dog quite so badly.

"Are they usually so persistent?" the omega says, eyes flicking to the door as there's more knocking.

I climb to my feet, stride to the door and swing it back, my gaze landing on another small omega who looks remarkably like the one in my room, no room service in sight.

The woman's gaze lands on me. Her eyes widen in horror, and she opens her mouth and screams.

In the next minute, Avery is by my side, pushing me into the room and placing herself firmly in the doorway.

"Isla," she says.

The sister.

"Avery!" the sister says, looking on the verge of a panic attack. "What the hell is going on? You said–"

"Because I hooked up, and I didn't want you to go all crazy about it, okay? But I need you to go away now, Isla, because I'm in the middle of having really wild, crazy sex and–"

"With him?"

"Of course, with him!"

"Avery," the sister says, her hands gripping the omega's

arms. She lowers her voice to a whisper, but I can still hear her words through the bond. "Is everything okay? Are you in trouble? Do I need to call the cops?"

"I'm just fine. More than fine. You have no idea what this man can do with his—"

"Okay," the sister says, taking a decided step backwards. "I don't need the details." Her eyes flick around her little sister's face. "Are you really sure you're okay?"

"Never better, you know I think I actually passed out when he—"

"Fine, I'm going. Just ..." The other woman points her finger, then wags it. "Just don't miss the flight."

"I won't," the omega waves, "enjoy basket weaving."

Avery closes the door, sagging against it with a sigh of relief.

"Wild, crazy sex, huh?" I say. "Want to fill me in on something?"

She shrugs. "I've no idea if we did or we didn't. I mean, can't you tell? Do your balls feel lighter?"

"Do my balls feel lighter?! That isn't a thing."

"It isn't?"

"No. Anyway, can't you tell?" I point towards her midsection, trying not to think about what I caught a glimpse of before the panties went on.

She rubs her thighs together. "I don't feel sticky."

I suppress a growl in my throat and the urge to rush at her and make her damn, damn, damn sticky. So sticky ...

She stares at me, her cheeks bright pink.

"I'm sorry," I mumble. "But you brought it up."

"Perhaps we should stick to safe topics of conversation."

I nod. "And maybe you could put some clothes on."

I glance down at my body, then back up at her.

"How exactly did your sister find us? Didn't you tell her you were in the spa?"

"Tracker on my phone. I have a habit of getting lost."

Before I can ask what the hell that means, there's another knock on the door.

Avery rolls her eyes.

"Oh Alpha," she yells out. "That feels so good! So so so goood! Just like that, just ... like ... that. I'm going to, I'm going to–"

"Would you like me to come back later, Sir?" a voice calls out from the other side of the door.

Avery squeals and jumps away from the door.

"Room service," I tell her with a grin as she runs off towards the bathroom.

I open the door, relieved this time to find one of the hotel's waiting staff, and allow him to wheel three trolleys of food into the room and lay it out across the table.

When the door clicks behind him, the omega pokes her head out of the bathroom door.

"Has he gone?"

"Yep."

"Did he say anything?"

"He was too professional."

Her eyes alight on all the breakfast dishes spread out across the table. I didn't know what she liked, so I ordered one of everything.

"I thought you were ordering a drink," she says.

"I thought you might need breakfast."

"You thought correctly," she says, padding towards the table and moaning as she examines a stack of pancakes.

"Help yourself," I say, gesturing.

She drags three dripping pancakes onto a plate and curls up in one of the chairs.

"You know, living with you might not be so bad if this is what breakfast is like every day."

"We have two private chefs. You can order whatever you like for breakfast."

She stares at me, her fork hovering halfway to her open mouth, maple syrup, dribbling onto the plate. "Are you serious?"

"Yes, we're very busy. There isn't a lot of time for cooking."

"Oh," she says, cramming the massive forkful of pancake between her waiting lips. "So, what exactly were you doing here in Vegas, Mr. very-busy Cruise Hamilton?"

"Speaking at an event."

She tilts her head to one side. "How did you end up at the roulette table? You never explained that bit."

I take the seat opposite her and pour out one very black, very bitter coffee. I slide it over to her, watching in horror as she adds four teaspoons of sugar. Then I pour myself a cup.

How did I end up at the roulette table?

"I don't remember exactly," I say. "There was some dinner after the event. It was boring. I drank too much. Left early. Spotted the table on my way up to the room."

"Do you remember what happened next?" she says, licking syrup off her fingers.

I take a sip of the coffee, the taste bitter against my tongue. I try to remember what happened next.

I have a vague memory of her bright sunshine laugh, the way her dress hugged her figure, the perfume of her scent. But after that ... after that ...

"No," I say.

"Me neither. Have you ever blacked out like that before?"

I shake my head. Not from alcohol anyway. "Have you?" I asked.

"Once. My high school dance. But that was because my date hooked up with the girl he was actually in love with, and I spent the evening licking my wounds, or rather nursing them with vodka, lots of vodka."

"He sounds like a jerk."

"He was." Her eyes flit around the table and she lunges for the bacon next. "This was such a good idea." Then she halts, noticing my plate is empty. "Aren't you eating?"

"Oh ... yeah," I say, realizing I've been watching her. I drag a bagel my way and pile it high with scrambled eggs. "What have you decided?" I ask, attempting to keep my voice neutral.

"About?"

"Our situation?"

She chews. "You met my sister, right? There is no way she's going to let me head off with a stranger. And my dad won't care how many companies you own. He is going to track you down and kill you."

"I can speak to them both. Make it clear that my intentions are pure and that there won't be any funny business."

"Funny business?" she says smiling in a way that is far too flirtatious and has me thinking that particular promise will be a very hard one to keep.

Chapter Four

Avery

"I think," I say, eyeing up the man opposite me – who is still wearing far too little clothes and smells more and more delicious as the minutes pass, "no matter what my sister or my dad or anyone else may think, we don't have many options here. And it'll only be for a few days, right?"

"Correct."

"Okay, then." I nod, trying to feel some conviction in this decision. After all, I've already made some stupidly insane decisions in the last 24-hours that have probably screwed up my life and any chance of future happiness, what's one more?

His shoulders sag a little. In relief? Because he was hoping I'd put up a fight and refuse to come?

"I'll need to let the pilot know we're flying one more."

"Pilot."

"I have the helicopter booked for this evening."

"This evening?" I say. "So soon?"

"I have a board meeting at 10am tomorrow morning."

"Can't you push it back? You're the CEO."

"No, I'm sorry, I can't, Avery. We have people flying in from across the world."

"But this is a personal emergency, surely?"

"CEOs don't do personal emergencies. It affects the share price."

"Oh ... okay." I take a deep breath. "Time to put on my big girl pants, then." I pat my mouth with my napkin, examining the Adonis sitting opposite me. "If I go get showered, do you think it would be possible to arrange some clothes for me?"

"Of course. Size 10?"

I raise an eyebrow. "Correct."

"What do you want?"

I sigh. "An outfit suitable for breaking the news to your sister and your best friend, that you've just accidentally married and bonded with a stranger. Whatever you think says: don't panic, this will all be fine."

"Pantsuit?"

"Sure, why not? I've never worn a pantsuit in my life. Maybe if I had worn them more often, I wouldn't be messing up quite as often as I do."

"Are you suggesting this current situation isn't a unique occurrence for you?"

I consider whether to lie to my new husband, but it's probably only fair that he knows exactly who he has mated to.

"I've never woken up married before, but I have a great habit of screwing up my life."

He frowns. "How?"

"I'm 28. I've been fired from three different waitressing jobs – and probably about to be fired from my fourth. I'm single, living at home and I don't own a pantsuit. Whereas you ..."

"I wasn't always successful. In fact, we failed a lot before we were successful. Failing is part of the process."

"Do you think this is part of the process?" I motion between the two of us. "Do you think we screwed this up so badly, that we get to meet our true loves afterwards?"

"No idea."

Me neither.

I have the urge to touch the bite mark on my throat. I manage to resist it until I'm safely locked in the bathroom. Then I let my fingertips trail over the deep teeth marks. It feels tender but electric, sending shivers through my body.

Like every other omega on the planet, I've dreamed about an alpha's bite – often in bed with my knotted dildo. This wasn't exactly what I had planned.

When I emerge from the bathroom, the alpha points to several zipped-up clothes bags hanging in the wardrobe and mumbles something about needing a shower himself.

I watch him stride into the bathroom, trying not to observe the very fine ass the man possesses. I mean, jeez, I think the man could crack eggs with those ass cheeks.

Then I go to investigate the clothes. There is more than one outfit. One cream pantsuit. A pair of jeans and a t-shirt. A light summer dress.

I spend a long time contemplating the pantsuit, before dragging the dress over my head. Who am I kidding?

I am not worthy of a pantsuit. I'm not that organized, or responsible. I definitely am not CEO wife material. And not just any CEO, a billionaire, known worldwide. Men like that have wives who run huge foundations and campaign on grown-up issues.

That is not me. I was fired from my last waitressing job for putting sugar in all the salt pots. It wasn't the first time.

I spend a few minutes fussing in front of the wardrobe, wishing I had my makeup bag with me and then remembering the alpha has seen me hyperventilating and green on the floor. He is probably cursing every known god that he ended up bonded to a messed-up omega like me.

I shake the thought from my head and fetch my phone. I've put off the inevitable long enough. I need to face up to the showdown.

I text my best friend, Jacks, telling her I need to meet with her and Isla in twenty minutes. I consider making the meeting venue somewhere public, somewhere Isla won't be able to yell at me, and Jacks won't get away with punching the alpha. But then I remember Cruise Hamilton is well known and the last thing we need is people snapping photos of us.

Jacks sends me back a picture of a half-formed straw basket.

I remind her that she hates arts and crafts as much as I do and that this is urgent.

Ten minutes later Isla is buzzing my phone, but I ignore it – this conversation needs to happen face-to-face. Instead, I go hammer on the bathroom door.

I think the alpha has been in there longer than I was. I hope he's not one of those dudes who spends all day fussing about his appearance, although to be fair to him, he is very much entitled to fuss. The man is stunning.

And anyway, how he spends his time is absolutely no business of mine, unless, of course, it means my bestie and my sister arriving just as he steps out of the shower, all naked, and wet and …

"Are you nearly done?" I call out, just as he opens the door and I practically fall into his very bare, very toned and very glistening chest. A large scar cuts across his left pec and another zigzags across his lower abdomen. It only adds to his appeal.

"I'm done," he says, as I force myself to take a step away from somewhere that was frankly a very … nice place to be.

"My sister and best friend will be here in ten minutes."

"Because?"

"I need to tell them what's going on and as we're unable to separate, you will have to stay with me."

"Right." He nods and strolls to the wardrobe, losing the towel in the process.

I squeak and turn around, giving him some privacy, even though I would happily stand and watch the man dress.

I chew my lip while I wait, rehearsing how exactly I'm going to break the news.

Turns out, I needn't have worried. I open the door to my sister and my friend exactly ten minutes later. My bestie – the one I've known since first day at kindie when some mean kid tried to steal my Barbie eraser and she punched him flat to the ground – takes one look at me and declares:

"You got hitched, didn't you?"

"H-h-h-how do you know?" I gasp.

She points to the confetti still littering the carpet.

"What?!" Isla says, wobbling in her sandals. "You're what?"

I pull them both into the room and Jacks' eyes land on the alpha hovering in the background.

"Cruise Hamilton!" she yelps.

"What?" Isla mutters, looking extremely pale.

I grab them both by the wrists, yank them into the bathroom, and slam the door behind me.

Jacks immediately pushes Isla onto a stool and shoves my sister's head between her knees.

"It's worse," I admit. Isla whimpers. "We're bonded too."

"Oh, holy Mary, mother of God," Isla mutters.

"I know," I say, my sister's panic rubbing off on me. "I've fucked up my life entirely."

"Fucked up?!" Jacks says, pinching Isla on the shoulder and giving me a 'pull-yourself-together' death stare. "How have you fucked up your life? That's Cruise Hamilton. He's a billionaire. Rich, hot, handsome. You've landed the fucking jackpot, Avery."

"She doesn't know him!" Isla says from between her knees.

"Exactly!" I squeal. "He could be an asshole, or a sick pervert, or a secret mass murderer."

"He isn't. His pack have given away over half of their wealth to good causes. And not just the trendy ones, but the ones like helping old people with dementia and single moms who can't pay their bills."

"Really?" Isla says, peering up at Jacks. Isla is a sucker for men with big hearts and good causes.

"Yes, really. You are one lucky bitch, Avery Loren. I wish I'd ditched the party last night."

"But we can't separate," I say, thinking I deserve a bit more sympathy than my bestie is offering up. "Apparently the bond is too strong so newly formed and separating is freaking painful."

Jacks and Isla both nod like they knew that already.

"You're going to have to hang out together 24/7 for like the next ten days."

"He wants me to go live in his pool house."

"Dad will have a heart attack! There's no way he'll let you go off and live in some strange alpha's house."

"Pool house," I correct, "and he has a pack. There are five of them apparently."

"Oh Lord!" Isla mutters.

"And they are all equally as hot as him," Jacks says with a grin, pointing towards the bathroom door.

"I don't know if I can do it," I admit. The dude seems nice enough. But living with him? Living with a stranger? Living with five strangers? Five alpha strangers?

"What? Hang out with the five hot and obscenely rich alphas? Oh no, however will you cope?"

"Jacks!" I cry. "I'm serious. You know me. One-night stands maybe one thing, but living together?"

"One-night stands?" Isla says.

"Don't listen to her bullshit, Isla. She's slept with precisely four dudes. She is not some femme fatale."

"Does four include the alpha out there or not?"

"Oh my God, yes," Jacks says, grabbing my hands. "What was he like? Is his dick as big as they say? Did you see stars when he bit you?"

"How big do they say his dick… hang on, no we haven't slept together."

"But you said–"

I shake my head. "No sex, as far as we can both remember anyway."

"You don't remember the sex?"

"There was no sex. And as for the biting and the wedding, neither of us remember that either."

"Are you sure you're definitely bonded?" Isla asks hopefully.

I sweep my hair to one side and show them my newly formed bite mark. They stare at it – Jacks with clear admiration, Isla with a slightly sick sheen.

"It's beautiful," Jacks says in awe.

"It's a whole heap of trouble, that's what it is," I mumble.

Jacks rests her hand on my shoulder. "Avery, you'll be fine. And if you're nervous, then just act confident. Before you know it, you'll be feeling confident too."

"I don't know," I say.

"I don't like the idea of you being all on your own," Isla adds.

"Hmmm," Jacks says, "you want me to come with you?"

"What?" I say. "You'd do that for me?"

"Live in a billionaire's house for a week? Hell, yeah. Of course, I will."

"But your jobs?" Isla says.

"Dave can shove his job up his ass," Jacks says. "I've always wanted to go to Rockview."

"I think it would make Dad feel better about it," Isla says, "to know you had a beta friend watching out for you."

I nod.

"It's agreed then. I'll head home with Isla and the others. Pack us both some stuff, go give Dave the finger, and then I will meet you in Rockview."

"You're not coming with me now?"

"Avery, I packed exactly three pairs of panties. I need to arrange someone to look after Colin the cat. And I need to help Isla break this news to your folks."

"You don't think I should do that on the phone?"

"No," Isla and Jacks say together.

Jacks squeezes my shoulder. "I can catch a flight tomorrow. It'll be one night alone. I'll come as quickly as I can."

"Right," I say. "One night alone with the hot alpha and his four pack mates. I can do that."

Chapter Five

Cruise

I help the omega up into the helicopter and follow her in afterwards, helping to fasten her safety belt and put on her ear protectors.

"I've never been in one of these before," she yells over the roar of the spinning blades. "Are you sure it's safe?"

"Perfectly."

I offer her my hand, and, hesitating for a moment, she takes it. I squeeze it gently and repeat to myself the same mantra I've been repeating over and over for the last five hours.

I am not enjoying this. I am not thinking sexy thoughts.

I am a good alpha. I can control myself.

I am ignoring how warm her little hand is and the way her bare thigh brushes against mine.

I am not breathing in mouthful after mouthful of her scent.

Instead, I am thinking about the shitstorm that awaits us.

I haven't called my packmates. Or messaged them. They have no idea that I am arriving home married, bonded and with an omega mate in tow.

I should have called. I should have messaged.

But this news is going to go down like a lead balloon and I haven't been able to bring myself to deliver it. Not when there are far more enticing distractions like the sweet omega.

I have screwed up big time.

I have fucked my packmates over.

I'm putting on a brave face for the omega. I'm pretending this will all be fine.

But will it?

Declan may be understanding. At least he won't knock my lights out.

Max and Jonah? No chance.

And as for Kent? He's never wanted an omega. He's always made that clear. Work is his life and omegas are too big a nuisance. Now I'll be moving such a nuisance into our pool house.

"What are your packmates like?"

Shit, is she following my thoughts?

I shift slightly on my seat.

What do I say? Ruthless, focused, determined. That's what the business media would have you believe.

But they're also loyal, principled and occasionally even funny.

"We've known each other a long time."

"You have? How long?"

"Fifteen years. We met at college. Jonah and Declan were studying math. Max computer science. Kent and I business."

"You're all nerds, then?"

"Depends what your definition of a nerd is," I say, aware I'm not some weedy little dork by any stretch of the imagination.

"What do you do for fun? Apart from hanging out at roulette tables and marrying women you've only just met?"

Fun? There hasn't been time for a lot of fun over the last few years.

"Erm ... I like to work out."

"Hmmm," she says, and for some reason the fact that answer doesn't impress her has me panicking.

"Reading," I add quickly, "I like reading."

"Me too," she says, her face brightening. "I love a good book. I made Jacks promise to bring all my favorite books with her even though she moaned she'd go over her luggage limit and would be charged extra."

"I'll pay for it. I'll pay for all your books to be shipped."

She laughs, clearly thinking I'm joking.

"What do you like to read?" she asks.

The company reports, competition analyzes and the business papers. "Erm, murder mysteries," I lie. I did read one about a year ago when the internet went out and there was nothing else to do but pick up a book.

"I read them occasionally."

"What do you read then?"

She turns and looks out of the window. "It's so pretty," she says.

Yeah, fuck she is. And I like her company. Is that weird? I've known her, what? A day, and those hours I've spent in her company haven't been awful. Usually, I can't stand being with anyone but my packmates.

Declan is the social one. Not me.

"Declan?" she asks, turning around to face me again.

"Yeah, I think you'll like him."

Declan. He's the one I'll tell first. Introduce her to him. Win him on side before I tackle the others.

She sinks slightly against my side, and it takes all my willpower not to wrap my arm around her and pull her in close.

Then again, maybe Kent is right. Maybe omegas are a huge distraction. I have a feeling this one will be in particular.

* * *

The omega coos and gasps for the entire flight, gaze locked on the dark landscape below us. But I'm too busy fretting about how to handle this situation with my packmates for window gazing.

Could I fake a migraine and tell them I'm heading for the pool house for peace and quiet, then sneak the omega inside with me? Handle the big reveal in the morning.

Or am I better off facing this head on, leading her straight into the house and spitting out the truth?

Or should I be composing a message right now, forewarning them of what is coming their way?

I still haven't made up my mind as the helicopter touches down on the piece of land just west of our home, but any choices are whipped firmly out of my hand by the appearance of Declan, waiting for me beside his car.

He grins and waves at me as I climb out of the helicopter, yelling, "I thought I'd come and meet you. I wanted to hear how the big speech ..."

His words trail off as he watches me guide the omega out of the helicopter after me.

He cocks an eyebrow at me.

"Hi," the omega says, holding out her hand to him before I've said a word. "I'm Avery."

Declan takes her hand in his, giving her one of his winning smiles, white teeth gleaming against his golden skin, his scent of cedar clear in the air. "Declan," he says.

"One of the packmates," she says.

"One of Cruise's packmates, yes."

He keeps smiling at the omega and then suddenly the smile slips, and he frowns. His eyes flip to me, back to the omega and then to me.

He sniffs. Avery peers up at me with an anxious look.

"We're bonded," I blurt out, not able to take the goddamn tension and needing this secret off my chest and in the open.

Declan blinks rapidly.

"I'm sorry," he says, still frowning, "I thought you just said–"

"I did. We're bonded."

Declan blinks some more and for a moment, about ten dozen different emotions seem to flicker over his face. Finally, he says, "How?"

I look at Avery and she looks at me.

"I didn't know you were dating anyone. Why keep a secret? Why didn't you–"

"We only met last night," Avery says. "We haven't been having some secret affair."

"You met last night!!" Declan says, a look of disbelief now planting itself across his face.

"I drank too much. Avery here drank too much. Neither of us exactly remembers what happened. But here we are."

"Bonded and married," Avery says with a little curtsy.

"You're married as well?"

"Yep."

"How is this possible?"

"Well, it seems Las Vegas officials really don't pay much attention to how sober their bride and grooms are. And it's pretty damn easy to grab a license, a few witnesses and–"

"No, I mean, how did this happen? Cruise is not the type of man to–"

"Well, I'm not the type of girl." Avery crosses her arms. Inwardly, I groan. This isn't the start I was hoping for. Declan was meant to be my easy win.

"Regardless of how this happened. It has. Avery and I are stuck together until the bond eases. She is going to be staying in our pool house until that happens. Her friend will be joining her tomorrow."

Declan is our chief schmoozer and negotiator. He's handled tense business deals, pissy investors and high-stakes altercations. He stares at us both for one whole minute and then he pulls his shit out of the bag.

"We'd be very happy to welcome you into our home," he says with an almost genuine smile. "And we'll take good care of you, I promise."

He guides her towards the waiting car and opens the door of the passenger seat for her, shutting the door once she's inside.

Then he grabs my elbow and hisses.

I brace myself, waiting for the berating I know I'm due.

"Fuck, man, she smells like nectar. And she's beautiful."

I swallow. "I know."

"But why didn't you warn us? I mean, shit, I would've

shaved and worn my best suit," he says, rubbing at the stubble on his chin.

"You know as well as I do, the girls love your just-got-out-of-bed look." He grins lazily. "I thought it would be better if I explained this face to face. Kent is going to be mad."

Declan nods. "Probably. But when he sees her ..."

"He doesn't want an omega."

"He's human and an alpha. We'll see."

"This is a temporary thing, Declan. Don't get your hopes up."

"Temporary?" Declan chuckles. "Your teeth marks are in her neck, man. This isn't temporary."

I go to argue with him, but he's already climbing in the driver's seat, and I'm left to bundle into the back.

They talk animatedly all the way on the short drive to our property, Declan asking the omega all the things I should have thought to ask her – where she lives, her family, her age, her birthday. Things a husband ought to know about his wife.

Chapter Six

Avery

"This isn't a house," I tell both alphas as I step out of the car and peer around. "This is a village. I mean how many properties are there exactly?"

Declan leans back against the car with a grin. He's as tall and as broad as his packmate although his skin darker, his eyes a golden brown and his hair chin length and wavy. "There's the main house. The pool house. A summer house out in the grounds. Two guest houses."

"And do you have omegas installed in each of those properties?" I ask in jest with a hint of suspicion.

"You're the first one," Declan says. "Do you want a tour?"

I peer at Cruise who's been awfully quiet ever since we left Vegas. "I'm actually really exhausted. Would it be really bad of me if I skipped the tour and introductions? Do you think we could do them in the morning when I'm hopefully less hungover and feeling more human?"

"Of course, I'll let your husband show you the way," he says with mischief. "And I'll see you in the morning."

"Goodnight," I say as Cruise motions for me to follow him around the main house, which looks more like a mansion than an actual house, and out towards the grounds at the back. A pool shimmers blue in the moonlight and beyond are the rolling lawns of what looks like a golf course.

Nestled beside the pool is another house. Much smaller than the main property but still at least twice as big as my parents' home.

"This is the pool house," he says.

We both stare up at the building, its windows all dark.

"Are we going in?" I ask.

"Right, yes," Cruise says, pushing down on the door handle and stepping inside, flicking on the lights. I swing my gaze around. It's better than the hotel suite. The decor is a mixture of whites and blues with seashells hanging on the walls and three large sofas positioned around the bifold doors, looking out towards the glistening pool. I can tell they've paid someone talented to design the place and, while everything looks eye-wateringly expensive, it's also somehow cozy. I can imagine snuggling up on one of the sofas. Possibly with the alpha.

Maybe Jacks is right, maybe I have lucked out. Then again, maybe that is not the way to be thinking about this situation.

It's clear to me why Cruise is feeling so uncomfortable. His packmates are going to think I am a gold digger. They are going to think I tricked him into bonding with me. After all, the man is filthy rich. What omega wouldn't want to live in a luxurious home like this?

Is that what Declan thinks? He seemed ... nice. I swallow. Very nice.

Lusting over your new husband's hot packmate is probably about as despicable as admiring his outrageously gorgeous properties. Then again, isn't that how packs work?

I flop down on the nearest available sofa. This is a lot and my head hurts all over again.

"Are you okay?" Cruise asks, shutting the door and pulling down the blinds.

"Like I said, just tired. I think I need a good night's sleep, and this will all be easier in the morning."

"Can I get you a drink or anything to eat before bed?"

I shake my head. "Just take me to the nearest bedroom please," I say. The alpha's eyes flash. "I mean, could you show me the way?"

"This way," he growls, the noise doing funny things to the bond in my stomach.

He leads me through into a giant bedroom with mellow lighting. A bed dominates the space, piled high with a mountain of different cushions, and a soft, plush carpet covers the floor. One wall contains a walk-in wardrobe and resting against the other is a vanity table most woman would kill for.

We both hover in the doorway.

"Is this okay?" he asks.

"This is more than okay. It looks amazing." Almost like a nest. Is it a nest? Did they build it as a nest?

He stares at me, and I remember he can read just about every thought spinning in my head. My cheeks sizzle.

"I'll leave you to ... get comfortable."

I bite my lip and nod.

He smells so good and the way his shirt strains across his chest is reminding me just how good he looks as well.

"I think I'm going to crawl straight between those sheets and fall asleep."

He nods. "I'll be over in the main house. If you need me, you can call."

"Oh," I say. "Whereabouts?"

"I'll show you." I follow him back down to the lounge and he points across the pool and out towards the humongous mansion. "That's my bedroom, up there," he says, pointing to a second-floor window.

"You don't think ..." I say, then hesitate.

"Yes?"

"That the distance will be too far?"

"You here, me there?" he asks. "It might be. I could stay here in the pool house. In one of the other rooms."

"I think that would be better."

"The bond is new," he says.

"And particularly strong."

"Here," he says, walking back towards the corridor. "I'll take this room here."

I peer further along the hallway. There're two rooms between his bedroom and mine.

"Hmmm," I say. "It's still a little far."

His eyes flirt across my face and I watch his Adam's apple bob in his throat as he swallows.

"I can take the room next door."

"Yes," I say. "I think it would be sensible for you to sleep next door."

Together we walk along the hallway, Cruise pausing at his door and me pausing at mine. The six feet between us feels infinite.

"Or maybe ..." I venture.

"Maybe?"

"As it's the first night–"

"And the bond is so fresh."

"And very strong."

"I could sleep on the floor in your room?" he suggests.

My shoulders sag with relief. "Yes, in my room. I think it's the sensible thing to do."

"Very sensible," he says, nodding and together we peer into the room and towards the giant bed.

"Well," I say, "I'm going to go brush my teeth."

"There's an en suite through there," he tells me.

When I return a few minutes later, he's made himself a bed on the floor right alongside mine.

"Looks comfy," I say. "Can a billionaire like you cope with sleeping on the floor?"

He snorts. "I'll be just fine."

He looks down at my bedtime outfit – the Bart Simpson nightie that I've had since my teens.

"It's comfortable," I say, as his gaze lands on the hole right by Bart's shorts. Other than Jacks and Isla, I hadn't exactly planned to spend the night with anyone when I'd packed for Vegas. I certainly hadn't packed nightwear worthy of a honeymoon.

"Hey," he says, "I like the Simpsons. Although, I was always more of a Lisa fan."

He stalks off towards the bathroom and after a moment's hesitation, I climb in between the covers of the bed. I don't know what position to lie in. On my back, arms and legs straight in a determined I-am-not-trying-to-seduce-you stance. Or my usual preferred position, face down, butt up.

I opt for the former.

He reappears a moment later in another pair of boxers and his t-shirt and I confess I'm a little disappointed not to earn another glimpse of that chest of his.

He switches off the light, plunging us both into darkness and I listen to him stumbling around, bashing into the bed with a yelp, until finally he finds his make-shift bed and settles down.

Then the room is silent except for our breaths and the distant whirr of the swimming pool.

I chew my lip and force myself to count sheep – ugly, smelly sheep. It's no use. My mind is much more interested on dwelling on the man laid out down on the floor beside me – the man I can hear tossing and turning. I wonder what his packmates are like. Will they hate me? Will they be friendly like Declan? Will they be as hot as Cruise?

"Hot?" Cruise says, the sound of his voice making me leap about a foot up into the air.

"Huh?"

"Are you hot? Too cold? Is the bed comfortable?"

I roll onto my side and peer down through the darkness, his gleaming eyes peering up at me.

"The bed's fine. How's yours?"

"Fine," he says. But I don't need the power of the bond to know it's not.

"This is silly. This bed is gigantic. You should just come sleep up here with me."

"I'm not sure that would be appropriate."

"We're married. I think it's allowed."

"I'm fine."

"You're clearly not."

"I tell you, I'm fine."

"Look," I say, scurrying to the far side of the bed, "there's plenty of room up here and, trust me, this bed is super comfortable, and I am like the princess and the pea. If there's one little bump in the bed, I would find it."

"I'm sure you'll be far more comfortable without me in the bed."

I am not sure about that.

"You're being silly. Just come up here, will you?" I say, reaching down to grab a handful of his t-shirt.

"Avery?" he says, hand capturing mine.

"Yes, Cruise?"

"We're newly bonded mates. I am repressing a lot of alpha instincts right now. I'm not sure I can trust myself if I climb into that bed with you."

"O-o-oh," I say, feeling my body warm as well as my cheeks. Do I want him to control himself? Images of him losing control and pinning me down on the bed flood my mind.

"Jesus," he says.

He unhooks my fingers from the fabric of his shirt.

I shake the images from my head and force myself to get a grip.

"Look, we're both adults. We're not horny teenagers. Okay, so I'm an omega and you're an," I gulp, "alpha. And, yes, we're newly bonded, but we are not our hormones, right? We are better than that. And also, I can build a barrier of cushions between us."

"I'm not sure cushions would stop me," he mutters.

"I've shared a bed with my sister countless times before and that girl walks and talks and does all sorts in her sleep. Trust me, cushions will work. And I won't be responsible for damaging your back."

I pull the cushions from the head of the bed and construct a wall down the center of the mattress, pilling them two high.

Begrudgingly, the alpha drags himself off the floor and climbs into the bed, the mattress sagging as he lowers his weight. I can't see him though. Not behind all those cushions.

Of course, I can smell him. But that is another problem altogether. One I can handle.

Surprisingly, I find his proximity – rather than pumping me up into a horny frenzy – has my eyelids sagging and my mouth pulling open in a wide yawn.

It has been a long day. I am still not over this mega hangover. And having him close is somehow comforting, subduing. Before I know it, I'm drifting off to sleep, confident that the alpha has nothing to worry about.

Chapter Seven

Avery

Like the day before, it takes me several minutes to work out where I am when I open my eyes the next morning. Except this time, I am not greeted by the pain of a thousand daggers stabbing into my skull. No, I find a strong arm wrapped around my waist, a hard body lying against my back and something even harder nudging my backside.

I wriggle and that hard something gets a whole lot harder and grinds against me.

Oh ... right, that would be my husband.

He's out for the count, his breath heavy in my ear and warm against my skin.

How exactly did we end up in this position? When I fell asleep last night, there was a wall of cushions between us. Now those cushions are nowhere to be seen.

Not that I'm complaining.

I inhale, sucking in his woody scent and letting a sensation of bliss ride through my body.

This feels pretty nice. More than nice. Dreamy. I would die a happy woman if I could wake up this way each day.

I sigh a little, sinking back against him and the alpha mutters something in his sleep before nuzzling my throat.

I freeze.

I should wake him up.

I should really wake him up.

I should not let him trail his lips down my neck, lower, and lower, towards the ...

Oh Lord!

He laps his tongue against the wound on my shoulder, sucking on the teeth marks.

I really ought to stop him now.

He murmurs, grinding a little harder against my backside and I get a very full idea of just how large and girthy this man is.

My eyes roll back in their sockets and slick flows down my thighs.

Immediately, the thick aroma of slick fills the room, and the alpha jolts awake behind me.

I hold my breath and don't move. Maybe he'll fall back to sleep, and I can slip away.

"Omega?"

"Erm, morning," I say as bright and breezily as I can, fully expecting him to whip his arm away.

He doesn't move. His cock is still pressed firmly against my ass, and his arm is tight around my body.

He sniffs. "Is that ...?"

He reaches a hand between my legs, gliding his finger up my leg and meeting the slick trailing down my thigh.

He growls, and, holy smoke, if that doesn't have me gushing even more slick right over his hand.

"Care to explain," he says in a voice so husky I wonder how I'm not orgasming.

"You were ... erm ... nuzzling my bite mark."

Silence.

"I was?"

"Yes."

"And that," he says, his mouth veering close to the wound again, "caused this?"

He swivels his fingers through the slick and, pulling his hand out from under the covers, holds them up to examine.

"Yes," I confirm.

His cock jerks behind me and I can't help but let out a needy sigh.

"Shit," he says.

"It was inevitable," I say.

"I should have remained on the floor," he mutters.

"Do you think that would have helped?"

He thinks. "Somehow, I don't think so. You smell so damn good, Omega."

He lifts his slick-coated finger into his mouth and sucks.

"Erm," I say, wriggling my ass in a brattish way against his cock. "Do you think you could put that mouth to better use?"

I don't have to ask the man twice. He has me flipped onto my back and caged by his ginormous body in mere nanoseconds.

I shiver from the top of my head to the tips of my toes in anticipation. He gazes down at me with lust-filled eyes and groans.

Except it isn't one of those I-want-you-so-badly groans.

"What?" I say in alarm.

"Bart Simpson is staring up at me with a whole lot of sass and I may have had some wild fantasies in my time," interesting, "but they've never included a yellow cartoon boy."

"Oh," I squeak, shimming my nightie up my body and over my head. "Better?" I ask, lying back down in just my panties.

His hot gaze trails slowly over my chest. "You have no fucking idea how much better," he says, this time with the right kind of groan. His gaze travels higher, lingering over his bite mark. "May I?" he asks.

"Please!" I whine.

He lowers his head, and I can't help a second whimper before he presses his lips on the fresh wound causing more bliss to spiral through my body.

"It's so perfect," he mumbles. "Looks so perfect – my teeth marks on your throat."

"Uh huh," I manage to mutter, as he swivels his wet tongue over the wound.

"How does it feel?" he growls.

"Please never stop doing this."

"Really? You don't want my mouth somewhere else?"

"No, just here."

"Really," he says, his breath hot against the tender wound. "Not here," he grinds his cock between my legs.

"Oh," I say, "right there would be pretty nice too."

"Nice?" he scoffs, before scooting down my body and ripping my panties in half.

"That was a little dramatic," I say.

"Just be glad I didn't do it to that ..."

"Nightie."

He harrumphs and I go to tell him my nightwear was

not chosen with him in mind, but then his mouth is on my pussy and all my logical thoughts turn to mush.

The man has a very talented, very skillful, very enthusiastic tongue. Is that how he seduced me into this whole situation?

"Who says I seduced you? Maybe it was the other way round."

"With my Bart Simpson nightie?" I say cynically.

"With your wickedly delicious scent. I haven't been able to stop thinking about how you'd taste."

"And?" I moan as he lathers my clit with long strokes of that tongue.

"Fucking delicious."

I giggle. "You alphas, you're always so over the top."

"I can be less enthusiastic about this if you'd like, Omega."

"No," I screech, grabbing a hold of his hair as he feigns jerking his head away. "I am not compl— oh God!" I scream, my spine arching as he shoots electricity through my body.

"There's no god involved in this situation, Omega. It's just you and me."

I am most definitely okay with that, especially when he circles my clit over and over again, then flicks me hard and I fly straight to heaven without passing go.

"Oh jeez," I moan as he continues sucking on me, forcing a second orgasm straight after the first. "Could you please fuck and knot me now?"

His tongue halts its frankly devilish work and he lifts his head to stare at me.

"I don't have a condom. Do you?"

"Me? No, why would I have a condom?"

"It wasn't a–"

"How can you not have a condom? Don't you live with four guys?"

"You're right," he says, nodding. "I can sprint over to the main house—"

"No!" I pant, "I need a knot now."

"Are you saying ..."

"I'm on birth control and I got tested after my last relationship."

"Relationship?" he says darkly.

"Can we talk about that later?" I ask, growing increasingly desperate for my mate to knot me. "But how about you—"

"I've always used protection."

"Really? Even in a long term—"

"Can we talk about *that* later?"

"Yes," I say enthusiastically. Enough talking, more rutting and knotting. Lots of rutting.

He growls, gripping my calf and forcing my knee up into my chest. It opens me right up for him and for a moment, he just stares right at my pussy like it's some incredible work of art.

"It is a work of art. It's fucking beautiful."

"See, overly dramatic."

"You're not good at taking a compliment, are you?"

"You know what I am good at taking," I say, wiggling my ass.

The very serious alpha actually chuckles at that and then he's lowering himself down, and we groan in unison as he sinks into me.

The man is big, like the rest of him. Very big, and he stretches me wide, sinking deeper and deeper.

I moan a little and he pauses, bending down to nuzzle at my bite mark some more.

"It's okay, Omega, you're doing so well. I know you can take me all."

Take him all? I thought I had taken him all!

"No, sweetheart, there's more."

I'm not sure he's right. I'm not sure I can take any more, but then the things he's doing to that bite mark has me writhing beneath him, and my walls relax, letting him penetrate deeper still.

"Good girl," he pants as he bottoms out. "Good girl."

My pussy throbs around him, becoming even more needy but he doesn't seem quite ready to move yet.

"This feels ..." he says trailing off.

"Hmmm," I agree. The man is big and heavy above me and I know we're meant to love that stuff as omegas, but half the time it's intimidated me. Not with him though, somehow the weight of him pressing me down into the mattress, his big cock deep in my pussy, is erotic as hell.

"Ready?" he whispers.

"Oh fuck, yes please," I whine, surprised by how crazy I sound, like I'm in heat or something.

He slides from me, taking his time about it and igniting every sensitive spot along my walls. Then he grinds back in. He's teasing me. And I don't hate it. With most men it's a wham-bam kind of thing, which, don't get me wrong, I've enjoyed, but this, this has me begging and pleading.

"Fuck me hard. Please alpha, fuck me hard. Knot me!"

"Not yet," he says firmly, "not yet little one. You're not ready for it yet."

"I am."

He shakes his head, continuing to grind and grind and I circle my hips encouraging him to give me more.

"Shit!" he says, "you really are a needy little thing."

"Uh huh," I agree. Very needy.

"Fine," he says, pulling out of me and slamming into me so hard, the bed bangs against the wall.

I see stars. Bright dazzling stars.

He does it again. And again, and again. Taking my breath away with each hard thrust and all I can do is cling to him and take it as my body winds higher and higher.

"Going to come for me, Omega?"

And there's no way I can't. It feels too good and soon, I'm jolting around on the bed like a live wire, my pussy clenching and sucking around him.

"Fuuuuuccckkk!" he says, and the quiet, reserved alpha comes noisily, all grunts and groans that have me spiraling again.

"Knot me!" I beg, needy for that stretch. Needing him to lock into my pussy and never leave.

He gathers me up in his arms, hands tight on my backside so I can't wriggle away. And then I feel the stretch. More stars, more lightning, more tastes of heaven.

It's not usually like that. Don't get me wrong, the knotting is always delicious. But there's usually some pain, some discomfort. Not with him. It's like his knot is designed for my pussy.

"Hmmm," he says, sucking on my bite mark. "It damn well was."

Chapter Eight

Cruise

Every alpha loves knotting an omega. It's what we were designed to do. Designed for breeding. For pumping her pussy full of seed and ensuring it's locked inside her.

And, yeah, sure, at the time it feels like nothing else. The best feeling there is in the whole entire goddamn world.

But the bit afterwards, well, I've always loathed that bit. Stuck with an omega who either has nothing to say or far too much. Unlike Declan, I've never been one for hugging and cuddling. Once I've knotted her, I want out.

It's why I've steered away from one-night stands and why my relationships have never lasted.

Not today though. Not with this girl. Not with the way my bond hums in my stomach and her sweet pussy convulses around my cock. Not with her sugary perfume in my nose and my teeth marks in her neck. Not with her strange thoughts swirling around her mind. The girl is crazy, her thoughts chaotic. It's fascinating. Like a hard slap around the face. Like waking up after years of walking around in a daze. Like seeing in color for the first time.

Like fresh air.

I lick at her wound. I can't help myself. I'm obsessed with how good it looks, with how good it tastes, with how it makes her shiver.

"Could you," she pauses to hum in contentment, "could you do that purring thing you did yesterday?"

"You liked that?"

"I'm an omega. You are my mate – for now anyway." I suppress a growl because, after all, she's right. Temporary, Cruise. This is just temporary. "I'm programmed to like it."

"Okay," I say, clearing my throat and making her giggle. The laughter dies on her lips though, when I begin to purr for her. Her body goes limp in my arms and melts against mine. If my cock wasn't locked in her pussy, I'd be fucking her all over again. In fact ...

I reach between her legs and stroke her clit.

This is possibly the best morning of my life and–

"Cruise!"

Of course, that means it has to be interrupted.

"Cruise, are you in there!"

Declan.

"If we kept quiet, do you think he'd go away?" the omega whispers, her voice all husky on account of all the screaming and moaning she's been doing.

"We can try."

"Cruise! Where are you, man? You know we have the board meeting this morning, right?"

"Shit!" I groan. I'd forgotten. Completely forgotten.

I don't forget things. That is not like me.

Footsteps echo down the hallway, pausing outside the bedroom door and then the handle rattles.

"Cruise, what the fuck?"

"I'm sick," I say, thinking of the first thing that enters my mind. He isn't going to believe it. I haven't taken a sick day in ten years.

"Bullshit!" Declan says. "Get your ass out here now! I'm already fending off Kent over at the house. He's about to rip you a new asshole."

"Declan," I say firmly. "I can't."

"Can't what?"

The omega shakes in my arms, biting her lip to stop from giggling despite my stern look.

"I can't get my ass out there." My knot is still rock hard and locked into the omega's pussy. Usually, it's deflated by now and I've made my escape, but my knot seems to be in agreement with me. It's happy just where it is and there's no sign of it deflating any time soon.

"Cruise, are you fucking the omega?"

I don't answer.

"Shit, you are, aren't you? You dirty bastard."

"That's my husband you're talking about," the omega calls out before I can stop her. "He's not a dirty bastard. He's a perfect gentleman, and this was entirely consensual."

"We're meant to be leaving for the board meeting in five minutes!"

"Not going to happen," the omega says.

"Cruise, put the omega down."

"I told you, I can't."

"She's very cute, and she smells delicious, but you–"

"His cock is knotted in my pussy."

Declan swears and I hear his forehead knock against the wood of the door. "Fuck, you knotted her?" he moans.

"Just tell the others I'm ill, will you?"

"You need to come tell them the truth."

"I will, just not right now. Not before the board meeting. Cover for me, Declan."

He huffs out air. "Okay, okay."

He doesn't move. "Declan?"

"Just give me a minute here, will you? I'm ..." He groans. "You're knotted to her, right now?"

"Yes."

He's silent, and then he asks quietly, "How does it feel?"

The omega peers up at my face.

"How do you think?"

"Tell me, Cruise, or I swear to god I won't help you out, man."

"How *does* it feel?" the omega asks with curiosity, her head tilting to one side.

Those dark eyes of hers could drive a man wild. Flirtatious, seductive.

I'm entranced by them.

"I'm not a poet," I say, holding her gaze. "I don't have the ability to describe it. But trust me when I say, I want to do this to you over and over again."

"I think I could get on board with that."

"You could, huh?" I say, finding her clit again and stroking that sensitive little nub of hers.

She's all swollen and sensitive and this simple touch has her moaning.

"Jesus Christ!" Declan groans.

We both glance towards the door.

"I forgot he was there," the omega whispers.

Me too. I am not a forgetful person. Not when it comes to my packmates.

"You sound so good, Omega," he whines. And I feel bad for my packmate. If it was me on the other side of the door, I'd be chewing my own knuckles. The omega's scent is all heightened and intense. It's enough to drive a man mad.

"She looks even better," I concede.

She smiles, her eyes drifting shut and her legs trembling as I continue to stroke her.

"Does he want to see?" she whispers so quietly I almost don't hear.

My hand freezes. She opens her eyes in alarm, her cheeks pinkening.

"I'm sorry, I didn't–"

"Are you serious?"

Her face flushes even redder. "It just sort of tumbled out, but, I mean, you know, being with a pack is every omega's ultimate fantasy."

Every omega wants a pack. That doesn't mean every omega gets one. Omegas are rare. But packs are even rarer.

She chews her lip, all sorts of images whizz through her mind. Hot images I want to make real. "But I don't want to–"

"Can I let him in?" I ask.

She nods, those dark eyes of hers turning even darker.

"Declan?" I call out, "are you still there?"

"I'm still here," he says woefully.

"The omega wants you to come in and watch as I make her come with my fingers."

The omega whimpers and I'm pretty sure I hear Declan fall to his knees.

"Are you messing with me, man?"

"She's very close," I say, "she's a sensitive little thing. Do you want to miss this?"

He has the door crashing open in the next second, slamming it shut behind him and staring towards the bed with wild eyes. He's dressed in his best suit, tie straight, jacket buttoned up, shoes shining, but his face is flushed, his usually neatly tamed curls messy around his face.

"Shiiiiiitttt," he groans as he takes in our combined bodies, his gaze falling eagerly to where I'm locked into her pussy.

She looks up at the other alpha in the room and with a mischievous smile, says, "Hi."

And I know it's far, far too early to be saying this, but I think I may be falling in love with my wife.

Chapter Nine

D^{eclan}

I am meant to be presenting at a major board meeting for our company in less than twenty minutes.

Instead, I'm standing in one of the bedrooms of our pool house staring down at my packmate knotted to an omega he married 48-hours ago and getting her off with his fingers.

Did I step into an alternative reality? Am I dreaming?

If I am, this is one of the best sex dreams of my life.

Because not only is the omega stunning – cute and curvy, wholesome looking if it weren't for those dark eyes and pouty lips – she also smells divine. Sounds divine too as he rubs at her clit and all these moans and whimpers fall from her lips.

Her legs shake on the bed and my packmate groans. I can imagine why. I bet that pussy of hers is milking his cock hard, especially when her skin flushes, her head falls backwards, and the pleasure seems to swim through her body.

"Fuuuuccckkk!" I mutter and I can't help but drop to my knees by the side of the bed to get a better look.

We haven't had a lot of time for omegas since our business took off and we hit the big time. We've been working our asses off keeping a company the size of a small country running effectively, dodging mothers who want to set us up plus gold-diggers and honey-traps. It's been easier just to say no to it all.

But is this what we've been missing out on?

The omega jolts on the bed as aftershocks claim her and I spy the wound on her neck the shape of my packmate's jaw, where he sunk his teeth and claimed her.

I don't think anything has ever made me harder, especially when he leans down to ring his tongue over the indents.

"Wow," I mutter, and the omega opens her eyes and looks up into mine.

"I know," she says dreamily, "your packmate is one very skilled man."

I chuckle. "He's a bit of a perfectionist. If he's going to do a job, he likes to do it right."

"Hmmm," she says. "I like that."

"I bet you do. Are you one of those spoiled little omegas who likes to get her way?"

"I wish," she says, with a little too much regret.

I glance up at Cruise, but I'm guessing he knows only slightly more about his new wife than I do.

"Not been spoiled enough, huh? Well, we'll have to put that right while you're staying with us, won't we?"

She considers me, biting her lip. "What did you have in mind?" she asks.

I have a whole host of ideas, many of them too X-rated to describe with words, but my thoughts are interrupted by the loud blare of my phone in my breast-pocket.

The board meeting.

I usually love these things. Correction, I live for them. I'm the salesman of the pack. The one that can sweet talk investors, schmooze with the big fish, and close the deal. Board meetings are my chance to shine.

Today, I'd rather boil my own balls.

"Duty calls?" the omega asks.

"Yeah," I say, running my finger around the collar of my shirt. A shirt that's feeling a million times tighter. How am I meant to get through this meeting when I know the image of the omega coming will be replaying around and around my mind? I'm going to have a permanent hard-on.

I take a deep exhale and lumber up to my feet.

I'm also going to have to cover for Cruise. There is no way in hell I'm going to be able to pry the man away from the omega. The way he's holding her tightly in his arms, like he won't be letting her go, tells me that. Shit, I've never seen him hold anyone like that before.

"I really hate to leave, little omega, but I've got to get to a board meeting," I say with the disappointment clear in my voice.

"You take your work very seriously," she says, with a little brattish pout.

"We all do," I say, glancing at Cruise – work clearly the last thing on his mind as he nibbles her throat.

Somehow, with a hell of a lot of determination, self-control and willpower, I drag myself out of the pool house and go to meet my other packmates waiting for me out front.

"What the hell took so long?" Kent asks, the lines of tension clear across his brow. "Where's Cruise?"

"And why the hell do you smell like that?" Max asks, coming right up close to me and sniffing.

I can spin a yarn – it's part of the game we play as businessmen. There were plenty of times I bent the truth in the early days of our corporation – convincing investors we had more backers than we did, portraying more confidence in our products than we had, pretending we were further along on our developments than we were.

This time, I choose the truth. This situation is too fucked up not to.

"Cruise is in a bed with an omega. He won't be coming to the meeting."

My three packmates – Kent, Max, and Jonah – all gape at me like I just spouted a load of ancient Arabic at them.

Max slaps my back and chuckles. "Yeah, good one, Declan."

"I'm serious," I say.

Max shakes his head with a big grin. "Cruise wouldn't miss a board meeting if his own mother was on her deathbed. He definitely wouldn't miss one for an omega."

I shrug. "Well, he is."

"Cruise?" Jonah says, adjusting his glasses on the bridge of his nose. "Where would Cruise even find an omega?"

"You should ask him," I mutter.

The lines on Kent's forehead grow deeper and steelier.

"Look, it's going to be fine. Jonah you can cover his slides in the presentation and between Max and I, we can field any questions."

"I'm going to wring his neck."

"There isn't time," Jonah says.

Kent's knuckles whiten. "As soon as we get back. As soon as we get back, I'm wringing his neck. And if the omega is still here, I'll be tossing her out too."

I peer over my shoulder towards the pool house.

Yeah, I don't think that is going to happen.

Chapter Ten

A^{very}

The alpha wasn't lying. He said he wants to knot me again and again and that is what we do, uninterrupted this time, for the next two hours.

It's like a heat, except I'm not all dazed out. I'm in the moment and very much loving that moment.

But by mid-morning, my stomach is rumbling like crazy, and the alpha is determined, despite my best efforts to convince him otherwise, to feed me.

"Get dressed," he tells me, "we're heading to the main house and I'm cooking you more pancakes."

"Can't we have one of those private chefs of yours deliver us food in bed?" I say, trailing my fingers down his chest.

"No."

"And the packmates?"

"Still at the board meeting."

"Fine," I huff, "but I'm jumping in the shower first."

He shakes his head and I incline mine.

"Is there a problem with me showering?" I ask.

"Yes," he says, "I like you smelling of me. I like you full of me," he adds with a growl.

I swallow. The man has an ability to say exceedingly hot things. "Okay, but just so you know, this isn't how our week-long marriage is going to go. I am not the obedient little housewife type."

"You couldn't be obedient for me?"

I lift my eyebrow. "If you ask me to pick up your boxers and scrub the toilets—"

"How about if I told you to drop to your knees and open your mouth?"

I swallow again. "I thought we were making pancakes."

"We are. I'm just curious."

"Well, until you give the order, you'll have to remain curious."

"Hmmm," he says in a way that suggests he's mighty tempted to give that order right now. However, my stomach growls at him and he nudges me out of bed.

The main house is even more impressive inside than it is outside. We walk through the doors and straight into a vast open-plan space, so cavernous it reminds me more of a cathedral than a house, the ceiling high above me and the Rockview sunshine streaming through the endless windows of glass.

A huge Neapolitan Mastiff comes padding down the hallway towards us. I gasp and Cruise steps in front of me, bending down to greet the dog.

"It's okay, Avery, he may look tough, but he's a massive softie."

"He's gorgeous," I say, stepping around the alpha and crouching down so my face is level with the dog's droopy face. "And handsome."

I pause for a moment, letting the dog sniff my face eagerly and then I reach out and scrub under his ears. "Aren't you quite the distinguished gentleman?" I say to him as he closes his eyes in pleasure.

"Gentleman?" Cruise says. "Barney is pushing fifteen and spends most of his time farting."

I look up at Cruise. "Are you telling me, Mr. Hamilton, that you have never farted in your life?"

"Not as much as Barney here."

"Don't you listen to the grumpy alpha, Barney. You're delightful."

"Come on," Cruise says, taking my elbow and dragging me to my feet. "If you don't stop now, he'll never let you go."

"I'm fine with that."

"Yes, but you need to eat." He pulls me along to the kitchen, the dog plodding after us.

In the doorway, I stand for a good few minutes swinging my head backwards and forward, as Barney settles himself down on a mat in the corner.

It's also gigantic with a mixture of sleek lines and complicated gadgets and a large solid-looking dining table – big enough to seat at least eighteen.

"Hamilton," Cruise says directing his voice towards the black cube nestling in one corner, "I need the recipe for pancakes."

The Hamilton device lights up, and a robotic voice lists the ingredients as the alpha fishes out egg cartons and milk from the fridge.

When he's done, he turns around to find me standing there with my hands on my hips.

"You don't know how to make pancakes?"

"No."

"It's really easy."

"Omega, I can build a computer from scratch and write a code for just about anything you can imagine."

"But you can't make pancakes?"

"I'm sure I can make pancakes."

"Hand it over," I say, motioning towards the ingredients.

"I can follow a recipe."

"We don't need one. Mixing bowl and wooden spoon please."

"Hamilton: Mixing bowl and wooden spoon."

"Mixing bowl: cupboards under the grill. Wooden spoon: main cutlery drawer," the robotic voice answers.

"Seriously," I say. "You couldn't just look?"

"It's much more efficient to ask Hamilton. He knows where everything is stored in this house."

"How convenient for any robbers who break in." I roll my eyes and hop up onto the counter. "Hamilton: tell me where the safe is."

The device blinks red. "Voice not recognized. I am not authorized to answer this question."

The alpha grins. "Our security system is top-notch."

"Hamilton. If a robber breaks in, where should I be sure not to have them search for a safe."

The device whirrs, its lights blinking.

"You know, it listens to your conversations," I say.

"You know we designed this tech and that is an urban myth."

"It's not. Jacks has one of these things in her apartment and the other day we had this long conversation about our friend Bilbo. The next day dildo adverts were all that flashed up on her phone."

"She was probably shopping for dildos without telling you."

"She tells me everything."

"Including her masturbation habits?"

"Everything," I say with emphasis.

He places a bowl, a spoon and the ingredients on the counter next to me.

"Tell me, those private chefs – are they human or robots?"

"Humans."

"But I bet you have robots here, don't you?"

"Not ones that can cook food – although we're working on that."

"Sex robots," I ask, narrowing my eyes. "There are dudes all over the internet claiming you tech guys are designing robots to replace women."

"We do not have a sex robot."

"But you have a robot?"

He sighs. "Hamilton: send OGE 300 into the kitchen."

There's a distant whirring noise that grows louder and louder and then a tiny little circular robot glides into the kitchen. Barney lifts his head from his paws and barks at it in disgust.

"What does he do?"

"It cleans the floors."

"And?"

"That's all."

I watch as the robot glides across the floor backward and forward avoiding chairs, the counter and the door.

"He is so cute," I say, watching as he bumbles through the legs of a chair.

"Cute?"

"You should name him. Give him a little bowtie." The alpha shakes his head like I'm insane. "I bet you would sell twice as many. Hamilton: order OGE a bowtie."

"Ordering a bowtie. What color would you like?"

"Hamilton cancel order," the alpha snaps.

"So," I say, "Hamilton won't open the safe for me, but I could get him to order me anything I wanted." The alpha scowls at me. "Like a yacht. Or a diamond. I bet you haven't set a spending limit."

The alpha whips out his phone and types out a message.

"What are you doing?"

"Making a note to review our security."

I smile and pull the bowl towards me, dumping a load of flour inside. Then I fetch an egg and lift it to my head, smacking the shell against my forehead.

"What are you doing?" the alpha asks in disbelief.

"Cracking the egg," I say, breaking it in half and letting the insides slop into the bowl.

"That is not how you break an egg."

"It is in our family."

He stares at me like I am definitely insane. I bet he is regretting this marriage and bonding even more than he was before.

"It's just a silly thing my dad started when we were little. He always cracked the egg on our heads. And now that's how we do it."

The robot comes zooming towards us, bumping against the alpha's feet. Barney barks again but doesn't bother to come and defend his master. He reaches down and switches him off.

I stir the mixture, adding in the milk.

"So, tell me Cruise Hamilton, how much trouble are you going to be in for missing this meeting?"

He leans backwards and crosses his arms over his chest.

I'm guessing that means a lot.

Chapter Eleven

Kent

"Just relax," Declan whispers tersely to me as we make our way through the Hamilton building and up to the board room. "You look like someone stuck a rod up your ass. It's making everyone nervous."

I grind my teeth. "I'm going to kill him."

"I know you said that. But put it to one side. There will be enough rumors circulating about his absence without you adding fuel to the fire."

He's right. So I try. Try to loosen up my shoulders and blow the fury away. But it doesn't work. As Jonah talks the board through our latest investment and expansion plans, I can feel my shoulders winding tighter and tighter. I can't stop my leg from jiggling under the table and my knuckles bleach white through the taut skin of my fists.

What the hell is he thinking?

Women are trouble. Omegas even more so. We learned that the hard way early on in our success and we've wisely kept away from them ever since.

Now Cruise is ditching board meetings for a chance to roll around in bed with some girl. A girl he's brought back to the house.

We don't do that. It isn't part of the plan.

"Kent?"

Declan elbows me and I peer across the board room to find Robert Wiseman addressing me.

"Yes, Robert," I say, forcing my leg to still.

"You're not in agreement with these plans?"

"I'm 100 percent in agreement with these plans. I don't know why you would think otherwise."

Robert taps his pen against the table and shakes his head. "You sure don't look happy about them."

"Just a bit of a headache today."

"Maybe you're coming down with whatever Cruise has caught," Janice Preer says, sending Robert a knowing look.

"Perhaps," I say, managing a pat smile.

Declan pats me on the shoulder. "You know how this business works, folks, if we're not all in agreement it doesn't happen. This is a pack business after all."

I tune out as my packmates answer more questions, Declan working his magic to charm them all and Jonah bewildering them with all the data and numbers.

When it comes to the vote at the close of the meeting, I'm hardly aware of the proceedings, Declan having to nudge me again, so I raise my hand at the appropriate time. Then we're shaking hands and saying goodbyes.

Declan flops down in the chair when the last board member leaves, grinning from ear to ear.

"That went well."

Max laughs. "Was there any doubt?"

Without Cruise there, yes it was. He could have cost us that vote.

"How about we crack open the Jack Daniels and celebrate?" Declan suggests, but I'm already heading for the door.

"Where are you going?" Max calls.

"Back to the house."

"But we have–"

"I don't give a damn."

This girl is bound to be trouble and I need her out of the house, out of our lives, before she digs her claws into Cruise and causes a whole heap more trouble.

I growl as I storm through the building, ignoring the various 'Good morning Mr. Hamiltons'.

I could expect this of Declan, maybe Max too. But Cruise? He doesn't even like sex that much. Or women. He's almost as obsessed with the business and the numbers as I am. This is his love, his passion. Building an empire. And a legacy. Transforming the world.

Not some girl.

As I reach the foyer, I can hear my packmates chasing after me. I don't wait for them. I head straight for my car and speed out of the executive parking lot.

When I reach the house forty minutes later, I fly out of the car, not even bothering to slam the door shut behind me, and through the front door. There I halt in my tracks.

It's the scent. Sugary. Sweet. Vivid. So bright I can almost see it hovering in the air. It hits me square in the sinuses, penetrates right through to my nervous system.

I huff out air through my nostrils, wetting my tongue to dislodge the taste and shaking my head.

Sound permeates in the direction of the kitchen. Music and ... giggling.

A light feminine sound that irritates my skin.

I lower my head like a bull about to charge and stride in that direction.

The sight that greets me from the kitchen doorway has me halting in my tracks a second time.

Cruise is standing by the stove, unshaven, a massive fuck-off grin on his face, wearing a t-shirt and shorts. I haven't seen the dude in a pair of shorts since college. He has a frying pan in one hand.

A small woman stands behind him. Her body leaned right into his, one arm wrapped around his waist, the other curled around his hand.

"Ready?" the woman asks with a tease.

"You know I can do this myself."

"We've already lost two precious pancakes to the floor, Alpha. Just admit you need me to show you how."

"Show me how," he says in a flirtatious voice I don't think I've ever heard my packmate use.

I glance down towards the floor, finding Barney in his bed. He lifts his brows.

"One, two, three," the woman says, and together they jerk the pan upwards, the pancake flying high up into the air, flipping over 180 degrees and then falling. The woman screeches and they yank the frying pan left, the pancake hitting the base.

"Yes!" she says, holding out her hand for him to high five. Cruise turns slightly to reach her hand and in doing so, spots me in the doorway.

"Cruise, a word please," I say stiffly.

The smile on the woman's face falls away.

"Avery," Cruise says. "This is my packmate, Kent. Kent, this is Avery."

I don't say a word, refusing to meet her eye even when she says, "Nice to meet you."

"Cruise, a word."

He considers me for a minute. Obviously debating whether to give me that word. Then he nods curtly.

"Think you can manage the rest?" he asks the omega.

"Possibly. I may also have eaten them all in about a minute flat."

Cruise actually chuckles and motions his head towards the doorway. We step out of the kitchen, and I begin to walk further down the hallway in the direction of my office, somewhere we won't be overheard, when Cruise lands his hand on my shoulder.

"That's far enough," he says.

"What?" I say as I hear three other cars pull up on the drive and our packmates bundle through into the house.

"I said, that's far enough," he repeats.

"I'd prefer we had this conversation somewhere private," I hiss.

Cruise simply stares at me as Declan, Jonah and Max come to a stop by my side.

"This is as good a place as any. Say what you have to say, Kent."

"And that's it? That's your reaction? No 'sorry I bailed and screwed you all over for some chick'. Are you for real? You realize Jonah had to pick up all your slides and field all your questions."

"It was no problem," Jonah says, holding up his hand.

"It made us look stupid. Divided. I can guarantee half the board will be on their phones to each other discussing this. Right now."

"I am sorry. I would have been there if I could."

I consider swinging back my fist and smacking my pack-mate square on that perfectly chiseled jaw of his. But I am too damn shocked by the nerve of the man.

"And what exactly was stopping you?"

Cruise scratches the back of his neck and peers through the gap in the doorway towards the omega. She's sitting on the countertop, legs swinging, ladling a piece of pancake streaming with maple syrup towards her mouth.

She tips back her head and captures the running sauce between her lips, licking them with a soft groan before taking the whole piece in her mouth.

For a moment the five of us just stare. Then I remember I'm fucking mad.

"Women are trouble. You've known her, what? A day? And you're already ditching one of the most important meetings of our career."

"You're exaggerating," Cruise says.

I take a step towards him, and Declan grabs the back of my suit jacket.

"Just tell him, Cruise," he says, attempting to hold me back.

Cruise takes a steadying breath, and, continuing to scratch his neck, looks at us all with sheepish eyes.

My stomach drops.

What the hell?

"I bit her."

"Is she threatening to sue you?" Jonah asks, adjusting his glasses.

"A claiming bite. We're bonded."

More silence. Only the soft moans of the omega enjoying her pancakes and the angry beat of my heart.

"You *what?!*" Max finally chokes out as I break free from Declan and swing my fist right into Cruise's face.

His head snaps backward, then forwards, and he charges towards me.

"Stop it!" Declan says.

But we don't. He locks his arms around my waist, attempting to tackle me to the floor, and I pummel my fists into his back. In the next moment, the other three are there too, attempting to pry us apart. Max receives a smack on his cheek in the process and Jonah a knee to the groin. And then we're all fighting, tumbling to the floor in a tangle of wrestling alpha bodies.

Someone smacks me in the ribs, someone else rips my jacket, and I receive a foot to the shin. In return, I hit someone in the gut and deliver someone else a dead leg.

"Ahem." It's that scent again. Sweet, tantalizing, sugary.

Everyone freezes.

I peer up, my arm locked around Declan's neck.

"Is everything all right here?" The omega stands above us all, licking syrup from her fingertips. She's dressed in one of Cruise's t-shirts – which she's tied around her middle revealing a flash of soft stomach – and a pair of teeny tiny shorts that hug her ass and leave her legs bare.

Declan and Cruise manage to clamber to their feet almost immediately, Cruise looking even more sheepish. Jonah and Max follow quickly after, looking at the omega with clear interest.

I take my time, brushing off dirt from my ripped suit as I do.

I swallow blood and wipe the back of my hand over my mouth.

Then I glare right at the omega, meeting a pair of amused dark eyes.

"I don't know who the hell you are or how you pulled this off, but I am going to find out."

"Pulled what off?" she asks all feigned innocence.

My gaze falls to the very vivid bite mark on her shoulder. All new and raw. It has my cock twitching and that makes me all the more angry.

"That!" I say, pointing to the mark before storming away.

The little con artist may have fooled my packmate but not me.

Chapter Twelve

Avery

The four remaining alphas line up before me, each in a state of disarray. Cruise has a bruise blooming across his cheek. Blood trails from the corner of Declan's mouth, his teeth all red. The third alpha has long fair hair that I assume was tied back neatly and is now a tangle about his face. And the glasses of the fourth and final alpha perch on the bridge of his nose at a peculiar angle. All of their shirts are pulled from their pants, buttons missing, ties askew.

They look like a bunch of naughty schoolboys who just got caught pinching candy from the teacher's desk.

"There are pancakes if any of you are feeling hungry after your ..." I suppress a giggle and point to the floor.

Then I turn and return to the kitchen, the sound of four large alphas bundling after me.

I could get used to that. I could probably get used to the

sight of five alphas wrestling around on the floor too, if they hadn't been fighting about me.

I tuck it away as future fantasy material. I'll revise it. In my fantasy version, the alphas will be fighting over who gets to give me the next foot massage or put the bins out.

Cruise raises an eyebrow at me, and I pick up the plate of pancakes and thrust them forward.

"They're really good," I say. "Cruise made them."

"Cruise?" Declan says, glancing at his packmate.

Cruise shrugs one shoulder and hooks a pancake off the plate, rolling it between his fingers.

"Would you like one, erm …?" I ask the large alpha with the long hair.

"Max," the alpha says, obediently taking a pancake too, eyes locked on my face in a way that has me blushing and moving on to the final packmate.

"And you?"

The alpha adjusts his glasses, making them slightly less wonky on his nose, then he takes a pancake too. "I'm Jonah. And you are?"

"Avery."

"Avery," the two packmates say together in a way that has my insides spinning.

"And how did you meet, Cruise, Avery?" Max asks, his intense eyes not leaving my face.

"In Las Vegas."

Max peers over at Cruise who is fiddling with the coffee machine. "And you just decided …"

"I know what your packmate thinks. And although he is clearly a giant asshole with no manners and a temper problem, I can see his point. You're rich, and famous and," I gulp, "good looking. I bet you must have omegas falling over themselves just to get within three feet of you."

"I bet you have alphas falling over themselves to meet *you*, Avery," Max says without a hint of sarcasm.

"Not exactly." I screw up my face. "But honestly, neither of us even remember how this happened. I guess we were both drunk and got carried away in the moment or something. I mean, I've done some crazy stuff in my life, but nothing this crazy. To date. Anyway. I'd say that this must be the official most crazy Avery-thing I've done so far, replacing all previous records."

"What crazy stuff?" Jonah asks.

Heat crawls up my neck towards my cheeks. Damn it. I walked straight into that. "You'd probably have to get me very drunk again for me to tell you."

"Hmmm," Declan says with what I think is a twinkle in his eye.

"Cruise doesn't usually drink," Jonah says, observing his packmate as he sets two cups of coffee on the counter and returns to the machine.

"Me neither," I sigh, "I'm a disastrous drunk. As you can see." I hold out my hands. "But really, this wasn't part of some master plan. I'm hopeless at planning. Ask my sister. If she hadn't reminded me, I'd have turned up at the airport without my ticket." I swing my gaze around the three packmates, wondering if they are in any way convinced. "I didn't even know who Cruise was."

Declan laughs. "I bet that dented his ego."

"No," Cruise says, placing a cup down in front of me. "It was refreshing."

"Anyway," I say, ignoring the way his confession pleases all those omega instincts, "I'll only be here for a week, until the bond wears off, and I'll keep out of your hair and–"

"Keep Cruise from attending any meetings," Declan says with a grin, making my cheeks sizzle.

"He didn't tell me he had a big meeting," I mumble.

"I wouldn't have been able to go anyway given our ..."

"I could have come with you."

"I'm sure he spent his time much more productively," Declan says, reaching across the counter to retrieve the sugar and whispering in my ear as he does. "Making you come."

I wasn't kidding about my craziness. I have a habit of landing myself in stupid trouble. Nearly always of my own making. Right this second is no exception because those words, and the way he says them, full of heat, has slick trickling into my panties.

Honestly, what is wrong with me? Is it the fresh mating bond? I'm like a slick tap.

The aroma of my slick is pretty unmistakable, and all four alphas must smell it, because all four alphas bristle. The tension in the air electric.

"Well, it was nice meeting you all," I squeak. "But I guess I'd better do as I say and get out of your way now so you can return to whatever you have to do and–"

"Have you tasted that?" Max asks Cruise in a growl so deep, I have to concentrate damn hard not to slick some more.

"Yes," Cruise says simply, holding his packmate's gaze.

"She taste as good as she smells? As good as she looks?"

"Better," Cruise says.

Max's eyes snap towards me and the heat in his expression is enough to have my knees buckling.

I've never been around a pack before. I'm an average omega. Not some rich spoiled one from the upper reaches of Rockview society. Any packs back home are snapped up quickly by the kind of omegas who can tuck their legs behind their heads and have family money enough to purchase yachts as wedding gifts. Packs have no interest in the likes of me.

Of course, that hasn't stopped me dreaming of a pack, even though I know I'll most probably end up marrying a nice beta guy. Or if I'm lucky, a lone wolf alpha type. I'm perfectly okay with that. Packs and all that come with them are a really really nice dream and all, but I bet the reality is like what I witnessed in the hall. Fighting and squabbling. Although, having said that, the fighting was really hot – and completely childish. But also hot. Very hot.

As is being in the presence of four alphas who – am I imagining this? – look like they may want to eat me?

Oh, they want to eat you all right! Cruise says through the bond, and I squeal and race as fast as my little legs will carry me to the safety of the pool house.

Chapter Thirteen

Avery

Except the pool house isn't really safe. Especially when the alpha is forced to follow after me by the strength of the bond. Especially when his scent fills the air, mingling with the smell of ... erm ... sex. Especially when the bedroom is dominated by the giant bed with its tangled sheets and it's very hard not to relive everything we were doing here a few hours ago.

"I need to call my sister," I say, retreating to the room furthest from the bedroom, and opening all the windows.

"My packmates haven't finished talking with me. We're going to have to go back over there."

"After I've spoken to my sister," I tell him. I just need a moment to clear my head and regain my senses. My very sensible older sister is the person to help me do that.

I sink down onto a chair and check my messages.

There's several from Isla, demanding to know whether I am still alive or not, one from Jacks telling me she's about to board her flight to Rockview, and one from my parents congratulating me on the new job.

I call my sister.

"New job?" I say when she answers.

"I had to tell them something."

"So, what did you tell them exactly?"

"That you were scouted in the casino for a part in a film, shooting out in Rockview. That you'd be there for a few weeks and that Jacks was heading out to chaperone you."

"And they bought that?"

"They grilled me half to death, but I held firm to my story. You owe me one."

"You're a tougher woman than me." I fold like a stack of cards as soon as my dad twists the interrogation lamp my way.

"I know," Isla says. "So how are things going? Are you okay? I've spent half the night worrying about you."

Guilt swims through my gut. I can just imagine Isla pacing around her bedroom, conjuring ever increasingly awful scenarios in her head, when in reality I've spent the last few hours either curled up with an extremely hot alpha or being knotted by him.

I suppress a little whimper at the thought.

"I'm just fine. They are behaving like perfect gentlemen," I say, which is sort of true if you ignore the way the alpha fucked me over the side of the bed while yanking on my hair, the little ruckus in the hallway, and the way one of the alphas had called me a scam artist to my face. All things I decide are best kept secret from Isla.

"What are they like?" she says, with more curiosity now. "I've been Googling them. Their reputation is confusing.

Some paint them as ruthless, cut-throat business moguls who would toss their mothers under the bus for a deal. Others as nerdy, socially inept geeks."

"I don't think they're either of those things."

"So, what have you been doing all day? Are they at least keeping you entertained?"

"Oh, you know," I say, hearing the alpha shuffling on the other side of the closed door.

"I don't like the idea that they've shut you up in some cupboard–"

"Cupboard?" I laugh. "You've been reading too much mafia romance again, Isla. Like I said, gentlemen. Perfect manners."

"Hmmm," she says. "They haven't tried anything funny, have they? Just because you accidentally bonded to their packmate doesn't mean–"

"Maybe I'd want them to try something funny," I murmur.

"Avery," my sister warns.

"What?" I say, feeling rebellious. This isn't the way this conversation is meant to be going. She is meant to be persuading me against funny business. Not tempting me into it.

"I know what you're like. You jump in head first with your heart on a platter and end up with your feelings all smashing to pieces."

"I do not!"

"Alexander Cheesam."

"That was high school."

"Your coach."

"It was a phase."

"Henry Smith."

"I hardly shed a tear when he ended things."

"Lies."

"I'm not going to get emotionally involved. But you're not here, Isla. You try being in close proximity to five very hot alphas. They smell like ..." I groan.

"Oh God," she says. "When does Jacks get there?"

"Later this afternoon."

"I'm calling her right now with instructions to watch you like a hawk."

"I am a grown adult, Isla. I don't need someone babysitting me."

"Says the girl who accidentally got herself bonded to an alpha she had only just met!" my sister says with exasperation. "These are rich men, Avery. They'll be entitled and spoiled. Used to having their own way. Used to using people and disposing of them. Be careful."

I peer towards the door. Is that what Cruise is doing? Using me for sex while I'm here, then as soon as the bond weakens, he'll be packing my bags and tossing me out the front door.

Does it matter if he does? In the meantime, I get to live in luxury and enjoy the best sex of my life.

"I'll bear that in mind, Isla," I say, promising to keep in touch and hanging up.

I let my phone drop onto my lap and my head fall back against the cushions of the chair.

"Are you all right in there?" Cruise calls out from the other side of the door.

"Who? Me?" I say.

There's a pause. "Is there anyone else in there with you?"

"No."

"Then you."

"I'm fine."

I stretch, feeling a little sore in places that haven't felt sore in some time and pad towards the door. When I open it, an alpha falls backward into the room, landing with a thud by my feet.

I peer down at him. "Were you listening to my conversation?"

"I can read the thoughts in your head," he reminds me.

"Right," I say, my cheeks blazing for about the millionth time this day as I try to recall all the embarrassing thoughts that have been swimming through my head.

"You're worried I'm using you for sex – or at least your sister is. But you're not sure you mind."

"Are you? Using me for sex?" I ask as he continues to peer up at me.

"I hadn't planned on it. I planned on being a good alpha, a gentleman," he says, his eyes twinkling with mischief, "but it's pretty hard."

My eyes flick down to his groin where it most definitely is hard. "And why's that?" I ask, resting one hand on my hip.

He groans a little, gaze floating down my body. "You're pretty hot, little omega, you smell wet and sweet and delicious, and the thoughts that spin around your head are dirty as hell."

"Like this one?" I ask, sending him an image of the idea his position lying on the floor is generating in my head.

"Fuuuuuck!" he says. "Take off those ridiculous little shorts and your panties and get down here now."

I shiver. We should be talking about his packmates. We should also be talking more about the 'using-each-other-for-sex' thing.

"It can wait, Omega. Do as you're told."

I give him my best bratty look and take my time sliding

my shorts and then my panties down my legs. He watches with an intensity that has me throbbing between my legs, and he licks his lips.

When I'm bare, he reaches his hands up in the air and beckons me down. I step toward him and kneel on the plush carpet. Immediately, he takes a hold of my thighs and drags me forward until I'm hovering directly above his head.

"Sit on my face, Omega," he barks, and I lower myself down. He uses his strong arms to stop me crushing him, holding me so I hover right above his mouth, his breath warm against my most intimate parts.

"This view is ..." he mutters.

"It's not half bad from up here either," I sigh, gazing down at his muscular body before me.

He lowers me closer, right down on his mouth and spends a good minute French-kissing my pussy with such enthusiasm I lose the ability to breathe. In fact, I don't think I've ever met a man do anything to my pussy with such enthusiasm.

He growls, his mouth vibrating against me, making my eyes roll back in their sockets, and then he lifts me a little higher and begins sweeping his tongue through my folds, backwards and forwards, until my legs are shaking, and I'm gushing slick right into his face.

I feel like an actual princess sat up here on his face like it's some kind of throne – a very pleasurable, dirty throne.

He flicks at my clit and just as I'm about to tumble right over the edge, he leaves me hanging and fucks me with his tongue.

I go slightly wild, unable to help but grind myself against his mouth, begging him to make me come. His fingers dig more tightly into my thighs, and I can see how hard he is through his pants.

Tears stream down my cheeks, my skin flushes hot and if I don't come soon, I might combust.

But he seems hellbent on torturing me, playing with my clit again before he goes back to sucking and kissing my folds.

"Alpha, please! Please make me come."

"Little mate," he murmurs into my pussy, "you're mine. You do as I say, and you come when I tell you."

I can't help it. It's something about those words – far too fucking hot. I come loud and messy, bolting around on top of his face like I'm riding a bucking bronco.

When it ends, I'm all breathless and dizzy and he lifts me off his face and scrabbles up onto his knees.

"I didn't say you could come," he says.

"I couldn't help it," I moan.

"An omega should do as her alpha says," he tells me firmly.

"So, what will you do about it?" I say, hoping this is going in a certain direction.

He examines my flushed face. "Spank you."

I whimper and he knows there's nothing I would like more.

"Shit, you really are a dirty girl." He shakes his head. "On your hands and knees."

I pout and do as I'm told, my backside pointed right in his direction.

He spends a few minutes simply squeezing and palming my ass, then without warning he slaps me across my left ass cheek.

It sends a delicious jolt through my pussy, and I moan.

"Harder," I whisper.

"Harder?" he says. He rubs his palm over the place he's

just hit me, then strikes me again, this time with a little more force and I call out as another jolt spins through my core.

"You like that?" he chuckles. "It's meant to be a punishment."

"Bad girls tend to enjoy their punishments."

"You're not a bad girl. You're a very very good one." He smacks me twice more, even harder this time, so I'm knocked forward and the combination of my smarting cheek and the thrill to my pussy is divine.

He slaps me three more times until I'm dribbling slick. Then his mouth is back between my thighs. Only this time all his attention is focused on a completely different hole. Which is ... new. And ... nice. Very nice. So nice, when he thrusts his fingers into my pussy and commands me to come, I do. Just as noisy. Just as messy as the last time.

Chapter Fourteen

K ent

My usually sensible packmate has not done his homework. He's been so dazzled by the cute little thing with his teeth marks in her neck, he's failed to engage his brain. No, his dick is firmly in control and running the show.

Means I'm going to have to do his homework for him. Especially as I can already hear the others waxing lyrical about how damn good she smells. Especially when Declan reveals the little thing had let him watch as our packmate made her come.

Thinking with their dicks the lot of them.

I'm going to find out who she really is.

I walk into the office and find Barney laid out across the floor. He lifts his head when I walk in and gives a yap of excitement.

"Yeah, it's me," I tell him. "Where were you earlier

when I could have used your help, huh? You're meant to look out for your dad, you know."

He's looking older these days and certainly doesn't have the energy he used to. No jumping around, attempting to knock me over when I return home. More sleeping than walkies these days. But just as loyal as always.

Barney lumbers to his feet as I walk across the office to my desk. As I lower down onto my chair, he comes to sit on my feet, laying his head in my lap.

"Really?" I ask him.

He lifts his brows in reply and gives me the puppy dog eyes.

"You know that doesn't work so well when you're an old boy, right?"

He stares at me, knowing full well that it does. I sigh dramatically and stroke his ears, and soon his eyes are drifting shut and he's dozing.

I smile down at him, then remember why I'm here.

The girl.

It takes less than a minute to search for her online and discover all her social media profiles. She's used her real name, which almost seems amateurish. Then again, she needed a form of identification for the wedding, and they aren't as easy to forge as people will have you believe.

Yeah, she really is Avery Loren.

I skim through her Insta first. A series of photos of her with her family. A sister a few years older. A mom and dad. Plenty of cousins.

I have to confess the girl is beautiful. Her eyes dark and mesmerizing. Her lips full and pink. Her skin smooth. I pause on one, her face all lit up by a dazzling spotlight. I enlarge it so it's full screen, look for the signs that she's retouched the picture, or maybe retouched her actual face. I can't find any. I stare at her photo some more and she stares right back at me with those eyes.

Then I click it away with a huff.

Barney opens his eyes and appraises me.

"Don't you say a word," I warn him. "I'm not one bit interested in her." Even if she reminds me of those old movie starlets I found dead hot as a kid – still find deadly hot now.

Barney sniffs and I keep scrolling.

There are endless pictures of her pet cat.

"See," I mutter to Barney. "She has cats. What more do I need to say?"

I hate cats. They smell bad, scratch up your furniture and trip you over on the stairs. But I feel a tad guilty for these thoughts when I find the tributes written to her feline who obviously passed a year back.

I keep scrolling. These aren't the photos women so often send me – links to their Instas that include endless shots of them in very little clothing, sometimes in their underwear or a swimsuit. Often a close up of their ass.

I've been receiving those kinds of photos for years and years. At first, it was a thrill, knowing women wanted me. Now I have an automatic program set up which sends them all straight to the trash can where they belong. Those women don't want me. They want my money.

I keep scrolling backwards and all of a sudden, some dude starts appearing in the photos. My spine stiffens. Barney lifts his head from my lap, sensing something's wrong.

"He looks like a jerk," I say. "Bad taste in men as well as pets." The dude's smiling too much, posing too much, swanky clothes, hands all over the omega. She doesn't look so happy in the first few pictures. There's a deadness in her eyes. But as I keep scrolling back in time, she looks happier and happier, gazing at the man like he's the goddamn moon, dark eyes shining. Kind of the way she was looking at Cruise.

I flick forward again. To the pictures of them at the end, before the man vanishes from her Insta all together. Sad eyes.

Why hasn't she deleted all these photos? Erased the dickhead from her life?

I scroll back again, searching for other men, other clues.

There are a handful of boyfriends. But nothing else of interest.

I flop back on my seat.

Barney lifts his paw and rests it on my knee.

"I just don't trust her," I tell him. "Accidentally bonding and marrying in Vegas? It's bullshit, right?" Barney watches my mouth moving. "Right?" I repeat, patting his paw.

He barks in reply.

"Yeah, I knew you'd agree with me. We're not so easily fooled are we, boy. But it's fine. She'll reveal herself. They always do. We just have to wait. Be patient. Then Cruise will come to his senses."

Chapter Fifteen

Jonah

There are two places Kent will be. The gym. Or the office. He's the most focused out of us. The most determined. He thinks, lives and breathes our business, only pausing to pound the treadmill and lift a few weights.

I try the gym first, thinking he might be taking out his frustrations on the punching bag. It's empty so I pad along to his office next. From behind the door, I hear him pounding his keyboard.

I guess he's still angry.

I knock on the door and walk in. Barney trots over to me, licking my hand and then heading out the door. I don't blame him; Kent's bad mood is palpable.

"Are you okay?" I ask as he continues to abuse his keyboard, his eyes not leaving the computer screen in front of him.

"Fine."

"Don't need patching up at all?" I ask, examining the slice above his eyebrow.

"I said I'm fine."

I sigh. "Right. I'm sure your keyboard agrees."

"What?" he says in irritation, looking up at me. I hold his gaze and he flings his hands up in the air. "She's a scam artist."

"We don't know that."

"She is. The whole waking-up-married-in-Vegas thing only ever happens in chicks' romance novels. Or because one half of the marital party manipulated things to happen."

I lift my glasses from my face and examine the lenses, then rub them clean with the hem of my shirt.

"You could be right."

"I am right," he huffs. "I'm always fucking right."

I swallow my irritation. Kent is a good guy but when he's in a mood, he can be arrogant and requires handling with care.

"If you are," I continue, "it doesn't change the matter that Cruise has bonded her – and judging by his uncharacteristic behavior – rather taken with her too."

Kent snorts. "He's not. He's just thinking with his dick and not his head."

I place my glasses back on my nose. I disagree. Cruise likes sex – all alphas do – but he's never loved it. He's certainly never thought with his cock as Kent so eloquently puts it. Not even back in our college days when hormones and egos were running high. This is different. I've never seen him look so gooey-eyed.

"This needs handling with care," I tell Kent. "If you go threatening to throw his newly bonded omega out of the house, he's going to do more than punch you."

Kent scoffs a second time.

"It could be worse, Kent. Do you want him leaving the pack?"

Kent stares at me. "He wouldn't do that."

"Are you sure?"

"Then what do you suggest?"

"That we do what we always do when faced with an impassable situation, we formulate a plan. Come on, I suggest we discuss this with the others."

Reluctantly, Kent rises from his office chair and follows me back down the corridor to the kitchen where the others are waiting.

The omega's sweet honey aroma hangs heavy in the room and the remnants of the pancakes she was making are scattered across the counter.

Kent makes a show of snorting and rubbing his nose. "It stinks in here," he says.

"You don't like it?" Declan says with a chuckle. "Man, it smells fucking amazing."

"It's too sweet, too strong."

This time I scoff. A lot of omegas smell overly floral for my tastes, overly perfumed, a little on the manufactured side. Avery's scent smells natural, genuine, like stepping into a meadow.

"Kent's agreed to formulating a plan," I tell the others, changing the subject.

Kent folds his arms across his chest and leans against the doorway.

"We don't need a fucking plan," Declan says, "she's only a girl."

"A scam artist," Kent repeats like a broken record.

"You really think so?" Max asks, disappointment shining in his eyes.

"Yes," Kent answers firmly.

"Immaterial," I say. "Whether she is or not, Cruise considers this situation temporary at the present time. The power of their bond will weaken in seven to ten days and then the omega will return home."

"They'll still be bonded," Declan mutters.

"And married," Max adds.

I dismiss that problem with a flick of my hand. "The marriage can be annulled."

"Can it be annulled if it's been consummated?" Declan asks with a grin.

Kent growls, grinding his molars together in a manner that, when he does that at the office, has our members of staff backing away.

"The bond is more of a problem," Max says, and I nod my agreement.

"But there are experimental procedures being trialed in Europe to reverse the bonding process."

"Ridiculous voodoo magic," Declan dismisses, then adds, "And probably freaking painful. Could you put the girl through that?"

"She got herself into this situation," Kent says.

"I already have our best people looking into this," I say, before another fistfight breaks out. "We'll find the most effective – and kindest," I add, cutting off any arguments from Declan, "procedure." I look at them all. "I'm more worried about how we get through the next few days."

"What do you mean?" Kent asks.

"Cruise is already sleeping with her," I adjust my glasses, trying not to picture that. "I for one find her scent pretty irresistible–"

"For fuck's sake," Kent says, shaking his head in disgust.

"I'm being realistic. One packmate bonding and rutting her is containable, if–"

"She's not a disease!" Declan protests.

"Fucking is!" Kent snaps.

"If we all get involved with this girl," I plow on, "then this situation will become more difficult. Possibly irreversible."

"You're being dramatic," Declan says. "Not to mention presumptuous. She's pretty occupied with Cruise right now. We may not be of any interest to her."

Max shakes his head. "Omegas want a pack. You know that as well as the rest of us. They want a pack of alphas rutting and knotting them."

We're all quiet for a moment and I'm certain I'm not the only one picturing that scene.

I blow out air.

"What I'm trying to say is, that unless we want to make this difficult situation even more difficult, we need to stay away from the omega."

"She's living in the pool house. Bonded to our packmate. You don't think he's going to take offense if we ignore and snub his mate?" Declan asks.

"She's not his mate," Kent mutters.

"I'm not saying you shouldn't talk to the omega. Just don't ..."

"Fuck her?" Max asks.

"Touch her."

Max rubs his hand over his face. "That sounds torturous."

"We don't need an omega," Kent says sternly. "That's been the agreement. That's always been the agreement. We don't need an omega fucking things up." He looks at each of us sternly in the eye. "Right?"

I nod. So does Max.

Declan shoves his hands in his pocket and stares down at the floor.

"Declan?" Kent says.

"She's fucking adorable."

"For fuck's sake, keep it in your pants, or we'll all be fucking screwed," Kent growls, "or are you incapable–"

"I'm capable," Declan snarls, "doesn't mean I'm happy about it."

I glance around my packmates. Kent's right. Our experience has shown us that omegas are troublesome. This one's only been here a day and look at the cracks already forming in our pack.

Chapter Sixteen

C ruise

After her second orgasm, the omega mewls and curls up into my side, all limp and sedated. I smile to myself, face sticky with her slick, chest full of a sense of pride. I gave her two ground-shaking orgasms she won't be forgetting any time soon.

"Ground-shaking, huh?" she murmurs.

"Are you saying they weren't, Omega?" I say, pinching one of her stiff nipples. "Because I'm certain every one of my packmates heard you coming over in the other house."

"Oh lord," she says, burying her face into my chest in embarrassment.

I grip her chin and lift her face so she's looking up at me.

"You're not really embarrassed, are you? You seemed to enjoy putting on a show for Declan earlier." She flushes that delicious pink that reminds me of strawberry ice-cream. "Don't lie now, Omega, or I may have to punish you again."

"I don't think I could physically take another punishment," she sighs, "you've destroyed me for all other men."

Good, I think, that satisfaction growing tenfold in my chest.

"So, does the idea that they heard you leave you mortified, or ..." I examine her face, eyes all droopy and dreamy, "or turned on?"

I'm not letting this go. I'm already confident of the answer but I want to hear it from her lips. Out loud. Because if I am right then that opens up a whole host of possibilities I haven't considered in a long, long time.

She bites her lip. "Turned on," she admits.

"You like being watched, do you, my little exhibitionist?"

"I didn't know that I did, but now I think so, yes."

"And do you ..." I take a deep inhale, trying to calm my racing heart, not letting my hopes rise. This is a messy situation, and I am probably getting carried away. "Do you like to be shared?"

Her eyes flash with something dark and I don't need her yes. However, regardless, I want it.

"It's always been a fantasy of mine. Honestly, Cruise, I don't think there is an omega alive who doesn't own that fantasy."

"But fantasy and reality are two different things. We can dream of a particular thing. But when it comes down to it, the reality isn't the same."

"I think I'd like to make that particular fantasy a reality."

I swallow. My heart is drumming like a rock star on speed now. "Would you like to make it a reality with us?"

"It probably wouldn't be very sensible," she says.

"Probably not," I say, noting that isn't a no.

"It would make our situation even more complicated."

"Probably."

"And your packmates may not want that."

"Trust me, they want it."

"Even Kent?"

"Kent will come around." He won't want to miss out on this opportunity.

An omega like Avery. Cute, funny, sweet-smelling, beautiful, with omega instincts so finely tuned she'd probably slick on command.

She squirms next to me. The idea turns her on. She smells wet all over again and I can't help but drag her up onto her hands and knees again.

Honestly, I should get so drunk I lose my memory more often, because so far, I have no complaints about this situation. None at all. Not even if my packmate is so angry at me he punched me in the face. No, I don't care. Because when I thrust into that tight, warm, pretty pussy of hers it's like heaven itself.

"I'm going to watch them fuck you, little mate," I say, half crazed now as I grip her hips and fuck her hard. "I'm going to feed you my cock while Declan fucks you from behind, just like this. And you're such a good girl you're going to take it, aren't you?"

"Yes, Alpha," she moans, half-crazed herself.

"And then I'm going to lick out that plump ass of yours, while Max dines on your pussy. Then you're going to ride my cock while Jonah plays with your clit. Fuck," I mutter, seeing the images of my words reflected back in her mind. I can't wait for that. I cannot wait.

* * *

Of course, there's one problem with my master plan. The best friend.

If I had my way, I'd be carrying the little omega straight up into the main house, laying her out on the bed in the master bedroom and inviting my packmates to feast on her.

But no sooner is my knot deflating, than the omega's phone is ringing.

"Leave it," I tell her, debating whether I need to throw some clothes on the little thing or can just carry her up all bare like she is.

"It's probably Jacks," the omega says, her face lighting up. She dives across the carpet and hits accept. "Are you here?"

I watch as she umms and ahhs into the cell phone, then hangs up.

"She's ten minutes away."

I do the math. Is that long enough—

"It isn't!" the omega squeals. "Besides, maybe we need to take a breath here."

"A breath?" I say. A breath is the last thing I want to do. The omega isn't even in heat and I'm practically in rut here. Hard. Ready. Obsessed.

I scratch the back of my neck.

Yeah, maybe a breath is a good thing.

"You've changed your mind?" I ask.

"No, but we should probably do this slowly, right?" She screws up her nose in an adorable expression. "As you may have noticed, I'm not exactly good at sensible and slow. And that usually lands me in trouble."

She points to the wound on her neck, and I growl, diving towards her.

"Oh lord," she says, as I wrap my hands around her waist and lap at the bite mark. "That's so good. Whose stupid idea was it to invite Jacks in the first place?" Then her spine stiffens and she pushes at my chest. "No, this isn't slow and sensible. I need to put some clothes on before Jacks arrives."

"I think it should be illegal for you to wear clothes. In fact, it's now a rule, little mate. You are forbidden from wearing clothes in this house."

"I wish you'd stop saying things like that. It's so hot!"

I growl again. I'm not known for my hot words, but there's something about the omega that brings the darker side of me rushing to the surface and demanding to be unleashed.

Somehow though, the omega finds some willpower and wriggles from my arms, trotting off down the hallway to find some clothes.

Like a dutiful dog, and because the bond tugs me that way, I follow, very willingly, after her.

"Jacks will be under instructions to report back to Isla. So, we need to act cool. Like there's nothing going on."

"That is going to be very hard when you're riding my cock and screaming my name, Omega. I think she'll be in no doubt what's going on."

"Shit!" she says, not even attempting to pretend we're going to be able to keep our hands off each other.

I go to the bathroom to wash my face and when I'm back I find her, looking decidedly flustered.

"She's here!" she says, and I groan. The omega smacks me on the arm. "Behave."

I nod, although I wonder how I'm going to be able to keep that promise.

How do bonded alphas get anything done? How do

they run successful businesses, lead nations and generally keep functioning normally? Because being bonded to an omega is one enormous distraction. This is why Kent has always been adamant that we don't need one. That's why I've always agreed. I'm far too ambitious to have time for omegas and eating pussy and rutting and knotting.

I screw up my eyes.

Is this what it's like to be an addict?

"She's really nice, I promise," the omega says, examining my pained expression.

"It's not that. I'm sure your friend is lovely." If a little on the direct side. "It's just ... you're very distracting."

"Ditto," she says.

"But I have a business to run."

She bristles a little. "And I do have a life. Friends, family, a job."

"Right," I say. Although waiting tables is not the same as running a multi-national company with employees across the globe. She glares at me. "I think I can hear the car."

She jolts and, to my surprise, takes my hand and leads me down the stairs, around the main house and to the drive yard where one of our cars is pulling up and my packmates are waiting.

"There's another one?" Kent says with a look of thunder. "How many omegas did you go round bonding?"

"Just me," Avery says brightly. "This is Jacks. She's here to keep an eye on me." She runs towards the car, diving in to hug her friend before she's even swung her legs out of the car.

"Why?" Declan asks me.

"She's an omega. On her own. She doesn't know me from Adam."

"And yet she bonded you," Kents says, shaking his head

and stomping back into the house, Barney trailing by his side.

Avery pulls her friend out of the car and swings her around to face the line of alphas.

"This is Jacks, everyone. Everyone, Jacks."

"Howdy," Jacks says, touching the peak of her baseball cap. "This is one hell of a pad you have here. Has *The Disaster* managed to get lost inside yet?"

Avery elbows her friend and hisses, "One time, Jacks, that happened one time."

"Disaster?" Jonah says, examining both the women through his glasses.

"That's what we call her."

"Because?"

Jacks chuckles, hugging her friend. "She has a habit of landing herself right in the middle of them. Case in point," she says, motioning to me and then Avery.

"I wouldn't consider this a disaster," I say.

Jacks keeps smiling but her gaze flicks from me to the omega.

"Come on," Avery says, taking Jacks by the hand. "Let me show you the pool house."

"How about my bag?"

"Jones will bring it," Max tells her.

Jacks lifts an eyebrow and lets Avery pull her along. I go to follow but Jonah puts his hand on my shoulder, stopping me in my tracks.

"Kent's still fuming," he says.

"I noticed but I think he'll get over it pretty quickly." Especially when I tell them all about that fantasy the omega is keen to indulge.

"You need to talk to him!"

A pain stabs violently in my gut and I peer after the omega.

"Cruise!!" she squeals, clutching at her belly.

"I will but–"

Declan shakes his head. "Why the hell did I pass the speaking gig over to you?"

"Because you're an asshole and know that I hate those things."

"If I'd taken it maybe I'd be in your shoes right now," he says wistfully, "with a damn good excuse not to leave that little cutie's side."

"Yeah," I say grinning. I'm not even going to deny this situation has its advantages.

I follow the two women as Avery skips around the pool house bubbling with excitement and then agree to give both of them a tour of the main house, ignoring the way I can hear Kent thumping away on his keyboard. In fact, I decide it's best to avoid the office entirely.

Unfortunately, Avery notices my attempt to steer them away from that end of the corridor.

"What's down there?" she says, standing on her tiptoes and attempting to peer over my shoulder as I attempt to guide her away by the crook of her elbow. "Is it the nest?" Her voice almost bubbles over with the thought of it and Jacks eyes us both.

"No, it's just our office."

"We can't see it?" Jacks asks.

"I think it's best that we don't disturb Kent right now. He's working."

"Kent's the grumpy one," Avery tells her friend, and I can't exactly argue with that. "Where is the nest then?" she asks me as I lead them down the hallway.

"We don't have one."

Avery's feet halt. "All these rooms – all these properties – and you don't have a nest?!"

"No. We don't need one."

"I think your omega would disagree."

"As you know," I say, "this pack doesn't have an omega."

"But when you get one–"

"We're not looking for an omega."

"Oh," Avery says, and Jacks' eyes flick between us again. "But you must spend time with omegas in heat, right? You need a nest for that."

"We don't spend time with omegas in heat. It's not really our thing."

Avery bursts into laughter which quickly dies when she sees my expression. "You're serious."

"I am."

"Isn't an omega in heat what all alphas live for?" Jacks asks, examining a piece of art on the wall.

"The ones who are ruled by their dicks," I scoff. Avery gives me a you're-one-to-talk look which I hope the friend misses.

"All men are ruled by their dicks," Jacks says, turning back to us. "It's a known fact." She points at the two of us. "Case in point."

"That was ... Our pack isn't like that."

"I can't imagine a packhouse without a nest," Avery mutters, shaking her head in shame, and I have a sudden urge to build her one. Right here and now. "My nest at home is small," she continues, "but I love it, and not just for a heat, I'd spend all my time curled up in there if I could."

"What's it like?" I ask.

I can see the image of it in my mind and I can't help imagining myself rutting her through heat in that little room, with its fairy lights and its one big bed littered with cushions and blankets.

Our feet slow as I keep imagining – the little thing all flushed and sticky, mewling for a knot and me having her every way possible – and she watches the scenario play out through our bond.

Jacks doesn't realize we've slowed until she's several yards ahead of us. Then she turns and finds us both staring into space, eyes glazed, cheeks flushed.

"Everything okay?" she asks with a puzzled expression.

I cough and do my best to disperse the erotic daydream away. "Fine," I say.

"Fine," Avery says, a little breathless.

"You look hot," Jacks says to her friend.

"I feel it." Avery waves her hand in front of her face. "Rockview is a hell of a lot warmer than home."

Which it may be, but there's AC blasting through the house. Kent especially likes it icy cold.

"How about a swim?" Jacks suggests. "The pool out there looks incredible."

"Can we?" Avery asks.

"Sure," I say. I'm in need of an ice-cold shower. A dive in the pool may be the next best thing.

Chapter Seventeen

Avery

"You're fucking, aren't you?" Jacks says with a huge smile as she sits on the bed and swings her legs.

"No?" I say. She can't possibly know that we are. It's not like it's written across my forehead.

"You are," she insists. "You have that look about you."

"What look?"

"So I'm right?" I don't answer. She laughs. "That look of satisfaction. Yeah, you look like one satisfied woman."

"Bullshit, I look exactly the same as I always do."

Jacks shakes her head. "Usually, you're a little skittish. Eyes a little wild."

I give her the finger. "Also bullshit."

"Stop being so coy and come tell me all about it."

"You won't go blabbing to Isla?"

She looks a little offended. "Avery, have I ever gone blabbing?" I shake my head. "Exactly. I cross my heart."

"Fine, we're fucking. A lot. Have been for most of the day."

"And?"

"And what?"

"It's good, right? Hence the," she points at my face, "blissed-out expression."

I walk over to the mirror and examine my face. Maybe my eyes do look a little brighter and there's color in my cheeks. Maybe sex with an alpha is good for the health and the complexion. "It's good, obviously. Otherwise, I wouldn't be doing it."

"Really? I thought if an alpha gives you a command, like lie down and let me fuck you, you don't have much choice in the matter."

"Jacks, you know that isn't how it works."

Jacks examines my face with more seriousness. "Yes, but I also know that you've been taken advantage of in the past. I should have come with you from the start."

"Jacks, that was a long time ago now."

"Not that long, Avery."

I walk away from the mirror and take her hand in mine. "I won't be screwing anyone I don't want to in this situation."

"Hmmm," Jacks says.

"What?"

"It's just the way you said that sounded like there might be other people you are considering screwing in this situation."

I will my cheeks not to sizzle, but they do anyway. There's no point denying it.

Jacks grins again. "The other packmates?"

"Yeah, the other packmates," I say in defeat.

"Ahhh, you lucky bitch! My best friend is fucking the wealthiest pack in the country, probably the world," Jacks screams, flopping back on the mattress and kicking her legs.

"Shush," I say, peering at the door. I can sense the alpha is not too far away. "I'm not screwing them yet."

"But you want to?"

I laugh and bury my face in my hands. Again, there is hardly any point in denying it. Jacks knows all my deepest, darkest fantasies, just like I know hers.

"I thought so. And trust me, you will be. Those men look like they want to devour you."

I shiver. "Really?"

"100%!"

"Cruise has basically said I should. In fact, he seems pretty into the idea."

"He's part of a pack. Of course they want to fuck you together. That's what packs do."

"I wouldn't know," I say. "I've never been with one, remember. I've never had that chance."

"Well, now you do. This is what you've always wanted."

"Isla would think it was a bad idea."

"*Pssk*," Jacks says waving her hand, "you don't think Isla would hawk her collection of Sylvanian Families figurines for the chance of sleeping with a pack?"

"True." Isla, like every other omega on the planet, has been dreaming of a pack since the day she presented as an omega. In fact, I remember her role playing such a scenario with said Sylvanian Families figurines. The little bunny girl got a *lot* of action! But girls like us – without family connections and wealth – we don't get the packs. We have to spend our days dodging the bad guys and hoping to find some nice dude among the many crappy ones. "But she also disapproves of this whole mess."

"It doesn't seem like that much of a mess to me," Jacks says. "Granted, it's not a conventional way of meeting your future husband – or husbands," she winks, "but who says it's any worse than any of the other ways? It's not like we've been having much luck with internet dating or anything else."

"True again," I say, flopping back on the bed and smiling wildly. "It just seems too good to be true." The smile fades on my face. It wouldn't be the first time that's happened.

Like the really sweet guy who took me on amazing dates and treated me like a princess, only for me to learn he had several other princesses on the go as well. Or the time I landed a waitressing position that paid twice as much as anywhere else, only to discover they wanted me to serve tables topless. Or when I thought I'd landed my dream job only to find it was a horrific nightmare, complete with nasty monsters.

Yeah, when something seems too good to be true, it almost always is. I just really hope this isn't one of those occasions. Because I really, really, really want to experience what it would be like to be with a pack. At least once in my lifetime.

"You don't think I'd regret it?" I ask Jacks.

"Regret sleeping with a pack of hot, alpha men? Personally, you know that's not my thing. But for you, Avery, it most definitely is. Why would you regret it? Besides, I have a sneaky suspicion this 'accidental bonding'," Jacks makes inverted commas with her fingers, "is going to lead to something more permanent."

"One, it was accidental. No," I make my own pair of

inverted commas, "about it. And two, it won't. In a few days' time, the bond will release and you and I will be flying home."

"Okay," Jacks says, swinging her legs, "I'll humor you, and we'll pretend that's going to happen, then you still get to enjoy the very hot sex with the very hot alphas. What's the problem?"

"Feelings."

"Feelings," Jacks repeats.

I lower my voice to a whisper, even though the alpha can hear everything through the bond anyway. "You know that's why I've never been able to do the one-night stand thing."

Jacks rolls her eyes. "If you've started sleeping with Mister Hunk already, I'm assuming it'll be more than a one-night stand." I whack her on the shoulder. "Avery," she says with more seriousness again, "if you truly believe this isn't going to go anywhere, then you need to be careful. Leave your feelings at the door and enjoy the five alpha cocks. Don't let yourself get hurt."

"You know I'm really crappy at that." It's why we had to leave *Les Mis* halfway through the performance. And why Jacks refuses to watch any kind of reality TV with me – those tear-jerky back stories have me sobbing. And why I've had my heart broken more times than I deserve considering the small number of relationships I've actually had.

"Avery, you can tie yourself up in knots about this – pun fucking intended," she lifts her hand for me to five high, "or you can make the most of this crazy situation and enjoy yourself."

I nod. "Okay, you're right."

"Of course I am."

"That just leaves the ... er ... practical considerations."

Jacks lifts an eyebrow. "Go on ..."

"I've never been with more than one guy before, Jacks. I'm not sure how it works technically."

"Avery Loren, don't pretend like you haven't watched a bucket load of omega pack porn."

"Cross my heart and hope to die, I haven't."

"How about those books you read?"

"They don't really provide a step-by-step guide."

"I'm sure the alphas will be more than willing to demonstrate and lead you through a step-by-step process." Jacks chuckles and I punch her shoulder a second time.

"Jacks, I'm serious. I don't want to go in there unprepared especially when my nether regions are involved."

Jacks snorts. "I don't know why you're asking me, Avery. When it comes to men, you have a lot more experience than me. Plus, I'm a beta. I can't take one knot. Let alone two."

"There are betas who can train to take a kno—"

"La la la," Jacks says, placing her hands firmly over her ears and crossing her legs. "I don't want to know."

"Jacks," I say, yanking her hands away. "I'm serious. I need to study up."

"Fine!" Jacks says, pulling up her phone and typing away. She holds the screen towards me. "One omega, three alphas, triple penetration. You wanna watch?"

I nod my head eagerly and Jacks hits play, then immediately hits mute when her cell starts to emit a series of really loud moans.

We sit side by side watching the screen.

"Is this meant to be a turn on?" Jacks says, screwing up her nose.

"It's not designed for gay women," I point out.

"You saying you like it? That girl does not look like she is enjoying herself."

"She's trying her best. She's not the greatest actress."

"The dude looks like he's hammering a nail into the wall."

"I think this was designed for men."

"Wanna try something else?"

"Not yet. I want to see how exactly they're making this work." Jacks twists the screen around and we tilt our heads. "Can you zoom in?"

Jacks goes to do that when there's a loud knock on the door.

I scream and Jacks stuffs the phone in her pocket.

The door opens and Cruise pokes his head inside.

"Everything okay in here, ladies?"

Jacks and I sit side by side on the bed looking guilty as hell, my cheeks so pink I must look like a flamingo.

"Absolutely fine," I say.

"Just doing some research," Jacks says.

Cruise looks at us with suspicion and I wonder how much he saw through the bond.

"Do you think you could pause your ... research," he smirks, "and join us for dinner?"

"Us?" I ask.

"My pack," he says.

I look at Jacks and she nudges me.

"Yes," I say. "Yes, I'd love to."

Chapter Eighteen

Max

Pack dinner is unofficially mandatory. You don't miss it. But it seems all the rules are being thrown out the window today. After all, Cruise missed an important board meeting – practically criminal. Therefore, I shouldn't be surprised that when we sit down to dinner, Kent's chair remains empty. He's locked up in his office somewhere sulking about the omega. I tried talking to him. Jonah tried talking to him. We have our plan. We're in agreement to not let ourselves become tangled up with the girl. That doesn't mean we have to be rude.

Unfortunately, she's chosen the seat next to mine, opposite Cruise, Declan on her other side and Jonah next to Cruise. She smells divine and with her dark hair pinned up, I have the perfect view of that bite mark on her throat.

I don't think I've seen anything so perfect in my life. Something I want to touch. To lick. To suck.

To replicate.

This may be tougher than I thought. Perhaps Kent has the right idea after all.

I comb my fingers through my hair and try to focus on the conversation and not the bite mark on the omega's throat.

"So, what's for dinner?" the omega's friend asks, sitting at one end of the table and observing us all with obvious amusement.

"Freddricho knocked up a variety of dishes because we didn't know what you'd like," Declan tells her.

"Avery likes variety and choice," Jacks says, picking up her wine glass and taking a long sip. The omega throws her a look.

"You're not picky then?" I ask. Omegas can be sensitive when it comes to taste and smell. I reminded Freddricho of this earlier, going over the dishes he'd chosen on the list and reminding him to go easy on the garlic and spice.

Of course, my actual experience with omegas is old. Years and years old now. But I remember ...

I remember some omegas will slick on an alpha's command. I know some can take more than one knot in the throes of a heat. I know some are practically addicted to the taste of their alphas' come.

I know far more than I wish I did right now. I am mighty curious to discover if all these things are true of this particular omega.

I wonder if this little omega can do any of those things.

I rub at my head. I need to get control of my thoughts.

"What do you like to eat?" I ask her.

She touches the wound on her neck absent-mindedly,

an action that has all our alpha scents spiking. Her nose twitches, her pupils widen a little and she rubs her thighs together under the table.

The idea of eating in my office, like Kent, is looking more and more appealing.

"I'm not exactly fussy–"

"See!" Jacks says, raising her wine glass.

"I'll eat just about anything."

"You must have a favorite," Declan says.

She smiles. "My mom's mac and cheese."

"That sounds good," I say.

She smiles at me. "It is."

"You still live at home, right?"

"Yes, I'm saving up to get my own place, but rental deposits are huge. I think I'll be ninety by the time I can afford my own place."

"How much do you need?" Cruise says. "I'll write you a check."

She rolls her eyes. "I wasn't asking for–"

"Don't believe a word she says. She secretly loves living at home," her friend says. "She could have moved in with me years ago. But she likes having her meals cooked for her and her washing laundered."

The omega's cheeks pinken.

"You're a spoiled little omega after all?" Declan says, leaning towards her.

"I do my own washing," she says. "And I work six days a week. I'm not that spoiled."

"Well, we could fix that," Declan whispers. "Every omega deserves to be spoiled."

"Every woman does," Jacks points out.

"Maybe we all secretly want to be spoiled a little,"

Avery says. She prods Declan with her finger. "Even alphas."

"Alphas are pretty hard to spoil," I say.

Jacks laughs. "They are not. Give them an omega in heat and they're pretty damn spoiled."

I glance at my packmates. She's not wrong. An omega in heat is heavenly. Heavenly and something we've avoided for several years, because an omega who isn't trouble is hard to find. The piece of heaven, in our experience, has too often come with a cost attached.

"We should've taken you out for a meal," Declan says, quickly changing the subject. "It sounds like you both need spoiling."

"And this is our first time in Rockview," Jacks says.

"Really?" I say, turning to the omega.

"Yep, never been here before."

"Then we should've taken you for a tour and then dinner," Declan says. "Showed you the ocean."

"And have every paper printing our picture and running stupid stories the next day!" Jonah says, shaking his head.

Jacks lowers her glass to the table. "They don't print an awful lot about your personal lives."

"Because we work damn hard to keep them private," Cruise says.

"Anyone would believe your pack live like celibate monks." She grins. "You must have really good people."

"We're careful who we associate with," Jonah says.

We all turn and look at the omega.

"What?" she says.

The dining room door draws back and for a moment I think Kent has relented and is joining us, but then Freddricho walks through, balancing a tray laden high with dishes on his shoulder. He arranges all the plates out in front of the omega, explaining to her in detail which each one is and encouraging her to try them.

We watch her place forkful after forkful of food between her pouty lips, umming and ahhing her pleasure.

It's more erotic than most porn I've watched.

Can I feign a headache and leave dinner early?

Unfortunately, she's turning to me and engaging me in conversation before I have the chance to make my excuses.

"Cruise tells me you're the mastermind behind the Hamilton α-phone?"

"He is being generous. We were all behind the design of that phone."

"And he is being modest," Cruise says, waving his fork towards me. "It was your bright idea. Made our fortunes."

"Do you have one?" I can't help but ask her.

"Of course! Doesn't everyone have one?"

"63% of Americans do," Jonah tells her. "We'd like to increase that to 100."

"There are some people you'll never get on a smart phone," Avery says. "My grandma still struggles to use her landline. I've tried to teach her how to use a cell because it would be nice to video call and stuff, but she ends up pressing all the buttons and turning the thing off every time."

"We're developing simpler, more intuitive tech," I tell her. "Phones that will be easier to use for those who struggle with technology. In fact, that was why Cruise was in Vegas. He was presenting to potential new investors about our plans." I lower my knife and fork. "Why were you there, Avery?"

Kent's convinced she's a scam artist. I might as well test that theory while I'm sitting next to her.

"My cousin's bachelorette party."

"On a Monday night?" Declan scoffs.

"Vegas is expensive," Avery says, attempting to saw through a piece of bread. "It's like half the price if you go on a weekday."

"Then why go to Vegas at all?"

Avery shrugs. "Bride's choice and you can't argue with the bride. Especially when you're one of her bridesmaids. Or at least I was. I've probably been fired given the circumstances."

"I'm sorry," I say.

"Oh, don't be. She has like six others and she was threatening to put us in bright orange dresses. I love the girl, but orange is not my color."

"It's not anyone's color," Jacks pipes up.

"I don't know," Declan winks at the omega. "Cruise looks pretty good in orange."

"I imagine Cruise looks pretty good in anything," Jacks mutters.

"Is your cousin an omega too?" Jonah asks her.

"Yes, all the girls in our family are."

"And is she marrying into a pack?"

Jacks laughs and Avery frowns. "Erm no. She's marrying her childhood sweetheart."

"An alpha?" I say frowning. Most alphas are in packs. The ones who aren't are generally assholes. Or worse.

"No, he's a beta. They started dating back in high school before Stacey's designation presented."

"And they're getting married?" I say, taken aback.

She pauses her sawing and turns to look at me, her dark eyes meeting mine. "Of course, they love each other."

"But he's a beta," Declan scoffs.

"So?" Avery says defensively, resuming her sawing with renewed vigor.

"He doesn't have a knot."

Avery frowns. "You think knots are more important to omegas than love?"

Declan glances around the table as if searching for help. But he walked himself into that trap, he can walk himself out.

"No," he says slowly, "but an omega in heat needs a knot. She needs an alpha who can rut her through it."

"An omega doesn't need anything," Avery says, slamming her knife so hard through the bread roll it skids off her plate and across the table. Jacks catches it and tosses it back. "That's just mistruths alphas like to propagate."

Declan's mouth falls open. He looks as flabbergasted as I feel by that statement. "You're kidding, right? That isn't a mistruth. In fact, it's a fundamental truth. An omega needs a knot in a heat, otherwise it's painful and–"

"Are you actually mansplaining what it's like to be an omega to me, Declan Hamilton?" she says, pointing her knife in his direction.

He drops his gaze sheepishly to his dinner. "No ... but ..."

"No, buts. I've been through plenty of heats alone and I'm still sitting here to tell the tale, aren't I? I didn't die from lack of an alpha's knot."

"Shit!" Cruise mutters, staring at the omega like she just shot him through the heart.

I look at her too. Did this little thing really endure a heat on her own? More than one? My heart aches for her. I can't imagine how agonizing that must have been.

"She has a knotted dildo. That vibrates," her friend says into the silence.

"Yes, thank you Jacks," Avery says, slapping butter onto her bread.

All the omegas I've ever met would never consider going through a heat alone. Why would they? Why would she?

"Why?" I ask softly. "Why would you go through a heat alone?"

She shrugs, continuing to butter her roll even though it's now smothered in the stuff.

"Sometimes I didn't have a choice. Sometimes I had a choice, and the options were ..."

"Shit!" Jacks finishes for her. "There are a lot of assholes out there." She narrows her eyes and glares at us. "Plus, perverts whose ultimate fantasy is to sleep with an omega in heat."

"Oh God," Avery says, finally lifting the roll to her lips. "They are the worst."

Cruise's hands ball into fists on the tabletop. "Want to give me any names?"

"What? No!" Avery says.

"I will," Jacks says. "But be warned it's a long list."

"Doesn't matter," he says, meeting my eye. I nod. I may be determined to keep my hands off the little omega, but I still want to see that list. We've become very effective over the years at making any enemies, rivals or nuisances suffer.

"Anyway," Avery says. "My cousin is seriously loved up and very happy. Not every omega needs an alpha."

"Or a pack," Jacks adds, and I can't help but notice the way Avery shuffles on her seat.

It's hard to believe this is some scam.

Then again ...

Either way, I'm sticking to our plan.

Chapter Nineteen

Cruise

"Good morning, Alpha," a sultry voice says as I open my eyes the next morning. I find myself nose to nose with the omega, her dark eyes still a little sleepy. Shit, I could get used to waking up this way, her warm soft body wrapped around mine, her honey-comb scent swimming through the air.

"Hmmm, good morning," I say, dragging her even closer and nuzzling her neck. "How did you sleep?"

She giggles. "Not very well."

"Not very well, huh? Why was that?"

"A very hot, very horny alpha was in my bed."

"Are you complaining? You didn't seem to be complaining last night." Anything but, she spent most of the night begging me for more.

For an omega who loves a knot quite as much as this one

does, I'm finding it hard imagining her suffering through a heat without one. Not something that will be happening again. I made her promise that last night. Next time she has a heat – whenever she has a heat – she'll be picking up the phone to me and I'll be there in a heartbeat.

Fuck, the idea of her in heat!

I groan and she wriggles against me.

"Seeing as we didn't sleep much last night, could we spend the day in bed?" she purrs.

I roll on top of the little thing and pin her arms above her head.

"You want to catch up on sleep?" I say, grinding my way inside her, and loving the way her thighs fall open for me and she moans. It's like she was built for me and me for her. We fit so perfectly together.

"I had some other ideas."

I chuckle. "As good as that sounds, Avery," I say, circling my hips and making her moan some more, "if I miss another day of work rutting you, my packmates might actually skin me alive."

"They could join us," she says, then blushes furiously as I stop grinding into her pussy. "I mean, you said that is what you wanted."

"More than you could know," I say, fucking her harder now and loving the way she writhes beneath me, her scent soaring, her thighs and pussy all sticky with slick. "You liked them then? You had a good time at dinner?"

"Y-y-y-yes," she murmurs. "But ..."

I stop again and she wails. "But what?"

"Alpha," she pleads, rocking her hips, encouraging me to move again.

"But what, Avery?"

She bites her lip and meets my eye. "I've never been with more than one man before. Hence, the ... you know ..."

"Porn?"

"Research," she stresses.

I release her wrists and lower myself down kissing all the way up her neck. "You're worried about it? Are you going off the idea?"

"No!" she says in a way that has my pulse jumping. "But what if I can't?"

"You can."

"You don't know that."

I chuckle. "I do, little one. I've felt your pussy caressing my knot enough times to know what it can do." I reach down beneath the two of us, cupping her ass cheek in my hand and then finding her other hole. I plunge a finger inside her. This time she groans, her body turning to putty. Turns out this little omega likes my cock in her pussy and my finger in her ass. In fact, she likes it a lot and I've been testing her there. Adding a finger at a time, stretching her wider each time. "And as for here, little one, I think you're ready."

I fuck her some more until she's coming. Her pussy milking my cock, her ass squeezing around my finger.

"You want my cock here too, sweetheart?" I ask her, licking my tongue around and around my bite mark.

She inhales.

I wait for her answer.

I really want to fuck her in the ass. But only if that's what she wants too.

"Yes," she whispers eventually.

"You're sure? We don't have to if you don't–"

"Alpha," she says. "I've been waiting for you to ask me."

My tongue stills and I lift my head to look down into her face. "You have, have you?"

She nods with one of those beautiful smiles stretched across her face.

I slip out of her, harder than fucking ever, and take a hold of her thighs, maneuvering them until they're hooked over my shoulders and her pelvis is rolled forward, her pussy and her ass on full display. It's one hell of a sight.

I'm already drenched in her slick, but I spend a few moments stroking at her hole again, until she's moaning and more slick comes dribbling from her. Then I smooth the arousal over my cock.

"You sure you want this, sweetheart?" I ask, not even sure what the hell I'll do if she's changed her mind.

"Please Alpha," she says in a way that has me plunging inside.

She's even tighter here, so tight all the air rushes from my lungs and ecstasy swims from my groin right across my body.

"Ffffuuuucccckkk," I stutter out, "that feels so... Are you okay, sweetheart? Am I hurting you?"

She shakes her head, wild tears streaming down her cheeks. I kiss them, lick them away, feeling all her emotion, all her pleasure reflected back at me through the bond. It's powerful, so strong, so addictive. But I want more. I want her coming.

I stroke at her clit as I fuck her ass and soon, she's tumbling, that shot of ecstasy shooting straight through my veins too, so we're coming together, making declarations and promises I'm not sure either of us can keep.

* * *

Somehow, we drag ourselves out of bed and join Jacks for breakfast in the pool house kitchen.

"I need to go into the office," I tell Avery and Jacks.

The omega's cheeks are still flushed from all the orgasms I gave her this morning and she is humming to herself with contentment as she digs her spoon into a grapefruit.

Work is the last thing I want to do right now. I want to fling her over my shoulder and take her back to bed, but there are a hell of a lot of angry messages from Kent on my phone and I want to go some way to making things right with my packmate.

"The office?" Avery says, looking up at me. "I assume you want me to come with you?"

I nod. If I'm going, then she'll have to come too.

"Won't that start a lot of tongues wagging?"

"We can use the back entrance."

Jacks sniggers and Avery throws her a look. "What? It's your honeymoon. No judgment from me if you want to explore each other's back entrances."

Avery's cheeks glow and I growl. I can't help myself. Exploring Avery's back entrance this morning was probably the best moment of my life.

Avery rests her chin on her fist and gives me the same unimpressed look she just gave her friend.

"Sorry," I mouth sheepishly, and she smiles in return.

"Jeez," Jacks says, "you two are more domestic than Avery's parents and they've been married forever."

Avery drops her gaze back to her grapefruit. "I'm happy to go to your office. I'd like to see where you work."

"It's your honeymoon!" Jacks protests.

Maybe she's right. Maybe I should forget about work and focus on the omega. Deal with Kent later. Then again, going to the office is the perfect excuse to present the omega right under my packmates' noses. I saw how hard Declan, Max and Jonah were fighting their desires last night. Heck, it was all over their scents. It's only a matter of time before they fall for her charms and then ...

"Technically, yes, but–" I say.

"I really don't mind," Avery says, ducking as juice squirts from the grapefruit into the air, narrowly missing her eye. "I can bring my book and amuse myself. How about you, Jacks?"

"I'll come too," she says. "I'm intrigued about the Hamilton building. Is it true you have beanbags, trampolines and foosball tables?"

"No," I say.

A look of disappointment falls over her face but then she shrugs. "Oh well, I'm still happy to come."

"What should I wear?" Avery asks me.

A number of inappropriate ideas flash through my mind and she raises her eyebrow a second time.

"Whatever you want," I say, then add with a grin, "Just no Bart Simpson."

She giggles and Jacks looks between us, shaking her head.

* * *

Jacks whistles when we step out of the private elevator and into the office I share with Declan at the top of the Hamilton building. Avery halts by the doors, her mouth falling open.

"The view ..." she mutters.

Declan's already at his desk, but he stands up and walks towards us all.

"Impressed?" he asks.

The omega nods. "The city's so vast ... and the harbor, and the ocean ..."

Jacks walks up to the glass, breathing on it and then wiping away the mist with her sleeve. "Which boat is yours?"

"It's not there at the moment," Declan says, casually. "It's moored in the Caribbean."

"Of course," Jacks says, shaking her head in disbelief. "How many houses do you guys own exactly?"

Declan shrugs with a cocky grin. "Don't know. Lost count."

I stroll over to my desk and switch on my computer.

"Help yourselves to coffee, ladies," I say, waving towards the machine. "And make yourselves comfortable." I point towards the armchairs. Avery flops herself down in one and pulls out a book from her handbag. I settle into my seat, acknowledging that a day in the office is going to be a hell of a lot better than it usually is with Avery around, my bond humming in my core.

Jacks continues to examine the view from the window, then asks if she can go explore the rest of the building.

"I'm telling you," I say, "the trampoline bullcrap is just that: bullcrap."

"I'm still intrigued," she says, "wanna come, Avery?"

"Can't," Avery says, pointing to her stomach and then to me.

"Ahh, yeah, right. I'll come find you at lunch, then. You going to be okay?"

Avery lifts up her book. "I got to a really juicy bit. I'll be fine."

Jacks kisses her crown and disappears into the elevator. The doors close, leaving the three of us alone.

I focus in on the screen of my laptop. I have correspondence I need to catch up on and several reports I need to review and action.

My eyes keep straying to the little omega across the office, though. She's hooked her legs over the arm of the chair and swings them back and forth as she stares engrossed in her book, her eyes rocking side to side over the page.

Usually, there's a threat of anxiety bubbling in my throat while I work, alert for the next crisis, on edge for the next fire we're going to need to extinguish, ready for the next difficult decision. Not today. As I sit back in my chair and read through my emails, I realize I've never felt this calm at work before. This content.

I should be shitting myself. I've screwed things up.

Only this doesn't feel like a screw up. It doesn't feel like a screw up at all.

Chapter Twenty

Avery

I turn another page of my book, pretending to be riveted by the story within. It is a good story. But it's nothing to the two men on the other side of the office; their heavy, masculine scents swirling through the air and capturing all my attention.

I lift my book a little higher and peek at them over the top.

Both alphas have slung their jackets over the back of their chairs and sit in crisp shirts – Cruise's a light blue that complements his dark eyes, Declan's a white that shows off his golden tan.

Cruise has rolled up his sleeves showing off his strong forearms, and Declan's shirt is unbuttoned at the collar, revealing a flash of his sculpted chest.

Cruise jabs his finger at his keyboard in a way I find

rather hot, and Declan strokes his fingers through his beard in such a sensual way it should be illegal.

I rub my thighs together.

What is wrong with me? Guys in suits. Guys working desk jobs. That's not hot.

Firemen scooping people out of burning buildings are hot.

Soldiers running assault courses are hot.

Lumberjacks with their ginormous axes and equally ginormous muscles are hot.

"Lumberjacks?" Cruise says from the other side of the room, making me jump and nearly drop my book.

"What?"

"You find lumberjacks hot?"

"Lumberjacks?" Declan says, looking up from his work.

"Yeah, lumberjacks," Cruise says. "Avery finds them hot."

"So would you if you'd ever seen them chopping up wood," I tell him.

"You spend a lot of time watching lumberjacks chopping up wood?" Cruise asks with a slight growl.

"I've seen videos."

Declan grins. "Oh yeah, what kind of videos?"

"Not that kind," I tell him, lifting my book. "I have novels for that."

"Are there lots of lumberjacks in your books?" Declan asks.

"Cowboys," I say. "A girl has needs."

Declan lifts his hands. "I'm not judging."

I tilt my head. "Are you trying to tell me you don't watch porn?"

"I don't," Cruise says so earnestly I almost believe him. "I'm telling the truth," he protests, registering my skepticism through the bond. "I have a very vivid imagination. I don't need porn." He taps his fingertip against his forehead.

"And what kind of things does this imagination of yours conjure?" I ask, intrigued.

He holds my gaze, and I can see one very vivid fantasy of an omega squirming in heat, buried in the cushions and blankets of a nest, an alpha holding her down as he ruts her hard. The omega in question looks an awfully lot like me and the alpha an awfully lot like Cruise. I have to confess, that is one fantasy I could totally get on board with.

I sigh.

"You like that?" he asks darkly.

"Uh huh," I say, biting my lip.

"What?" Declan calls out, a note of desperation in his voice. "What does she like?"

"The idea of me building her a nest and rutting her through her heat," Cruise says and a whimper escapes from my throat.

"Shit," Declan mutters. "Want to hear my favorite fantasy, little omega?"

My gaze snatches automatically to Cruise's packmate and I nod my head.

He rolls his chair a little away from his desk.

"In my fantasy, I have this cute little omega secretary–"

"Are you sure you *don't* have some cute little omega secretary?" I say, frowning.

"Oh, she's cute," Declan says, shrugging and making jealousy spike through my gut. "And the same age as my mom."

"Some men like that," I mutter.

"She's also happily married."

"Hmmm," I say.

"May I continue?" he asks.

I'm too damn curious to refuse him, even if the jealousy is still swimming through my body. I nod my head.

"I have this cute little omega secretary who does exactly as I tell her."

"That's it?" I say. Confusingly, I feel a little disappointed, especially after Cruise's red-hot fantasy.

"You didn't ask me what I like to tell this omega to do."

I roll my eyes. "What do you like to tell her to do?"

"I tell her to put down her pen and pad and take off her panties."

"Oh," I say, unable to drag my eyes from his face.

"Then I tell her to lean over my desk and lift up her skirt so I can see her plump little ass and her pretty pink pussy. And you know what, little omega?"

"What?"

"She does exactly as I say, parting her legs on my command. Then I fuck and knot her right there against my desk."

"Oh," I repeat, my blood warming.

"I think she likes that fantasy too," Cruise whispers.

"You do, do you, little one?"

I hesitate, then nod, lowering my book to the floor and rising from my chair. I take my loose hair in my hands and twist it into a bun, securing it with the band I had around my wrist. Then I stroll towards Declan picking up a pen and piece of paper from his desktop.

"Good morning, Mr. Hamilton," I say in an overly chirpy voice, "what tasks do you have for me today?"

Declan's eyes darken and he grins. He folds his arms over his chest and strokes his chin.

"You mean, besides filing and answering my calls?"

I pout at him. "Anything you want, Mr. Hamilton."

"Anything?" he growls.

"I'm happy to help," I purr.

"Then take off those panties, Miss Loren. They must be ruined already. We can all smell how wet you are."

I rest the pen and paper back down on the desk. Then, reaching under the skirt of my dress, I grab the silky material of my underwear and shimmy them down my legs, stepping out of them and leaving them discarded on the floor.

"I like a tidy office, Miss Loren," Declan says. "Pass those to me."

I bend down to retrieve them, ensuring as I do, I give the alpha a flash of what's under my skirt.

He growls and when I pass over the panties, he snatches them from my hands, stuffing them inside a drawer. Then he sweeps his arm over the surface of his desk, sending his laptop and papers crashing to the ground.

"Against the desk, Miss Loren, and pull up your skirt. I'm going to fuck you now."

I peer towards Cruise, to see if he has any complaint about this turn of events.

"What are you waiting for, Miss Loren?" he says. "Do as the alpha says."

"Yes, Sir," I chime, shimmying around the desk, and bending over its surface.

Declan growls again and I feel the heat and weight of his body against mine. "Skirt up, Omega."

I reach around and tug it up, the cool air from the AC brushing over my backside.

Declan squeezes my ass and then whispers in my ear. "You're going to have to be quiet for me, little Omega. Can you do that?"

"Yes, Sir," I reply, wiggling my ass against him and feeling his hard cock through his pants.

"Good girl," he says, and I hear his zipper one moment, and feel the hot press of his cockhead the next.

Slick glides from my hole and I mewl. But he doesn't thrust inside me like he'd promised. Instead, he hooks one finger under the elastic of my hair and yanks it out, my hair falling loose around my shoulders. He gathers it up in his hand, twisting it around his fist and yanking my head upwards.

"Going to fuck you hard."

He grips my hip with his free hand and plunges inside me, the force of his body pushing me up onto the tips of my toes.

"Fuuuucccckkkk," he growls.

He tugs on my hair a little and the sting at my scalp and his heavy cock inside me is the perfect combination.

At first, I manage to keep my promise, smothering the moans bubbling in my throat as he thrusts into me and the desk groans and creaks beneath us. But then I catch Cruise's eyes, watching us intently, dark and full of longing and lust.

I can feel how turned on he is through the bond as well, how ... proud he is of me.

It's too much. I can't help the little scream that comes rushing out of my mouth.

"Quiet, little Omega, I have people working right outside the door," Declan whispers.

"Hmmm," I say, trying my best to temper down the urge to scream again. It feels too good. I'd imagined being with a pack a million times. But I never realized how erotic being watched like this would be.

Declan leans over me as he continues to fuck me and, removing his hand from my hip, wraps it over my mouth.

"Shhh, little one, there's a good girl."

I cry out again, this time his palm smothering the noise.

"I should have known you'd be a wild little one. I could see it in your eyes. A feral little omega who's desperate for cock and a knot."

"Yes," I moan into his hand, "a knot."

"Not yet though, need you coming first. Going to come for me?" he asks, tugging my head right back.

It sends me toppling right over the edge and I buck and jolt on the desk as waves of pleasure swim through my body.

"Is she milking your cock?" Cruise calls out to Declan.

"Yeah, like a good omega should," Declan says, and then he comes too, grunting loudly as he empties into me and his knot expands, stretching me wide.

"Oh God," I whimper as another orgasm hits me.

This was hot and we've barely scratched the surface of being together.

Chapter Twenty-One

Declan

I settle back down on my seat, taking the omega with me, my cock still knotted in her pussy.

"That was a million times better than the actual fantasy," I tell her.

"Hmmm," she says, closing her eyes as I nuzzle that bite mark on her throat. "And how many omegas have you fucked in total over your desk?"

"You're the first, sweetheart."

"Betas?"

"Nope."

"Why do I find that hard to believe?"

"I share an office with him. I can confirm it's true," Cruise says.

I lift my head from the omega's neck and peer over at him. We're a pack. In theory, there should be no jealousy and no competition between us. That doesn't mean there isn't. Cruise seemed eager for us to share this little omega he's found, that doesn't mean that reality will hit him in a different way.

The man, however, to my relief, looks fucking elated.

Something I'm not sure the others will feel.

"I'm still not sure I buy it," the omega says, her pussy pulsing around my knot. "I bet you have women lining up to throw themselves over your desk. That would be pretty hard to resist."

"You're pretty hard to resist, Avery," I tell her, licking my tongue over the bite mark this time and making her shiver deliciously. "I was meant to be keeping my hands off you."

Her spine stiffens, and she turns her head to look at me over her shoulder.

"Why?"

I groan. "I'm an alpha. We're all alphas. We get pretty possessive, pretty obsessive, pretty damn quick once we start fucking an omega, and this isn't some permanent arrangement, is it? You'll be leaving us as soon as the effects of the bond with Cruise wear off."

The omega swivels her gaze around to Cruise.

He stares back at her, his jaw and shoulders tight. Neither of them says a word.

I kiss the wound, feeling the dents Cruise's teeth has made in her skin against my lips. If I'd bitten an omega like Avery, I wouldn't be able to let her go. I'd want her sitting knotted on my lap like this for the rest of my days.

But I'm the sappy one of the pack – that's what they've always told me. Cruise, he's always been more level-headed. And as for Kent ...

"I like your hands on me," Avery whispers eventually. "I

like both your hands on me. That probably isn't very sensible – as you've said. You alphas may get possessive and obsessive, but us omegas, we get attached and dependent pretty darn quick too. Then again, I've never been very good at doing the sensible thing. I tend to follow my heart and not my head."

"I like that about you," Cruise says softly.

"It lands me in trouble," she says, smiling at him, then wriggling herself in my lap. "Another case in point."

I go to tell her that I'd be happy to land in this type of trouble with her for the next ten days, but before I get a chance, there's a knock on the office door.

"Mr. Declan Hamilton," my actual secretary says from the other side of the door.

"Shit," Avery says in my lap.

"Shush," I whisper to her. Then much louder, I say, "What is it, Mary?"

"You have a meeting with the innovation team starting now."

"Push it back five minutes," I say, then looking down at the omega add, "actually make that fifteen." Who am I kidding, my knot isn't deflating any time soon. I'm still pumping seed into this omega like she's in heat.

Ahhh heat ...

Avery elbows me.

"What?" I say.

"She asked you if you wanted her to print out some report."

I clear my throat and peer down at my laptop on the office floor. The screen is cracked.

"Yes, please, Mary. And can you send tech support up here too?"

"Certainly," she says and then we hear her footsteps

retreat from the door.

"Do you think she knew?" Avery squeaks.

"Probably. You're a pretty noisy little thing."

"I can't help it," she says.

"I like it," Cruise tells her. "I want to know when my omega is enjoying herself."

His omega?

Is that the bond talking or Cruise?

Although, as I nuzzle the little thing's throat some more and more of those noises come tumbling out of her mouth, I realize I'm beginning to think of her as ours.

Shit, Avery wasn't wrong, this is a heap of trouble.

The friend returns just before lunch by which time Avery is back on her own seat with her book, although without her panties.

She asked for them back. I said no. She argued a bit but when I reminded her how much easier it would be for me to eat out her pussy without the panties she relented.

I'm looking forward to delivering on that promise as soon as the occasion arises.

The friend glances around at us all with suspicion. I don't blame her. There is the definite scent of sex in the air – clear to any alpha or omega. Hopefully not so clear to a beta like Jacks.

"There were no trampolines," she says with disgust.

"I told you," Cruise says.

"Or foosball tables or beanbags. In fact, the only remotely interesting place was the innovation lab. But they weren't even wearing white coats in there. It was just a load of dudes glued to their computers."

"Why was it interesting then?" Avery asks, closing her book.

"They had some of the new products on display."

"Secret products," I say.

"Like what?" Avery asks.

"The latest Hamilton smartphone."

"It's beautiful," Jacks says. "You should come see it."

Avery looks across at Cruise.

"I'll take you there this afternoon. Although, we're going to need a cover story about who you are."

"I told them I was a tax inspector."

I groan. "Terrific." We'll have staff leaking stories to the press in no time.

"So, do you guys actually do lunch?" Avery asks. "Or are you too busy and important?"

"Far too busy and important for eating," I say. "But for you we can be persuaded to take a break. What do you fancy?"

She raises an eyebrow at me, and I may not be bonded to the girl, but I can take a guess.

"I'd kill for a cheeseburger, right now." Jacks says.

What follows is a lengthy discussion in which Avery and her friend argue backward and forward over the best lunch options. In the end, Cruise tells them he's taking them to the best sandwich store in the city in such a way that shuts down the debate.

"Are you coming too?" Avery asks, looking through her eyelashes at me.

"I'll catch you up. I have something I need to do first."

I wait for the three of them to leave, then fall back in my chair.

I feel like a complete douchebag and also fucking elated.

I've been wanting to fuck a girl over my desk since I got into business school.

But the freaking HR consequences of that have stopped me from making that fantasy a reality.

The consequences could be even more catastrophic when it comes to Avery, and yet I hadn't been able to resist.

The girl is like sugar. Sweet. Addictive. Causing a buzz in my body.

I smile to myself, shaking my head.

I don't regret it. In fact, I will be eating her pussy like I promised and fucking her over my desk again this afternoon – who am I kidding.

But my packmates – they are going to be pissed. Pissed, angry, betrayed.

Reluctantly, I drag myself to my feet and head across the floor to Max's office.

He's on the phone when I walk in and I take a seat and wait, foot tapping against the floor.

"What?" Max says as he replaces the receiver. "You look nervous. I hate it when you're fucking nervous. What happened?"

"Erm ..."

He narrows his eyes. "That bad?"

"Depends on your view."

"And in yours?"

"Fucking amazing."

His shoulders relax a fraction, then tighten again. "And in mine?"

I inhale. "I fucked the omega."

Max stares at me for a long, long moment. I try to read his expression, try to determine if he's going to strangle or forgive me.

"You did? Wh-when? How?"

"How? You need me to give you biology lessons–"

"Declan," he warns.

"In our office, over my desk, about an hour ago."

"Over ... your ... desk."

I lean over my knees, my foot still jiggling. "Yes."

A flurry of expressions flitter across his face – anger, betrayal, amazement, lust.

"Do you hate me?" I say.

"Hate you?" He smiles half-heartedly. "No, man. It was a fucking stupid plan. One we were never going to be able to stick to. You knew that. I knew that."

"But once Kent and Jonah get an idea in their heads ..."

"Yeah." He scrubs his hand down his face. "Shit, I wonder if I can convince Cruise to come work in my office this afternoon and bring the omega with him."

"Nah, I've already promised the omega I'd eat her out this afternoon. I'm so fucking desperate to taste her."

"Maybe I'll come watch that show," he says.

"You know, I think she'd like that. The omega is a little actress. Likes to perform. Likes to be watched."

"Does she now?" he says, eyes darkening. Then he shakes his head. "Jonah will be pissed. Kent will be ..."

"Apocalyptic?"

"Worse."

"Shit."

"You really think she is a scam artist like Kent says?" he asks.

"No," I say with conviction. "I think she's the real deal, Max. One hundred percent."

I know girls fake it all the time. But that was no fraud. The way she came, the way her pussy pulsed around me, that was no damn act.

It was the real thing.

Chapter Twenty-Two

Avery

After possibly the strangest lunch of my life (is it really possible to get turned on by a man eating a sandwich? The answer to that is, yes, yes it is. Especially when he's giving me I-want-to-fuck-you eyes as I attempt to force down my own lunch), Jacks drags me to a quiet corner of the alpha's office where we can attempt a private conversation.

Not that any conversation is truly private. Cruise can hear us through the bond and anyway, an alpha's hearing is especially astute. I'm sure they can hear every word. It doesn't stop Jacks.

"I did a bit more research for you," she hisses, tugging out her phone. I throw her a quizzical look. "About the you-know-what?" she says, motioning to the two alphas I'm sure are pretending to be engrossed in their work.

"Oh that," I say, pulling her closer and leaning my head right up close to hers. "And?"

"And you owe me, Avery. This was not ... how I imagined spending my time here in Rockview. But," she adds as I go to interrupt her, "as you are my best friend and I love you, I am prepared to make some very big sacrifices for you and your happiness. And if happiness comes in the shape of five very big, very well-endowed alphas, then so be it."

"I may already have made some progress in that department," I whisper right into her ear.

"What? How?"

"While you were exploring the building."

"In the office." Jacks shakes her head. "So, my research endeavors were all for nothing."

"No, no," I said. "We haven't got that far yet." I drop my voice even lower, although I can sense the tension from the alphas on the opposite side of this ginormous office. They're both straining to catch every word. "Declan and I did stuff while ... while ..."

"While?" Jacks says, her body also straining with tension now.

"While Cruise watched."

"Holy macaroni!" she yelps and Cruise jumps to his feet as Declan's head snaps up from his work.

"What?" Cruise says in alarm. "What's wrong?"

"Apparently nothing," Jacks says.

"Girl talk," I explain.

"I've always wondered what girls talk about," Declan says, a little dreamily, gazing towards me.

Jacks smirks. "Periods, cramps and–"

"Okay, okay," Declan says, the dreamy expression vanishing as he snaps his gaze back to his work.

"In fact, Avery was just telling me all about these new–"

"We don't need the details," Declan says, practically wrapping his arm around his head to block out our words.

"Jacks!" I giggle.

"Serves him right for eavesdropping," she says.

I catch Cruise's eyes as he lowers himself back to his seat. There's no use telling Jacks that Cruise won't be able to help listening in, although I hope he's polite enough to at least try.

"So how was it?" Jacks says. "I've never had a threesome."

"How about the time—"

"Doesn't count."

"Really good," I say, catching Cruise's gaze again over the top of Jacks' shoulder.

He winks at me, and I think that's even more sexy than the sandwich eating.

Sandwich eating, huh? he growls through the bond.

"Avery!" Jacks says, knocking against my shoulder.

"Huh?" I say, dragging my gaze away from the alpha.

"I said, what about the feelings?"

"The feelings? Hmmm, pretty damn good."

"Not the feelings in your pussy," Jacks says, wiping her hand down her face, "the ones in your heart. Are you doing all right on that front?" She does that thing where she scrutinizes my face.

"Yep, fine. I'm having fun like you told me to."

"And like you wanted ..."

"Yeah, totally wanted. It was super super hot, Jacks. And so, I'm definitely in need of that research. Dish it up."

Jacks narrows her eyes, scrutinizing me further, before she turns her attention back to her phone.

"Well, now that you're a pro at the anal stuff ..."

"What? Wait ... who says I'm a pro at anal?" I mouth.

"The two of you did. At breakfast."

"Did we?"

"Anyway," Jacks continues, "that's one of your options. One in the hoo hoo and one up your–"

"I knew that much, Jacks. I'm not completely stupid. I am more worried about the, you know, positions."

"Ahh right. I figured as much. I made some diagrams."

My shoulders sag in relief. "Thanks, Jacks."

"But ..." she hesitates.

"Yes?"

"You do know there are other ways of doing it too, right? Two, or even three cocks in one–"

"Yes, I knew that too."

"Right, good. Because I didn't know that was possible. I mean, three!"

I shrug. "I'm an omega. I'm designed for a pack to share me."

From across the room Cruise attempts to muffle a low growl.

"Jesus," Jacks mutters as my gaze swims towards him once again.

Jacks snaps her fingers in front of my face and I jolt, my focus returning to her. "Are you sure you're not going into heat?"

"Heat? No way. I'm not due one for a couple of months."

"You just seem awfully distracted. The way you get right before one starts."

"No, no. It's these men. They're really darn distracting."

Jacks peers over her shoulder and jolts herself when she finds both alphas glaring at us. "Definitely distracting," she mutters, reaching into her purse and pulling out a notepad. She flips over the cover, and I see a list of names I recognize.

"What's that?" I ask as Jacks keeps flipping.

"The list of names I promised to give Cruise."

"You're not seriously–" She glares at me. "Jacks, he wasn't serious."

"He was."

"Right," I say, rolling my eyes. "And what's he going to do with a list like that anyway?"

"This pack runs half the internet. I bet they can make a person's life very uncomfortable," she says sinisterly, and I decide I'm better off not knowing.

I turn my attention instead to the first drawing as she twists the pad my way. Across the lined page are what I think are three, maybe four, stick people. The number really depends if one is carrying a watermelon or being sucked off.

"What the hell is that?" I ask, pointing to a confusing scribble on the diagram.

"That's ..." Her eyes flick to the alphas and then she leans in to whisper in my ear.

I squint. "Oh, I see it now. That looks doable."

"Totally and you're pretty flexible anyway."

I nod and flip the page. "Nope," I say and flip again.

"Really? I thought that one looked kinda fun."

"Not if I don't want to crack a rib." I bring the pad up to my face and examine the next diagram. "What the hell is this? It looks like someone's juggling basketballs."

"That's you," she says.

"My tits are not that big!"

"Actually, Avery, they totally are. Then that's one alpha," she says, pointing to a stick man. "That's the second. That's the third, and that's the fourth."

"Four!"

She shrugs and I look closer. "Oh ... kay."

I flip over a few more pages. I'm not sure if looking at

these has me feeling excited by the possibilities or slightly terrified. Maybe a bit of both. At least I'm going to go into any developments armed with more knowledge.

"Thanks, Jacks," I say, kissing her cheek. "Can I keep these?"

"Are you going to study up?" she asks, ripping the pages out of her pad.

"Nope," I say, snatching them from her hand, folding them in half and stuffing them into my pocket. "I'm going to frame them."

Jacks scowls at me. "Are you dissing my artistic abilities?"

"Not at all. People pay a lot of money for erotic works of art like these."

"Asshole," Jacks mouths at me and I wrap her in my arms and give her another hug.

"An asshole that's very grateful."

"I just hope it comes in handy when you get there."

"*If* I get there," I remind her.

Two alphas may be on board, but two alphas do not a pack make.

Chapter Twenty-Three

Max

Unfortunately, I never get the chance to watch the little omega show. I'm dragged into some meeting and kept there all afternoon. By the time I emerge, fucking frustrated with a pair of testicles the size of basketballs, Cruise, Declan and Avery have left for the day.

I walk straight past their empty office and over to Jonah's. He's sitting at his desk, reading a report. He looks up when I enter.

"You ready to leave?" I ask him.

"Yes," he says, "but I'm going to stay here for as long as I can."

"Why?"

"There's less temptation here than at home."

Yeah, a lot less temptation. I consider informing him that Declan has already fallen foul of that temptation but decide that piece of information is better left delivered by the offender himself.

Instead, I wave him goodbye and make my way home.

The mansion is all lit up when I return home but eerily quiet and empty.

I head for my bedroom and switch on the lamp. I'll watch a film. Play a video game. Hell, I might even call my mom. Something to distract me from the omega.

The more I think about it, the more I consider this afternoon a lucky escape; fate intervening to stop me from doing something stupid.

I don't like the plan. I fucking hate the plan. But I can't deny it's a sensible one. The omega may smell like honey. She may be beautiful. She may have a smile and a laugh that make my insides spin. But what do we really know about her? And more importantly, she's leaving. A few more days and she'll be gone.

Better not to risk it.

I strip out of my suit and go take a long, cold shower. Something I hope will temper my dick's enthusiasm. It's freaking painful under the powerful blast. And my cock is about as pleased about the icy onslaught as the rest of my body. The effect doesn't last, though. No sooner am I drying off and stepping into a pair of sweatpants and tee, than my cock's stirring again. It's that scent. It's in the air.

I pick up the remote and flick through the film options. Then toss it onto the bed.

I switch on the game console, load up a game, peering out of the window while I wait.

The lights are on in the pool house, the blinds drawn. But there's a figure lying out on one of the loungers by the pool. I stroll over to the window for a better look. It's the omega's friend, scrolling on her phone.

My feet are heading out of my room, down the staircase and through to the pool before I know what I'm doing.

"Where's Avery?" I ask.

The friend yelps, tossing her phone up into the air before scrambling to catch it again. When it's safe in her hands, she lays a palm over her chest and sighs.

"You scared the crap out of me."

"Sorry," I say.

She places her phone down on her thigh.

"Avery's in there," she says, pointing to the pool house behind her. "With Cruise and Declan. They're trying to be discreet, but Avery doesn't really do discreet as you may have noticed."

"What do you mean?" I ask. Is Kent right after all?

"She's a free spirit. A wildflower. She doesn't do well with containment and ... quiet."

We're both quiet ourselves for a moment and sure enough we hear a scream of satisfaction carrying across the night's air.

"And there she is. On cue."

"You wanna come and watch TV in the main house?" I ask her.

"Uh huh." She swings her feet to the ground. "I love my best friend and all, and I'm pleased she's enjoying herself, but I do not need to hear that shit."

Me neither. Not if I hope to hang onto any of my sanity. Because that scream ... Yeah, I'd like to make her scream like that. I'd *really* like to make her scream like that. Over and over and over again–

"Max?" the friend says, right by my ear.

"Yeah?"

"Are we going in or not?"

I can't help but take a longing gaze towards the house.

Then I turn away and lead Jacks through to the den, somewhere I hope she won't cause any trouble.

"Can I get you anything? Drink? Snack?"

"You got a beer?"

"Sure." I stroll to the kitchen, trying damn hard not to listen out for any other tantalizing noises from the pool house. Grabbing a couple of beers from the fridge, I knock them against the side of the marble counter, the lids flying up into the air, and return to the den. I pass Jacks her beer and she takes a long swig, eyeing me as she does.

I settle down onto the couch next to hers. She's watching a football game. I love football but tonight it's all blurring lines and spinning balls. My mind is too busy on that scent and those noises.

"Can I ask you something?" Jacks says, knocking me out of my reverie.

"You can ask," I say. "I may not answer. Been stung too many times in media interviews to make that promise ever again."

"Fair," she says, taking a second gulp of beer. Mine's still untouched. "Any particular reason why you're in here with me, and not with them over there?"

"Who?" I say, feigning ignorance.

"Your packmates and my friend."

"I wasn't invited."

"Bullshit."

I stare at the screen.

I wonder what they're doing over there. What they're doing to the omega to make her scream in ecstasy like that. Are they – my hands dampen with sweat – are they taking her together? I screw up my eyes. It's a long, long, long time since we fucked an omega together. A whole lifetime ago.

I didn't know how much I'd missed it until now. Right

now. Knowing it could be happening only feet away and I'm sitting here watching some crappy football match instead.

"You should go say hi," Jacks continues. "Avery's super friendly. Always picking up new friends – sometimes to her own detriment. She once felt sorry for this loner kid at school who had really, really bad oral hygiene. She invited him to sit with us for lunch once and then he became obsessed. She ended up having to get a restraining order."

"Shit!" I say, my spine automatically stiffening at the thought of the omega in danger.

"It's okay. His folks finally invested in his dental care, and he ended up becoming a doctor. But what I mean is, you have very – exceptionally good – oral hygiene – and you're totally her type."

"I am?"

"Oh yeah. She loves the golden-haired bad boy types with the tats," she points to the inks trailing up both my forearms, "and the ..." she spins her finger around in my direction.

"The?"

"Muscles."

I flex my pecs automatically.

"Yeah, that would have her drooling."

I stare down at the bottle resting in my hands.

"But maybe she's not *your* type?" Jacks ventures.

"Oh, she's totally my type," I mutter.

"Glad to hear it. I don't understand how the girl is still single. I mean, she's hopeless, but adorable. Like a puppy. You can't help but fall in love with her."

And yeah, that's the problem. The last thing we need is to fall in love with Avery. She lives on the other side of the country. She'll be leaving.

"Why hasn't a pack snapped her up, then?"

"Well, there aren't a hell of a lot of packs back where we are from and the ones that do exist they're," she grimaces, "meh."

"Meh?"

"Snotty, rude, obnoxious. Avery and her sister tried the whole dating packs thing but where we're from those girls are not wealthy and connected enough. The packs want an omega who will help lift them socially, professionally, the whole she-bang."

"And Avery isn't connected or wealthy?"

Jacks lowers her beer and narrows her eyes at me. "No. Do you have a problem with that?"

"This pack isn't looking for an omega of any kind – wealthy or broke. Connected or ... unconnected."

Jack's eyes narrow further. "Sure," she says flatly.

"What does that mean?" I ask her.

"Every alpha wants an omega. Every pack wants an omega. You dudes live for that stuff."

"That's a hell of a stereotype."

"Not every stereotype is false. I'm also not blind. Or stupid. I've seen you drooling over her. And you said yourself she's your type."

This conversation is giving me a headache, and the omega's scent in my nose is making me irritable as hell.

I want to do something with that irritation.

Something like rut her hard.

"So, you don't care if she's broke, and she's your type. Why are you still sitting here with me?"

"Do you always solicit men for your friend?" I snap.

Jacks shrugs and turns her attention back to the game. I tune my attention back onto the screen too, but my heart is thumping in my throat, sweat trickling down my spine and my beer bottle shaking in my hands. Her scent spins in my nose and against my tongue and that scream rattles against my skull.

I take a swig of my beer. The bottle clashes against my teeth and Jacks side-eyes me.

I take out my phone. Check my messages, my eyes scanning over words I don't read.

What does she look like when she comes? Does she screw up her eyes? Or do her eyelids flicker? Does she blush and shake? Or does she go limp and placid?

And how does she taste? Like honey? That sweet? Or more musky, more real?

I lick my lips. I can almost taste that scent. Taste her.

My cock is so stiff in my pants it's almost fucking unbearable.

This is stupid. She might not even want me there. She might turn me away.

Okay, Jacks says I'm her type. Cruise and Declan say she likes to be shared and watched but that doesn't mean anything.

Except I can imagine it. I can imagine her on her hands and knees as I lick her out and Cruise feeds her his cock.

I almost come in my pants, like some inexperienced teenage geek.

I adjust the seat of my pants, grimacing at how damn uncomfortable I am.

The commentary on the football stops, the match cuts to a commercial break. For a moment the noise from the TV halts and another of those goddamn screams pierces through the air.

I jump to my feet and storm out of the den, out of the house, around the pool and bang my fist against the pool house door.

I wait precisely ten seconds and when nobody answers, I slam open the door and storm inside. My nose leads me straight to the master bedroom where I can hear female giggling from behind the door. I don't pause. I fling back the door and find the three of them in bed together.

Except they're not naked. Or tangled up.

No, the omega is dressed in what looks like PJs and is propped up against a pillow, sitting between my two pack-mates, a bowl of popcorn resting in her lap, the TV flickering on the far wall.

"Hey Max," she says. "We're watching a movie. Wanna come join us?"

"*Love Actually*," Declan says with a grin and a slight head tilt towards Cruise. It's a known fact that Cruise will only ever consent to watching political thrillers. Definitely not comedy. Definitely not *romantic* comedy.

"You're watching movies? Jacks said–"

"Jacks is sulking. She says she's watched this movie a billion times. But it's my favorite, and these two said they'd never seen it before." She pops a piece of corn between her pink lips.

I shake my head, feeling fucking confused. "But ... the screaming?" I murmur.

"Seems Avery here tends to get a little over-excited at certain parts of the movie."

"I can't help it. When Mark holds up those cards and confesses his feelings to Juliet, and when the Prime Minister goes searching for Natalie ..." She holds her hands to her chest and swoons.

I shift my weight from one foot to the other, staring at the three of them like an idiot. I'm going to fucking throttle Jacks.

"Have you seen *Love Actually*?" Avery asks me.

I clear my throat and find my voice. "Errr, no."

She pats the mattress. "Oh, you have to see it. We can rewind and start it again from the beginning."

"No!" Cruise and Declan say together.

Avery's face falls in a way that seems to cause me actual physical pain in my ribs. "I thought you were enjoying it."

Both my packmates reach for her, Cruise stroking his palm down her arm, Declan squeezing her hand.

"I'm loving it," Declan says.

"It's great," Cruise adds through gritted teeth.

"I'm just super keen to see how it ends," Declan adds.

She smiles again, somehow buying this act to please her. Or perhaps she's simply pleased my packmates want to please her.

I scrub my hand through my hair. I can feel it's getting a little too long.

"I'd ... better ... go."

"Go?" Avery says, disappointment marking her face a second time, that ache in my chest repeating all over again. "You're going?"

"He's not going," Declan says, diving over the bed to grab my arm and tug me down towards the mattress. "Are you, Max?"

I guess not.

"Here, you can take my place," Declan says with a look. "I'll go fill up the popcorn bowl. Avery has one hell of an appetite."

"Hey," she says, giggling and elbowing him. "I can't help it if you make the best popcorn in the land."

Declan's chest visibly puffs out and he scoops up the bowl, plants a kiss on the omega's cheek that has her blushing and leaves me the space beside her.

Cautiously, I maneuver myself into his spot on the mattress.

If I thought watching football with Jacks in the den was torturous, I expect sitting right next to the omega – her warm body leaning against me ever so slightly, her bare arm brushing mine, her scent so vivid my stomach grumbles – will be far, far worse. Agony itself.

Chapter Twenty-Four

Avery

I think I may be in heaven itself – bowl of popcorn in my lap, favorite movie on the TV, and three hot alphas surrounding me – one on either side and one laid out by my feet (like that isn't a fantasy I've perused).

I flip my eyes to Max on my left. I've hardly spoken to this packmate. He's the tallest and broadest, with long blonde hair and inks trailing up and down his arms. Arms that brush against mine every time he dives his hand into the bowl and scoops out a fistful of popcorn. Each time that action causes tingles to race across my skin and his proximity is making my cheeks hotter and my panties wetter.

I can't help it. It's not only the way the man looks – like he belongs in a fighting cage and not a suit – it's the way he smells too. Like pine forests.

I shove five more pieces of corn into my mouth. Not that

I'm hungry – just to stop myself from dribbling down my chin.

I need to get a grip.

Cruise may be keen on the whole sharing-me-with-his-pack business. I may be keen. Declan too. Doesn't mean the rest of his pack is. In fact, it's clear Kent is anything but and Jonah seems to be avoiding me since dinner last night.

Max may be equally disinterested. Here for the movie, not me. Although, the way his arm keeps brushing mine, the way his leg presses against me, doesn't feel accidental.

Does he know what that's doing to me? Can he smell what it's doing to me?

Max takes another handful of corn, throws it into his open mouth and drops his arm back to the mattress, his hand resting right by my hip. His knuckles graze against the skin there and on instinct, I wriggle.

From my peripheral vision, I see his eyes switch to me and I swallow.

Slowly, he shifts his hand, tickling his fingertips against me now. I bite my lip, eyes trained on the screen.

He strokes higher, to where the waistband of my pajama shorts meet the hem of my Cami top. He slides his fingers under the cotton material, connecting with the warm skin of my stomach. His hands are huge. I'm pretty sure they could circle my ribcage completely. And all of a sudden that's all I want them to do, biting my lip so hard I'm surprised I don't pierce the skin.

His hand travels higher, over my ribs and to the underside of my breast.

Here he halts, and the anticipation has a pulse pounding between my legs. But he only teases me for a moment, before caressing his coarse fingertips over the curve of my breast and finding the wrinkled skin of my nipple.

"No bra," he murmurs right by my ear.

I shake my head.

"Good," he says, pinching the already-stiff peak of my nipple between his forefinger and thumb, making my back arch, my head tip backwards, and a needy sigh fly from my mouth.

"I guess, we're not watching this movie anymore, then, Omega," Declan says from the end of the bed, pinching my toes.

"No," Max says firmly, "no more fucking movie."

"So got any suggestions on how we should pass the time instead?" Declan says.

Max leans towards me, squeezing my tit in his hand and growling.

"Like that, huh?" Declan chuckles. "You happy with that suggestion, Avery?"

"Very," I gasp as Max massages my breast and his other hand grips my hip and pulls me towards him. The popcorn bowl tumbles over, and corn litters over the mattress. I reach for the alpha, my own hands grappling at his t-shirt, feeling strong muscle beneath the soft fabric.

Max's mouth finds my neck and he licks a stripe down my throat, swirling over the bite mark at my shoulder. He growls even lower, tugging me right against his body and I can feel how hard he is through those gray sweatpants.

"Oh," I murmur.

"I've been hard all damn day smelling and thinking about you, little Omega," he says, before yanking down my Cami with his teeth and sucking the nipple he was just teasing into his mouth.

I mewl and rub my core against his erection. As I do, I

feel a pair of lips suck my left big toe into a wet mouth, and another pair of lips hit the back of my neck, strong hands gripping my waist.

And forget what I said earlier – forget whatever nonsense I've said before – because this is heaven. Three men – three alphas – sharing me, pleasing me. It can't get much more heavenly than this. Unless …

"I need to come," I moan. I'm wet and swollen and damn needy.

"Need to?" Declan mutters.

"Yes, nee—eeeeed," I squeal as Max jams his hand into my panties and rubs at my clit.

"Going to make you come in all the ways I can think of, little Omega. With my fingers," he flicks at me causing stars to crash across my vision, "with my mouth," he nips at my throat, "and with my cock." He grinds into me.

Yes, I want all of those. All at once. Right now.

I open my mouth. Then hesitate.

This is the dream. This is the slice of heaven.

Being with a pack – devoured by one. I want it so bad. But I'm also nervous. Can it really live up to the reality?

"Yes," Cruise says firmly. "It damn well can."

I peer over my shoulder at him, meeting those midnight eyes I'm beginning to rely on. Through the bond I can feel his confidence and reassurance.

"We're about to devour you together, Omega," he says. "Make you come so many times you won't know what day it is, what year it is, what is up, what is down or who you even are."

"Oh fuck," I say, as Max plunges two thick fingers into my pussy and massages the spot on my wall.

"You've never done this before?" Max asks gently by my ear. "Been with more than one alpha at a time?"

"No," I whisper back.

"But you want to?"

"Hell, yes," I gasp as his thumb connects with my clit and I think I might explode.

"Do you think you could take more than one of us? Shall we see?" He slides a third finger inside me, stretching me just a tad and then a fourth, drawing me open even more. "I think you could. I think you're built just like a good omega should be – capable of taking all her alphas. Of satisfying them all together."

I moan, writhing against his fingers, as Declan sucks my toes and Cruise rakes his teeth up and down my neck.

Max's thumb rubs at me, his fingers stroke at me and I come loud and noisy around his hand, flooding the sheets with slick.

The alphas don't give me a moment to recover. I'm flipped straight onto my back, my shorts and my top whipped away and Max's mouth on my pussy. I run my fingers through his hair, silky. The other two shift around us, Declan coming to kiss my mouth and Cruise my tits.

I'm coming again so quickly, I hardly have time to catch my breath.

"So fucking sensitive," Max says. "And you taste so good. So, fucking good." He groans, his lips vibrating against my clit and dipping me straight into another orgasm.

"Fuck, she really is," Declan says, nipping my earlobe. "I think we could keep her coming all night."

"I think that might actually kill me," I sigh, the pleasure still swirling through my body.

"Would be a nice way to die though, huh?" Declan says.

"Yeah," I whisper with a smile.

"Fuck, I'd happily die between these thighs," Max says, squeezing and then biting at them.

I smile even wider. Then that smile drops into a frown.

"What?" Cruise says, sensing my unhappiness almost immediately.

"You're all wearing clothes," I chide.

"You want them off?" Declan asks.

"Like yesterday."

Shirts, t-shirts, sweaters and pants fly across the room and then I'm rewarded with a truly heavenly sight. Three men surely sculpted in imitation of the gods themselves. Declan's dark hair hangs loose around his face and his muscular chest is covered in a thick rug of similarly dark hair I want to run my fingers through. Max is far lighter, dark inks scribbled all over his pale skin – inks I want to trace with my fingertips – and my tongue.

Then there's his cock. Just as long, just as thick as his packmates'.

Could I really fit more than one of those cocks inside me?

"Yes," Cruise says, firmly. "You most definitely can. But let Max have you to himself first. Okay, sweetheart?"

My eyes land back on Max, connecting with his green ones, heavy with lust.

"Okay," I say, rolling up onto my knees and reaching for him. He lowers one knee to the mattress, bringing his mouth to mine and kissing me deeply. I taste myself on his tongue and I shiver with desire.

He leans back, finding my gaze again. "Wanna ride me little one, because I'd love to see those tits of yours bouncing. Love to see you get yourself off on my cock." He takes his cock in his hand, running his fist up and down its length in a way that's frankly teasing. "Or are you a little princess, Avery, and want us to do all the work?"

I point to the bed. "Lie down, Alpha," I tell Max. He stares at me. "Please," I add, with a flutter of my eyelashes.

He huffs a little, still ruffled by an order from an omega. But then he lowers himself down, raising his arms and beckoning me closely. I crawl towards him and let him capture my waist. He lifts me into the air easily and positions me so I'm straddling his lap. His cock is right beneath me, stiff, dribbling pre-come and waiting for me.

I can't help a little needy whimper as I sink down onto him, more of those stars streaming across my vision as he brushes against all my sensitive places.

He groans as my pussy swallows him up, the bed shaking underneath us, his eyes falling shut as he loses himself to the feeling.

For a moment, I just stare at him, sort of spellbound by how good he looks, but then from somewhere behind me Cruise orders me to move and I lift myself up on my knees, his cock sliding along my walls, and then slamming back down, crying out because it feels too good for words.

I find a rhythm, one he dictates, using his strength to lift and lower me so I don't think I'm doing much of the work. It's just as well, because soon my legs turn to jelly and I'm too wild to know what the hell I'm doing, especially when he lifts his hips and slams into me from below, making everything twice as intense, a million times better.

His eyes open, and our gazes meet again, something crackling in the air between us, before his gaze falls to my tits and stay there.

"So fucking pretty," he groans. "These tits are so fucking pretty. Look at them bounce, look at them bounce as you bounce on my cock just like a good little omega should."

All my omega instincts light up. I never knew how

much it pleased me to be called a good omega, but I'd like them to call me it over and over again. And when he does, I come, clenching and convulsing violently around his big cock.

Such a good omega, I hear Cruise whisper in my head. "Going to be a really good omega for us now and let me fuck you too ..."

Chapter Twenty-Five

Cruise

I hold my breath, waiting on her reply.

"Yes," she says.

I watch her, grinding her pussy on Max's cock, her back arched, her breasts full, her beautiful neck elongated, my bite mark glistening on her throat.

How did this happen? How did such a beautiful creature land in my lap? What devil did I trade my soul with that night? What gods did I bargain with?

I have everything I could possibly want in my life. Success, money, a pack. I don't deserve any more than that. And yet, here she is, beckoning me towards her, those seductive dark eyes of hers alighting on my face, her pretty pink lips parting to say, "Cruise."

I crawl across the bed and pause beside them. Then

pressing my palm between her shoulder blades, I press her down onto Max until she's lying flat against his body.

I look down to where he's sunk deep inside her pussy and I line myself up above him, positioning my body over them to find the right angle.

"Ready?" I ask them both.

"Yes," they say together, and I grind myself inside her pussy. It's tight, Max is large, and he's already stretching her open. But she's an omega, she's built for this and with a little encouragement, with caresses and kisses, she relaxes, opening up and letting me thrust inside her. The three of us groan together. I can feel Max's cock against mine, hot and hard and as I slide out, we grind against one another, creating a different kind of friction.

"How does that feel, Omega?" Declan asks. "Are you okay?"

She can't answer. The feelings inside her are too intense. I can feel them through the bond.

"She likes it, don't you, sweetheart?" I say. "You like two alphas fucking you at once."

She whimpers, her hands tight on Max's shoulders. He grunts as I pound into her, increasing the pressure and the depth. I know she can take it. I know it's making her feel like nothing else has.

"Where did you come from, Omega? Where? Did you fall right out of heaven? A fallen little angel. So good, so precious, so damn beautiful."

"Cruise," she gasps, her fingernails sinking into Max's skin.

"Come again, sweetheart," Max growls. "Come again and then we'll knot you together. You want that, don't you?"

I want that too. It's something we've never done before. Sure, we've shared. Back in the old days we saw omegas through their heats. But that was long long ago. And not like this. Not together. We've never taken an omega together. Rutted an omega together. Knotted an omega together.

A whine plays in her throat, louder and louder until she's wailing, her skin hot and damp with sweat, her scent searing. She comes in that perfect way she does. Messy and loud, letting all three of us know just how good it feels.

Her pussy squeezes around the two of us, pushing us together and I cry out myself. My knot expanding of its own damn accord. Max grunts too and his knot grows, pressing up against mine, stretching our little omega wide open for us. I come, pumping seed deep inside my omega, and Max follows after me. His seed mixing with mine.

Fuck, when it comes time to breed this little omega, we are going to pump her full of come, have her belly rounding with it, have it streaming down her legs, creating a pack baby.

I press my lips to that bite mark, feel all her emotions through the bond, hold her in my arms, and in that moment I know, know it with all my heart and all my soul, I can't let her go. She's mine. My omega. Ours.

"Yours," she whispers through the bond.

* * *

Somehow the three of us manage to roll onto our sides, sticky, exhausted, happy.

Max strokes the damp hair from the omega's pretty face, his eyes locked on her. She's mesmerizing and he can't drag his gaze away.

Declan seems equally dazzled, lying out alongside the three of us, whispering again and again how amazing that looked, how he wants to fuck her with one of us next time.

"How was it for you?" I whisper into her ear, even though I know. I still want to hear her say it out loud. I'm an alpha. I have an ego I need stroking; plain and simple.

"So good," she says, her voice all raw and scratchy.

"Better than you imagined?"

"So much better. I don't know how I'm going to be content to sleep with just one alpha after this. I said you'd ruined me for all other men and now it's most definitely confirmed."

"Good," Max growls, "because you've ruined me for all other women."

She giggles.

And now you're ours, you won't be sleeping with any other men, I tell her through the bond.

She twists her head around to peer at me.

Your other packmates – Kent, Jonah?

I shake my head. I'm going to make them see reason. I will force them to. Avery is meant to be mine, meant to be ours. I'm not letting her go.

Her eyes flicker over my face and I feel hesitancy through the bond.

Hesitancy?

She confirmed she was ours. She said it loud and clear. She feels it too. There's no denying it.

"Can we talk about it later?" she asks out loud.

"Talk about what?" Declan asks.

"Avery's not going home. She's staying here with us. Because this is her home. This is her pack," I say.

The room is silent.

"Is that what Avery wants?" Declan asks.

"Yes," I answer for her, because I know it is, I feel it is. She wants it damn badly – a pack of her own. I can't understand the hesitancy.

"Avery?" Max asks her.

"This is all so fast–"

"Are you denying the way you feel, Omega?" I say, kissing my bite mark. I've never been so damn sure of anything in my life.

A mixture of emotions tumbles through her, and I try my hardest to capture and read them all.

"You're worried about our packmates?" I say.

She nods.

"Leaving your family. Your friends."

She nods a second time.

"You're worried about screwing up – of all the scrutiny Pack Hamilton's omega would bring."

"Yes," she says.

I hesitate. "You ... you don't think you're worthy of a pack."

She hesitates too. "Y-yes."

"Not worthy?" Declan says, propping himself up on his elbow to peer over Max at the omega. "Why would you think that? We're the ones not worthy."

"Oh God," she says, and I can feel how much she'd love to scurry away right now and not have this conversation. Instead, she's knotted to two of us and isn't going anywhere. "This is the first time I've been with a pack ... well, half a pack. And that's because I'm not exactly a catch. Which is fine. This has been the best sex of my life and I've really, really enjoyed it. But having me as a pack omega? Me?! I'm not glamorous. I tend to screw up. And I'm not connected or rich or–"

"We're plenty rich and connected. We don't need our omega to be," Declan says.

"No," Max agrees. "WE need someone genuine, kind,

sexy as hell. Someone light-hearted who will remind us there's more to life than work."

I stare at Max, unable to believe the words that just came out of his mouth.

"More to life than work?" Declan chuckles.

"Well, there is," Max says firmly. "I think we've forgotten that these last few years. Made sacrifices we shouldn't have."

"Like not having a pack omega?" Avery asks, her curiosity piqued.

"Like not having a pack omega."

"You were just too busy at work to find one or–"

"We weren't looking," Declan says.

"We were actively avoiding not looking."

"Why?" Avery asks.

"The business," I say, "we were too focused on the business and didn't want to be distracted by an omega." Which is not the whole truth but a big chunk of it.

"Hmmm," she says, her fingers tracing over Max's tattoos in an absentminded manner that's almost familiar.

"What?" I say, feeling that hesitation again.

"I wonder if an omega would only be a temporary distraction. Whether you'd all get bored pretty quick and return to your work, leaving your poor pack omega pretty rejected."

Declan laughs. "Temporary distraction? If we're talking about you, Avery, then no. I already know I want to spend as much time fucking and knotting you as I possibly can."

She sighs. "Well, that sounds ... nice."

"I can promise you it will be a hell of a lot nicer than nice."

"But that doesn't change the situation with your packmates."

"You don't need to worry about them," I say with certainty.

"Cruise," Avery says, "I really like you," happiness blooms in my chest, "but I'm not so desperate for a pack that I'm going to be with one when half the alphas don't want me."

"Right," I say, determined I'm going to make both Kent and Jonah see sense.

Because she's not leaving. Avery is going to be our pack omega.

Chapter Twenty-Six

Cruise

Unfortunately, my packmates are very adept at avoiding Avery and me over the next few days, which is a major problem. There's no way I can make them see how right Avery is for our pack unless they spend time in her company. And I can't convince Avery to stay when Kent and Jonah are doing their best to ignore her existence.

At least Jonah is polite about it. He makes an effort to say hello to the omega every morning and to ask about her plans for the day. But he's skipped the last two dinners, muttering about migraines and stomach aches and other made-up bullshit excuses.

Kent, on the other hand, won't look at her, speak to her, or even acknowledge her existence. It takes all my self-control not to smack his face. It won't help. It'll only make him all the more stubborn.

No, I'm going to need a more subtle plan if I hope to win my pack around to the idea of keeping Avery, of making her ours permanently. And I need to come up with one quickly, the bond binding us together is weakening each day that passes and soon she'll have no reason to stay.

I wait until Avery is safely soaking in the tub after another day at the office and turn to Max and Declan.

"I don't want her to go."

"You've said that. Multiple times," Declan says with a grin, lying out against the pillows on the bed. He's just had the omega sucking his cock and he looks mighty pleased about it.

"I'm serious."

"I know you are, and I happen to be in agreement with you. We shouldn't let her go."

Max swings his gaze between us. "Kent and Jonah–"

"Exactly," I say. "We need to win them around to this. We need to win them around to Avery."

"It wouldn't be hard if they actually spent time with her. Then they'd see what we see and there's no way they'd want to let her go."

"My thoughts exactly." I pace the room, stroking my chin. "We need to think of a way to get them together."

"We should start with Jonah," Declan says, leaning over his knees. "He's the weaker link."

"Yeah," Max agrees. "Have you seen the way he looks at her?"

"Any ideas?"

"It's not hard. Just put the woman in front of him. He's only human."

"But if he's acting like a jerk, Avery is not going to be interested."

"Jonah is way too much of a gentleman to act like a jerk."

"Right," I say, still pacing. "So how do we get them together?"

Declan's eyes begin to twinkle.

"What?" Max and I say together.

"What has the omega been doing solidly for the last few days?"

Bouncing on our cocks.

I lift an eyebrow.

Declan rolls his eyes at us. "No, not that! Jeez, get your minds out of the gutter, fellows." He chuckles, like his own mind hasn't been floating around in the gutter for the last four days straight. "Reading. She's been reading."

"So?" Max says.

Declan rolls his eyes a second time. "Who else likes to read? Who built a library in our house?"

I grin. Now I get it. Max nods his head, obviously understanding too.

"Have you shown her the library yet?" Max asks. "She's likely to orgasm as soon as she steps inside."

"No, I haven't." The library is located next to our offices in the east wing of the main house, somewhere I'd avoided on our tour on account of the grumpy packmate destroying keyboards.

"So, let's deposit her in the library for our scholarly packmate to find," Declan pronounces, a proud grin stretched across his face.

I scratch the back of my neck, considering his suggestion. It actually seems like a pretty good plan, certainly better than anything I've managed to come up with.

"We'll need to get rid of the friend," Max points out.

"Crap," Declan says, falling back against the cushions.

While Jacks has been leaving us alone in the bedroom, she's been locked to the omega's side at all other times.

"How about Miranda?" I suggest.

"Miranda?" Max frowns. "Miranda the gardener?"

"Yes, she's kinda hot and single."

"So?" Max says, frowning harder.

"She might be enough of a distraction for Jacks."

"Are you suggesting we pimp out our gardener?" Declan says, pretending to shake his head in shame.

"No, I'm suggesting Miranda might be Jacks' type and Jacks might be hers. I think we should dabble in a bit of match making."

"Us?" Max says pointing to his broad chest.

"Why not? If it works out, then Jacks will be a hella distracted."

"And how are we going to get them together?" Max asks.

"Yeah," I say, scratching the back of my neck. "That might be the tricky bit."

When Avery emerges from the bathroom a half hour later, wrapped in a large fluffy towel, we're all lounging on the bed casually.

Obviously, not casually enough, because she narrows her eyes. "What?" she asks.

"I'm sorry, sweetheart, but we have to catch up on some work this evening."

"Oh," she says with obvious disappointment. Our last few evenings have involved work of a completely different kind.

"We shouldn't be too long. Maybe you could amuse yourself in the library?"

"Library?" she squeaks, her eyes lighting up. "You have a library?"

Bingo!

"Yeah," I say, nonchalant, inspecting my fingernails. "You finished your book today, right? Maybe you could find another one in there."

Avery claps her hands in excitement. "Jacks is going to go wild about this!"

Declan frowns.

Another half an hour later, Avery and Jacks are following the three of us around the pool towards the main house. It's mid-summer, the evening bright with sunshine, the air warm and humid.

"Hey Jacks," Max says casually. "Do you like golf?"

"Nah, not really my thing. Why?"

"No reason," Max mutters, although the fact Miranda is a golf-fanatic was definitely his reasoning. His shoulders droop in defeat. He glances at me and shrugs.

If Avery's eyes lit up at the mere mention of the word library, they positively sparkle when we draw back the door and she walks inside, head tipping backwards as she examines the book shelves that reach right from the wooden floor all the way up to the tall, vaulted ceiling.

"It used to be the house ballroom," I explain. "But it's not like we throw any parties, so Jonah had it converted into a library a few years ago."

"Jonah created this?" she asks, spinning around and around.

"Yeah, it's his mission to fill the room completely."

"He's nearly succeeded," Jacks says with a chuckle.

"It's amazing." Avery sighs in a way that doesn't sound that far off an actual orgasm.

"You know you're never going to be able to drag her out of this room," Jacks says. She walks to the nearest shelf and begins examining the spines lined up in rows.

"I didn't think you were a bookworm like Avery," I say.

"I read the odd book," she says, picking a book off the shelf.

"But it's not really your thing?" I prompt.

"Jacks is more into her sports," Avery says, still spinning, seeming unable to decide where to start in this huge room. "In fact, sports *is* what she reads."

"Are you sure I couldn't interest you in a round of golf, then?" Max says.

Jacks peers out towards the windows and the carefully rolled lawns beyond. "Stupid sport."

Declan shifts uncomfortably on his feet.

We watch the two women browsing the bookshelves, hoping Jacks may lose interest in the next minute or two. Unfortunately, she finds a journal on football stats and drops down into one of the many armchairs, spreading the book across her lap.

"Is there any sightseeing you'd like to do while you're in Rockview, Jacks?" I try next. "You know the nightlife is renowned. I could give you a few recommendations, find someone to take you out tonight and show you around."

"Nah, I'm here to look after Avery. Especially with you guys working."

"I don't need looking after," Avery says from behind a book. "I'm perfectly fine and I have enough in here to entertain me for a lifetime."

Jacks gazes up from her journal and finds the three of us alphas glaring at her. She finally gets the damn hint.

"Unless of course you're trying to get rid of me."

Declan chuckles in a way, having known him fifteen years, I can tell is phony. "Of course not, we're very happy to have you here. Happy to have both of you here."

Jacks considers her friend for a moment who seems

completely oblivious to the conversation happening around her. "You know what I would like to do, though, go for a run. I've been cooped up the last few days and I need to get out and do some exercise. Are you sure you'd be all right if I left you for a bit, Avery?"

"Yeah, sure I will."

Declan jumps forward so quickly you'd think someone had poked him with a red-hot poker. "Stay there. I'll go call Miranda. She's our head gardener. She loves running. I'm sure she'd love to take you out, show you the best spot."

Jacks looks a little amused. "There's no need for that."

"We can't let you go off running on your own. Safer with a companion."

"Jacks is pretty good at looking after herself. She once tackled some dude who tried to mug us to the ground and kept him pinned there until the cops showed up."

"We're alphas," I say, "and looking after our family is paramount to what we do."

"Family?" Jacks says and Avery looks up from her book.

"We consider our friends, the people we work closely with, part of our family. We look after them. You shouldn't go out running alone. Besides, I think you'll get on with Miranda."

"Fine," Jacks says, hooking the book under her arm. "I'll go get changed."

Thank you, Avery says through the bond, smiling at me.

Declan heads off to collect Miranda and returns with her fifteen minutes later. She's dressed in tight running pants and a crop top, her short dark hair pinned back from her face. Jacks eyes nearly pop out of their sockets, and I congratulate myself on this master plan as the two of them walk off together, discussing running routes.

When they're out of earshot, the omega wags her finger

at Declan. "Jacks isn't stupid. She knows what you're up to."

"And what am I up to?" Declan says.

"I'm not entirely sure."

"I promise you, nothing," Declan says. "Now, will you be okay in here for a little bit while we go finish up that work? We'll be right next door."

Avery laughs. "Are you serious? Will I be okay? This is actual heaven."

Declan winks at me. Stage one of the plan complete.

Chapter Twenty-Seven

Jonah

I step into my library and immediately know the omega is there, her sweet, sugary scent engulfing me completely.

She lifts her eyes from the book she's perusing and finds me standing in the doorway.

"Oh, hi," she says brightly. "I hope you don't mind me invading your library. The others are working and Jacks ... actually I'm not sure where Jacks is." She looks at her watch. "She doesn't usually run this long."

I rub at my nose and adjust my glasses.

I should turn around and walk straight out of the room. This is my personal sanctuary. The place I come to escape the world, immersing myself in books to avoid the stress and strain of our lives.

But with the omega here?

Unfortunately, Avery is just my type. So much so I

wonder if she's real. If someone created her just for me, reached right into the depths of my mind and pulled out my fantasy woman. The last few days – trying my best to stay out of her way – have been agonizing.

I should make an excuse and remove myself from her presence. However, I find my feet don't move and my glasses seem to steam before my eyes.

I take them off and rub the fog with the hem of my shirt.

"Your collection of books is amazing," she says, smiling at me. "Better than the public library back at home."

It's the smile that does it. The thing that hooks me inside the room and has me walking towards her. Her smile lights up the room. I've heard people say that kind of thing all my life and not understood what they meant. Not until I met her. Her smile is like the sun emerging from behind a rain cloud, flooding you in rays, warming your skin and leaving you giddy.

"What are you reading?" I ask. Most mornings she's had a book clutched in her hand – mostly one of those books with a shirtless man on the cover. "My collection may be good, but I don't have many romance novels."

"Shakespeare," she says, lifting the book so I can see the cover. "This is a beautiful edition." She runs her hands over the gilded cover then lifts the book to her nose and inhales. "Don't you just love the smell of books?"

I do. But I think I love her scent a million times more.

She smells like a flower. A beautiful flower, her petals all open for me, beckoning me in to suckle on her nectar.

"Which Shakespeare?" I ask. Coming to stand closer and twisting my head to peer down at the book. "*Romeo and Juliet?*" Or perhaps his sonnets. The omega seems obsessed with romance.

"God, no, not *Romeo and Juliet*," she frowns.

"You don't like *Romeo and Juliet*?" I thought all women liked that play, especially the film version with Di Caprio. Just shows how much I know about women, despite all the reading.

"It's far too depressing, don't you think? There're enough crappy things happening in the world, enough heartache to endure, without having to read about it too." I tilt my head to look at her. "I only read books and watch films with happy endings. Stories that will leave me happy, not blue. And," and she adds, wagging a finger at me, "if you're going to tell me that it's not real literature, or that happy endings are corny, I would remind you that plenty of Shakespeare's plays have happy, nicely wrapped up endings and he was a genius."

I can't help but smile. "I cannot argue with that logic. Which is your favorite play then?"

"Hmmm." She considers her answer, tapping her fingers against the hardcover of the book, and I realize there's more to this omega than I thought. I feel a little ashamed. A waitress from nowhere, I didn't think she'd know much about Shakespeare. I'm an idiot. "Probably *Much Ado About Nothing*. It's so funny. I love the banter between Beatrice and Benedick. It's what I read romance novels for too, the banter." I lift an eyebrow. "Okay, maybe the spice too."

"I like that play," I admit.

"I think Beatrice would be such an amazing character to play," she says, her face breaking out into another of those smiles. "What I love about the play most, though," she says, "is that it could have been a tragedy, just like *Romeo and Juliet*. There's a bit in the middle where it's all going horribly wrong – when Claudio believes Hero has been unfaithful and then everyone thinks she's died of a broken heart. It could have ended so badly – just like *Romeo and Juliet*."

"Claudio is an asshole."

She laughs. "Most men are."

"Not all," I say, my feathers a little ruffled.

"Not all," she confesses. She closes the book and hugs it to her body. I ask her some questions about the books she likes and the plays she's read, and we discuss whether the books they made us read back at school were the right ones.

"I'd love to see a play while I'm here in Rockview," she says. "The Rockview company is amazing. I've watched some of their performances on YouTube, but it's not the same as watching them live."

"I'm sure Cruise would take you."

"Does Cruise like plays?"

I smile. I can't see my packmate sitting through some postmodern production or worse, some musical that takes itself too seriously. I should be the one to take her. I haven't found someone in my life I can discuss books with, see plays with.

But that would be a dangerous thing, even if it sounds like a tempting one.

"So, I told you mine, now it's your turn. Tell me yours," she says next.

"Excuse me?"

"Your favorite Shakespeare? No wait, don't tell me ... Hmmm ... you're a deep thinker." She taps her finger against her pretty pink lips. "*Hamlet?*" She sticks out her tongue and rolls her eyes.

"I take it you're not a fan."

"Hamlet is a mega asshole. The way he treats poor Ophelia."

"I agree, he's also an asshole."

"So, not *Hamlet*?"

"Not *Hamlet*." I walk over to the shelf and run my hand along the row of Shakespeare's plays. I found them in an old bookstore, tucked away in the back streets of London last time we visited. I couldn't help but buy them even if the bookseller knew exactly who I was and charged me far more than they were worth. I find the book I'm looking for and tuck my finger under the top of the spine, carefully sliding it from the shelf. Then I pass it to her.

She smooths her palm across the cover.

"*Romeo and Juliet*." She smiles and the room brightens that little bit more. "You like to torture yourself, then?"

She has no idea!

"I guess so. But it's the language more than anything. It's very beautiful."

She nods, then closes her eyes, reciting word perfect:

> *"Give me my Romeo; and, when he shall die,*
> *Take him and cut him out in little stars,*
> *And he will make the face of heaven so fine*
> *That all the world will be in love with night*
> *And pay no worship to the garish sun."*

She opens her eyes and blinks up at me. "It is enough to make you believe in love," she whispers.

"You don't believe in love?"

"I'm not the one who stopped looking for an omega. That sounds like giving up on love to me."

I shove my hands into my pockets. She's right, we gave up on that dream in favor of another.

"Love isn't everything."

"I don't think Shakespeare would agree. I think he'd argue it is."

"And what do you think?"

She sighs, walking to the nearest armchair and sinking into its belly. On her lap balances the two Shakespeare plays.

"I think love is complicated. Some people get lucky and end up as Hero in their story. Others get screwed by warring families and miscommunications and end up as Juliet. However, what I think is, if you asked Juliet, was it worth it? Do you regret it? She'd say no."

Exactly, love leads to heartbreak ... or worse. Better to stick to the safety of books.

"You can have those copies if you want," I say, unable to help myself. The alpha inside me has a strong need to please the little omega and gifting her books is harmless. Far less harmless than the other ways in which my alpha would like to please her.

"Thank you," she says, "but I couldn't ruin your collection. You have so many beautiful volumes. Although ..."

"Although," I say.

"Like you said, it lacks romance books. I'm guessing you are more into logic than romance and yet your favorite Shakespeare play is *Romeo and Juliet*. Very curious. I can't make you out."

"You shouldn't judge a book by its cover."

"You shouldn't," she says pointedly, making the tips of my ears burn.

"Although in reality it's impossible not to. Therefore, why not make those covers as beautiful as possible? Why not fill all my shelves with beautiful books."

"Although there is nothing worse than picking up a book with this amazing, most incredible looking cover and you get all excited for what's within, only to be well and truly disappointed when the story sucks."

I chuckle, settling myself down in an armchair next to hers. "Yeah, that too. And once again the metaphor applies to people as well."

"Ahh," she says. "This is why you've given up on omegas, then? Too many looked good on the outside but didn't live up to your standards."

"We haven't given up on omegas," I say quietly.

"It's okay. I can relate. I've dated several beautiful looking men who turned out to be ... well ... assholes."

"You understand, then?" I say, resting my elbows on the chair's arms. "Given your own experiences, why Kent and I are so hesitant about your bonding with Cruise?" The color drains from her face and she looks a little taken aback at my question. "You hardly know each other. You don't really know what lies beneath the cover."

She considers me for a moment, her hands fondling the books in her lap.

"I've had a little glimpse of the story, though, and what I've seen so far, I like."

"But you don't know if there's an unexpected twist, a concealed plot."

"No, but I think," a little color returns to her cheeks, "I'd like a little more time to read the story before I toss the book aside."

I link my hands and spin my thumbs around each other.

She smiles again. "You haven't told me what book you came in here for."

"Ahhh ..." I say.

She laughs. "Oh no. Don't tell me. Some book on engineering or architecture?"

"Are you calling me a nerd, Omega?" I tease.

She giggles. "There's nothing wrong with a nerd."

"There isn't? Because in most stories, the girl goes for the football hero, not the nerd."

"Not in all stories," she says. Her cheeks pinken that bit more. "And it helps if the nerd looks like a football hero."

The tips of my ears burn even hotter, and I straighten my glasses on the bridge of my nose. Is it my imagination or are they steaming up again?

"How about you, Avery?" If she finds me confusing, contradictory, then I confess, I'm just as confused about hers. "Were you a nerd at school? You read books. You like Shakespeare. Or were you the head cheerleader?" She certainly has the looks.

"I was never popular enough to be a cheerleader. Which was a good thing. I would certainly have fallen and broken my leg or cracked my skull."

I would certainly have fallen for her at school. I wouldn't have been able to help myself. I would have followed her around like a lost puppy.

In fact, I can feel myself falling now. I ought to leave.

"I hadn't decided what I wanted to read," I tell her. "I came in here to browse for a book." Or was I pulled here by that sweet, sweet scent? "Is there anything you would recommend?"

"I have about a billion books I could recommend you," she says with another flash of those smiles, "but unfortunately you don't have a single one."

"Perhaps I ought to expand my collection. Perhaps it is lacking in certain categories."

"It is."

I hesitate. I shouldn't ask this ... She'll probably say no ...

"There's ... there's a dedicated, independent romance bookstore in Rockview."

"Oh my gosh, you're right – Cupid's Bookshelf. I've seen it on Instagram."

"Would you ... would you like me ... to take you there?" Her smile grows impossibly wide, dazzling. "Help me to rectify this problem with my collection."

She claps her hands together and bounces on her seat. "Yes, please," she says and then she lunges towards me and wraps me in a hug. A warm, soft hug that smells of honey and nectar and a meadow of flowers.

Chapter Twenty-Eight

Kent

I'm waiting for him in the dark.

"You too," I hiss as he walks into his bedroom and reaches for the light.

He jolts.

"Jeez, Kent, you scared me half to death."

"I should beat the living crap out of you. I thought we agreed. I thought–"

"Yeah, well, not everyone is as perfect as you are, Kent. The girl is one hell of a temptation. One I don't regret falling for."

"You slept with her?" I growl, all sorts of emotions spinning in my gut – fury, betrayal, jealousy.

He's right. She is a temptation. She smells like nectar. A scent designed to entice. A scent promising sweetness and heaven, if only, only, you take just one, one tiny, miniscule, little taste.

"No," he says.

I'm standing with my back leaning against the wardrobe, and he comes to stand in front of me.

He smells of her. His skin reeks of that scent. There's a haze in his eyes like he's high. And his usually combed red hair is a mess. His skin flushed.

He either took a really strong fucking pill. Or he fucked her.

"You're lying."

"I didn't sleep with her. We simply talked." They simply talked and he looks like that? "She's lovely, Kent, truly lovely."

His words batter me like powerful fists, and I'm forced to look away from his face.

I ball my fists, so tight the skin strains across my knuckles, threatening to split.

He rests his hand on my shoulder.

"Kent," he says, "just because it happened with–"

"I don't want to talk about it."

"–it doesn't mean this isn't real. It doesn't mean that every woman out there is a scammer. Avery is genuine. We all feel it–"

"In your heart," I spit out with sarcasm. "Or your cock?"

"In my bones. At least come spend time with her, get to know her. Because if you don't, she'll be gone in a few days, and you'll have missed your chance – we all will have – and I'm not sure that Cruise will ever forgive you."

"She won't go. She has her claws sunk into all of you now. She'll be clinging on for as long as she can."

Jonah drops his hand and shakes his head. "Kent."

But I don't want to hear any more. I've heard, seen and

smelled enough. I storm out of his room, Barney trotting behind me as I stride towards the office.

This has gone far enough. I have let this go far enough. I growl at myself and Barney barks in concern. I stop, letting him catch up with me and stroke his head, reassuring him it's all fine.

He may be old, but he's not dumb. He knows something isn't right. The strange omega scent in the air. The way I've been avoiding my pack. He stares up at me with those soft brown eyes, full of concern.

"It's all right, boy," I tell him. "It's going to be okay. I'm going to sort this out and then things will be back to normal."

I hoped – no, I believed – I wouldn't have to resort to this course of action. I thought the girl would have let slip by now, dropped the act and given a hint of her real intentions. I thought my packmates would have come to their senses.

But she hasn't and neither have they. Lovesick stupid fools!

I'm not letting her break up our family.

I need them to see the truth.

"Come on, boy," I say, clicking my fingers. Barney follows me into the office, and I shut the door behind us.

I'm going to sort this out once and for all.

Chapter Twenty-Nine

Avery

Every morning I seem to wake up with one more alpha in my bed. This morning there are three, all crammed into what seemed like a giant's bed a few days ago but is now looking decidedly small, especially when I'm squished in the middle of a two-layered, alpha sandwich.

Not that I'm complaining. Being surrounded by this much alpha flesh is like some kind of dream. It's also confusing.

They are making me promises. They are bewildering me with their words and declarations.

But I'm not some naïve little omega with no life experience. I know men – I've dated enough of them – to know those promises, words and declarations often have an expiry date or just turn out to be big fat lies.

And even if these men believe what they're saying, even

if Jonah and I seem to have made friends last night – there is one packmate who isn't on board and I'm not stupid enough to believe that isn't one hell of a problem.

As amazing as this has been, I'm preparing myself for the inevitable – my homeward trip in a couple of days' time.

Maybe even sooner given the way my bond sits in my stomach this morning.

Lighter, less intense. I can still feel Cruise there, clear as day. But the binds aren't as intense.

Carefully, I lift limbs, roll alphas and wriggle out of the bed, shimming a pair of panties up my legs and one of the alpha's t-shirts over my head.

At the doorway, I creak open the door and pause. I take a steadying breath and step into the hallway, just one little step. I brace myself for the yank of pain in my stomach.

Nothing.

I sigh with relief and take another step.

Still nothing.

The bond has released.

Gingerly, I walk down the hallway, waiting for a sudden surge of pain to strike me. It doesn't and I go in search of Jacks. I received a message last night that she'd gone out for drinks with Miranda after their run. When I find her room empty, I creep back to the bedroom and check my phone, finding a message sent in the early hours of the morning.

Jacks: Don't wait up. Winky face.

I type her back a message.

Avery: Call me when you untangle yourself from the bedsheets.

I glance at the three alphas in my bed. They are all out for the count. The temptation is too great. I snap a photo on my phone. I need at least one little memento to take home with me, to remind myself this wasn't all some crazy fever dream.

Once I've brewed myself a coffee, I walk out into the sunshine, throwing back my head and letting my face soak up the sun. I'm going to miss this too. It rains nine days out of ten back home.

I settle myself down on a lounger, sipping my coffee and Barney comes trotting out of the main house, towards me.

"Well, hello, there, handsome," I say, as he comes to sit beside me. "Aren't we looking especially distinguished today?"

He butts his nose against my palm, making it abundantly clear he's after ear tickles, not compliments.

"Okay, okay," I tell him, settling my cup down on the ground. "How can I resist you, when you're so very beautiful?"

I tickle his snout, then stroke the soft fur between his eyes before tickling under his large floppy ears. He drools in pleasure, long gloopy strings of it streaming from his jaws.

"Don't worry," I tell him. "I can relate. Being an omega is pretty messy business too."

"Ruff," he says in reply, and I laugh, bending my head forward so our brows meet and scrubbing a little harder.

"Not you too," a gruff voice says.

I look up and find the grumpy packmate, Kent, standing out in the sunshine. It's the first time I've seen him in days. Although, I've been able to smell him of course. His scent is in the air and on his packmates' skin all the time. Dark and swirling and pretty darn mysterious. A bit like the alpha himself. Actually, a lot like the alpha himself.

"Me?" I ask.

"Barney," he clarifies, clicking his fingers. The dog peers over his shoulder at the alpha and then trots towards him obediently. "First my packmates. Now my dog. You really are working hard."

"*Your* dog?" I ask.

Barney comes to sit beside Kent's legs and the alpha reaches down to pat the animal's head.

"Yeah, mine. I found him abandoned in some parking lot when he was a puppy. Half starved. I didn't want a dog. But, hey–"

"The eyes?" I ask.

"Yeah, the eyes." He pats the dog again with obvious affection.

I tilt my head to one side. "So, you didn't want a dog and you don't want an omega?"

"Are you trying to say it's the same thing?" he scoffs.

I shake my head. I'm just trying to figure him out. The man standing between me and future happiness.

Should I be trying my darn hardest to win him around? Should I be fighting for a place in this pack? I look into his steely eyes, and I don't think I'd ever convince him of anything.

Besides, isn't it an alpha's job to woo the omega? Not the other way around.

Inwardly, I sigh and pick up my cup of coffee, taking a long gulp.

He watches me with suspicion, like any moment I might cast a net his way and drag him towards me. Does he really think I'm a master seductress? It's almost laughable. If he knew how many times I've screwed up dates – getting the time wrong, or the venue, or wearing inappropriate footwear (heels to a bowling alley – yikes) or forgetting the dude's name, or spilling my drink all over myself or him or both of us. Yeah, I wish I was some master seductress.

"How old is Barney?" I ask.

He hesitates like he's not sure he wants to engage in conversation, but I have a feeling if this man has a weak spot, it's going to be his dog. I can relate, I could talk about Fluffy for hours if asked (another reason a date ended badly – but the dude did ask!).

"15."

"He really is a distinguished older gentleman then."

"Weren't you just moaning about his dribbling?"

I narrow my eyes at the alpha. How long was he there watching the two of us exactly?

"No complaints. My cat used to do the same. Although, I have to admit the volume of drool wasn't as vast."

Barney swings his gaze between us and then drops down onto his belly, resting his head on his front paws.

"It's walkies time," Kent says with authority.

Barney closes his eyes.

I can't help giggling. "I think that may be a no."

Kent crouches down and strokes his large palm right down Barney's spine in a way that makes me feel just a little jealous.

"Where do you take him for walks?" I ask.

"In the old days, everywhere. He required a hell of a lot of walking."

"He's a big dog."

"Yep, but these days, a wander round the grounds is enough for him. If I can encourage the lazy scoundrel."

"Oh, he's not lazy," I say, unable to help scuttling off my lounger and towards Barney, crouching down to scratch the crown of his head. "He's just conserving his energy."

From the corner of my eye, I see the alpha's nostrils twitch and I realize we're less than a foot apart now. The closest we've ever been.

Up close his scent is even more intriguing, like the deepest darkest chocolate.

"For what?" the alpha scoffs. "For more naps?"

"For protecting his owner from the big, scary omega," I joke, keeping my eyes fixed on Barney.

Kent scoffs harder this time. "You're not big. You're tiny."

"I'm 5ft 2 thank you very much."

"Exactly."

"But I am scary," I say, venturing to look up at him. I find him gazing right at me and he jolts in alarm to be caught staring.

He frowns. "I'm not scared of you."

"You're scared of something."

He stares at me for a long, long minute, my heart beating louder and louder in my ears as he does. He has the kind of eyes – the kind of stare – that would melt the panties right off most women.

"I'm scared of what you'll do to this pack."

"I could make this pack happy," I whisper. I could. I know I could. And I'm pretty sure they could make me happy in return. If only he'd give it a try. "What ..." I say, trying to find my voice, which is darn hard because I may not be scary, but this big brooding alpha definitely is, "what if it was fate that brought Cruise and me together in Vegas?"

"Or what if it was some clever, underhand ploy by a gold-digging omega," he says, snapping back upright.

"Why are you so determined to believe that?"

"Experience," he says and when I roll my eyes, he adds, "and what omega would be careless enough to find herself bonded to a man she doesn't know? She wouldn't be. Her family and friends would never let it happen."

I stand up slowly. "You're right," I say. "Perfectly right."

There's no use arguing with him. In some ways he's right. No sensible omega with her head on straight and her life pulled together would end up in such a ridiculous situation. I'm really, really darn lucky it worked out well for me. Okay, Cruise has one giant dickhead of a packmate – the alpha stood right in front of me – but the man I actually bonded to could have been a dickhead too. Or worse. A lot, lot worse.

"The bond's released," Kent says stiffly, looking me up and down.

"Seems to have," I reply.

"Then you'll be leaving soon," he says, his voice devoid of emotion.

Barney lifts his head and peers up at his master, standing there rigid as a soldier, his jaw tight.

"Yes," I say, "yes, I will."

I know when I'm beat.

Chapter Thirty

Avery

I watch the brooding alpha and his dog disappear around the side of the house and flop back on the sun lounger, my heart pounding in my chest, my stomach churning with unease. How does that man have the ability to make me feel this way? Confused, anxious, slightly – okay, very – turned on. But most of all, sad.

"You okay, sweetie?" I open my eyes and find my best friend standing over me, blocking the sun and casting me in shadow.

I shrug, hugging my knees and she drops down on the lounger next to me and rubs her palm over my shoulders.

"Shit, I should never have left you. What happened? Did those bastards–"

"No, no, nothing bad has happened."

"Then what's up?"

"Kent."

"Kent?"

"The grumpy one."

"Ahh him. What did he do?" she asks darkly.

"Nothing. That's it. Jonah and I talked last night and ... I don't know, he's very sweet. He's offered to take me to this really cute bookstore in the city today."

"I'm lost here, Avery."

I sigh. "I guess I felt like last night I may have won Jonah round, that maybe there was a chance I could stay here."

"That's good then. Isn't it? That sounds hopeful to me."

"Yeah, but then there's Kent. He's never going to come round. He's determined to believe the worst about me."

"Jerk!" Jacks says, cracking her knuckles in a menacing manner.

"It is what it is," I say, sighing again and resting my cheek on my knees.

"Ahh Avery," Jacks says. "I warned you to be careful with your feelings."

"I know but I'm hopeless at that."

"Not hopeless. Just open-hearted and trusting. It's what I love about you. It's what that jerk would love about you too if he gave you half a chance."

I manage a little smile. "Anyway, enough about me and my woes. Tell me what happened last night." I take her hand in mine, knitting our fingers together.

Jacks slides the sunglasses she's wearing – sunglasses I don't recognize as her own – onto the top of her head. Her mascara's a little smudged but her cheeks are rosy and her eyes dreamy.

"Shit, Avery, I've never met anyone like her before. She was ..."

"So, you had fun?" I ask, squeezing her hand.

"A lot of fun. Lots and lots of fun." Jacks gazes off into the distance, the side of her mouth lifting into half a smile.

"Jacks, that's amazing!" I say, sitting up straight.

Jacks flips her gaze back to mine and when she sees the eager expression on my face, one of panic swims over hers. "Now don't get all excited, Avery. It was one date – actually it wasn't even technically a date and–"

"Plus one stay-the-night," I say eagerly.

"One-night stand," Jacks corrects.

"I've never seen you look so ..."

"Look so what?"

"Dreamy." I grin at my best friend.

"I don't," she insists, dragging her hand down her face. "I look like shit."

"So, you have no intention of seeing her again."

"I ... we didn't ..."

"She works here."

"Yeah, she does," Jacks says, beaming again.

I squeeze her hand and squeal. "This is so exciting."

She jumps to her feet. "Avery!" she warns.

"It's okay. It's okay. I won't start making wedding plans for you yet."

"Wedding? Too early, Avery."

"You said getting hitched early might be a good way of finding a partner."

"That was you, not me." She rubs my shoulder again. "It's different for you. You have the bond and all that brings. I'm a beta. Finding my soulmate is a lot harder."

"I think it's hard no matter who or what you are," I say.

Jacks kisses the crown of my head. "That alpha is a jerk, but he'll come round, Ave. I know he will."

"Yeah," I say, but I'm not so sure.

Chapter Thirty-One

Cruise

I wake up and the first thing I realize is the bond has released. It's no longer a tight padlock in my stomach. Now it's a lighter, freer kind of bind.

The second thing I realize is that the omega is missing.

I open my eyes and jolt upright on the bed.

Declan groans next to me and turns over. Max is lying out on my other side. Both asleep.

No omega.

I scramble out of the bed, climbing over Declan.

"Fuck, man, what are you doing?" he groans, swiping at me.

"She's not here," I say. "The omega is not here."

"Relax, Cruise. She probably went to pee."

I crash out of the bedroom and towards the bathroom. I swing back the door. Empty.

"Avery," I yell, fear and apprehension bubbling in my gut. She's been right there by my side for days. Safe. Sound. Within touching distance.

I don't like this. I don't like this at all.

"Avery," I shout again, rushing into each of the bedrooms and looking for her there. Where the hell is she?

I race down the stairs, still calling her name and almost collide straight into Jacks. She's dressed in some ill-fitting clothes and she's wearing sunglasses that aren't her own.

She lifts them from her nose and her eyes travel down my body, halting at my groin.

Her eyes widen and then she cackles.

"Fuck me. No wonder Avery hasn't wanted to leave the bedroom in days. That is one hell of a big—"

"Where is she?" I growl.

Her eyes jump back up to my face. "Who?" she says, and is that guilt stretched across her features?

"Avery," I snarl.

"Oh ... Avery," she says, relief flooding over her face. "Out by the pool."

I feel relief flood my own body. She's out by the pool. Here. Right here. Not gone.

"She likes the sunshine," Jacks continues. "She's like one of those greenhouse plants. She was never designed for cooler weather. She needs sunshine and a warm climate. Somewhere like Rockview."

"I agree," I say.

"Good," Jacks says with a nod of her head. She starts to step towards the staircase.

"Wait," I say, "who did you think I meant?"

"What?"

"Who did you think I was looking for?"

"Erm, Miranda," she mumbles.

"Miranda?" I say. "Why? What have you done with her?"

"*Me* done with *her*?" she says, then hurries up the stairs before I can ask her more.

I stare down at my body. I'm very naked. The cleaners are probably already here and the housekeeper but fuck it. I need to check if Avery really is outside.

I step out into the sunshine.

"Here you are," I say with relief, when I find her curled up with an empty coffee cup, her eyes closed, her face flooded with light.

"Huh?" she says, opening her eyes to look up at me.

As always, the sight of her eyes stuns me for a fraction of time. It's easy to forget just how beautiful they are. To believe I've simply exaggerated their effect when we're apart. But then I come face to face with them once again and they whip my breath right away.

"For a moment, I thought you'd gone."

"No, I'm right here," she says, with a half-smile.

"What's wrong?" I ask, dropping down next to her on the lounger and dragging her towards me. She comes willingly, curling up against me.

"Nothing," she says. "Just thinking."

"About?"

"What happens next. The bond's released …"

Fear strikes through me, something I immediately try to hide through our bond. Is she considering leaving? We want her to stay. We've made that clear. But she's never been convinced. Kent's stupid reluctance has seen to that.

"It's loosened." The words come flying out of my mouth before I even know what I'm saying. "Not released. It'll be a few more days before it's released altogether."

"What does that mean?" she asks.

"It means we're afforded a little more distance from each other but not a lot," I lie. "We still need to remain close to one another." I cross my fingers and toes that she believes me, that she hasn't been researching this stuff, and that she doesn't realize what I'm saying is completely untrue.

"Oh," she says and am I deceiving myself or is that relief in her voice? She snuggles against me. "I'm not quite ready to leave yet."

"Good," I say, "because I need you to do me a favor."

"If you mean suck your cock, Alpha," she says with one of those seductive smiles, "you know I consider that a privilege not a favor."

I groan a little. "I'm holding you to that, but no, this is something which requires clothes."

"Shame." She sighs.

"There's a tech awards ceremony happening this weekend. Our company is sponsoring the event, which means our pack will be expected to attend. In fact, we're due to make a speech and hand out several of the awards."

She pulls away from me and sits up a little straighter. "Oh."

"Would you attend with us? The bond means I'd need you there," I lie again.

"You'd sneak me in somehow?" she asks with a frown. "Like we've been doing at your office?"

I take her hand in mine, running the pads of my fingers over her knuckles.

"No, I'd like you to come as our date."

"Date?" she yelps.

"Yes, date."

"But this is some industry event, right?"

"Yes."

"There'll be people there."

"Yes, there will be people there."

"With cell phones and cameras."

"Yes. There will also be members of the press."

She stares at me. "So, everyone will know about us."

"They'll know as much as we tell them. What that is, is up to you. We can tell them you're our date for the evening. Or we can tell them you're our mate." I squeeze her hands. "I'm serious about this, Avery. I'm serious about us." I need to show her just how serious. I need to show Kent too. No more hiding away.

She twines her fingers through mine and gazes down at our hands. "Cruise, Kent was just out here. He's not coming round to this. He's not going to change his mind."

"Give him a chance."

"I think he's had plenty."

"Come to this event with us. He'll be there. Let him get to know you properly." She's quiet for a moment, stroking my fingers. "One more chance, Avery, please."

She considers my request, her emotions tumbling through our bond. I can feel how much she wants this. I can feel how unsure she is, how determined she is not to get her hopes up, not to be hurt.

"Okay." She looks up at me, shaking her hair away from her face. "Is this some fancy do?"

"It's at the Crystalheim ballroom in the city."

"Oh lord!"

"Do you need us to buy you a dress, sweetheart?"

"No, I have a dress," she says, sternly, "but I do need you to let me bring Jacks." I maintain a straight face, but she feels my reservations through the bond anyway. "I need someone making sure I don't drink too much, or say the wrong thing, or get lost in that massive hotel."

"You'll have us for that. We'll be taking very good care of you."

"But you have no idea of the trouble I'm capable of landing myself in."

"I think I have a fair idea," I point out, raising an eyebrow.

"Trust me, I need Jacks there."

"Okay," I say reluctantly. "Maybe she could bring Miranda?" That would hopefully keep the woman distracted.

Avery smiles knowingly. "Good idea." She nuzzles her head under my chin. "Jonah promised to take me to a bookstore today."

"Yeah, he sent me a message about it last night. Told me my presence was required. Seems you've won him around – just like you will Kent," I add.

"Hmmm," she says unconvinced. "But the bond's loosened now so you don't have to come if you don't want to."

I consider this. I've liked being with the little omega 24/7. It seems kind of crazy to me. The idea of being locked to someone else's side continually always freaked me the hell out. I thought it would be intrusive, suffocating, overwhelming. It's been none of those things. It's been freaking awesome. She has the ability to blow away all the dark thoughts in my mind, to make me feel happier, lighter, someone who might actually be worthy of her.

Separating from her today, even for an hour or two, sends a sickness swimming in my stomach. But I know Jonah needs space to be with Avery alone. He's more quiet than the rest of us. Sometimes even a little shy. I'm more than willing to step aside for his sake and Avery's.

Yeah, and if I'm honest, mine too.

I need her to stay.

Chapter Thirty-Two

Jonah

One hour in the omega's company and I find myself standing in the middle of a very pink, very sweet-smelling bookstore on a Friday morning. A weekday. A day I'd usually spend in the office. That I'd always spend in the office.

This woman is going to turn our world upside down. Exactly what we wanted to avoid.

In our lives, we have order, routine, success. A lot of success. But do we have happiness?

I plunge my hands deep in my pockets watching as the omega talks excitedly to the bookstore owner, swapping recommendations between themselves.

I thought we were happy. How could we not be? How could five men with untold wealth – who could afford to buy anything they wanted in the world – who could afford to fund a flight out of this world – not be happy? It seemed wrong even to consider it.

Now, though, I realize I wasn't happy, because never before have I experienced this buzz deep in my stomach. Not when our first Hamilton phone took off. Not when we made our first million. Or billion. Or I bought my mom and dad their dream home. Or took my grandma to see the Northern lights just like she wanted. Not when we made the cover of *Life* magazine or received an invitation to the White House.

No, this feeling was never there before. Now it's humming and buzzing, spreading through my veins and making me feel alive.

And it's her. All her.

She peers over her shoulder and beckons me over.

"Rebecca and I have made a list of the romance books all libraries should feature."

I nod, picking up the paper, feeling the store owner's eyes on me. You think I would be used to people staring and gaping at me like this by now, but it's something I've never gotten used to. I may have the body of an alpha these days but back in school I was skinny and scrawny, with inch-thick glasses and too many freckles. No one ever looked my way. It still feels strange.

"Are you happy with this list, Avery?" I ask her. "Or are there any more you'd like to add?"

"There's already twenty books on the list!" she says, laughing.

"I want my library to be the best in the world," I say with a hint of jest but also quite a large helping of seriousness. "If there are more books that should be on this list, add them in please."

"Okay," she says, taking the list from me and tapping

her pen against her lips. She thinks for a minute, her dark eyes darting left and right, and then scribbles some more titles down on the piece of paper.

"Oh, those are good ones," the store owner says, then looking to me, adds, "your wife has really good taste in books."

"I'm not his wife," Avery says, eyes fixated on her list.

"Sorry, girlfriend."

"I'm not his—"

"How long have you been running this store?"

"Two years," the owner says, her chest puffing out in pride.

"How's business?" I ask, adjusting my glasses.

"They were named best independent bookstore last year," Avery says, "and they are always all over social media. I'm so pleased I finally got to visit. They have so many special editions you can't get anywhere else."

"Are you going to buy some? For yourself?" I ask.

She places her pen on the counter. "I'm going to do a bit of window shopping while Rebecca rings all these books through," she says, handing the owner the list.

The woman laughs. "It may take me some time – there are fifty books on this list now."

"Is that too many?" Avery asks, gaze darting to mine.

I lay my hand on my chest. "I feel rather ashamed that my library was so seriously sub-standard. I'm pleased to address this shortcoming."

Avery smiles at me and it makes me giddy. Is this what it's like to have a crush? A big overwhelming crush?

And if it is, then what am I going to do about it? Cruise would like Avery to be our pack omega. He says she would like that too. But the question is, would she like me?

I shift on my feet and adjust my glasses.

I was an awkward teenager. But things changed when I gained my alpha designation, when I grew into the man I am now, when I started to gain success in the business world. It's been a long time since I felt unconfident about a situation. Since I've felt like that younger man again.

Avery wanders away from me towards a stand of beautiful books, their pages sprayed in beautiful designs, their covers gleaming with gold and silvers. She runs her fingertips over the covers.

"These are gorgeous. Oh!" She lifts one from the display carefully like it's a newborn baby, cradling it in her hands. "This is my favorite book by this author. I think I may have read it at least five times and it still makes me cry every time they get together at the end."

"Are you going to buy it?"

She turns the cover open and her eyes light up when she finds an illustration inside. "Wow."

"It is beautiful," I say.

She carefully turns the pages, clearly not wanting to smudge or crease them. Then gently she lowers it back to the display with a hum.

"You're not going to purchase it?" I ask, confused. She seemed to like it. Am I so very bad at reading women?

"Not this time," she says with a pat smile, moving further along the display.

"But it's your favorite book," I say. "And a special edition. Don't you like the design?"

"It's very nice."

I frown. "I don't understand." She looks up, meeting my eyes, and blood swooshes through my body.

She chews on her lip, and her cheeks pinken. The blood

swooshes further south. I feel even more like a confused teenager, about to develop an erection in a bookstore. It doesn't help that her scent is sweet on the end of my tongue.

"It's a little ... on the pricey side," she whispers.

I gape at her. It takes me a moment to comprehend. Money hasn't been an issue, a concern, or a worry for many years. We can't spend or give it away fast enough, more and more of it keeps coming our way. I stopped looking at price tags a long time ago. I can't even remember the last time I struggled to afford something.

"Of course, how rude of me," I say, certain my own cheeks are now glowing like hers. "I will purchase it for you."

"No ... I mean ... I wasn't digging for you to buy it for me.

"I would like to." I cough and straighten my glasses. "I would like to buy you a gift. As a thank you for helping me today."

"I'm not really helping you though, am I? This was a treat for me, not for you."

"The others aren't interested in books so much. It's nice to find someone who is happy to accompany me to a store."

"Even a romance bookstore?"

"I have neglected the genre and intend to educate myself."

The omega reaches up on her tiptoes and kisses my cheek. "You're very sweet," she whispers. Is that a good thing? Do I want to be considered sweet? But then she threads her arm through mine, and I think it must be a good thing to have her warm body pressed against mine. "Come on, let's see if this store has any omega pack romances."

* * *

I instruct the bookstore owner to have all the books wrapped up and sent to the house, then with my shades and baseball cap firmly secured, I walk Avery via the back streets of Rockview to our office, two of our bodyguards pacing a discreet distance behind us, her arm still hooked through mine.

"This really is a beautiful city," she says, pausing to peer in at another window display.

"The sunshine helps."

"And that sea breeze." She closes her eyes, inhales and then sighs. "I love the way it smells." Then her eyes flick open and those cheeks of hers heat again.

"What?" I ask.

"Oh ... nothing."

"Avery," I ask with concern.

"It's just your scent. It's really rather nice too."

"It is?" I ask, taken aback. Of course, I've had omegas tell me that before, but I've suspected they weren't genuine in their compliments. Avery's seems genuine.

"Like orange blossom."

"It's rather unusual for an alpha," I confess.

"Perhaps, but I like it. It's too cold back home to grow orange trees but my parents once took us on vacation, and we stayed right by an orange grove. The smell was heavenly. I've never forgotten how good it smelled." Her eyes float shut again as if she's remembering and then open slowly, meeting mine.

I would like to kiss her. But can I? Should I? Something in her own honey scent suggests she wants me to. But perhaps that is simply wishful thinking on my own account.

We reach the office far too quickly after that and with regret I take her up to meet Cruise for lunch in his office.

It's obvious the two have found even this slight separation difficult and I can't help the jealousy I feel when she greets him with an enthusiastic smile and a lingering kiss.

In fact, I can't help thinking about that kiss and the way it must feel, the way it must taste, while we pursue the lunch options, so that when Cruise's secretary comes to take our orders, I'm still undecided.

"I'd go for the chicken," Avery says, leaning closer to me. "I had it yesterday and it was delicious."

I order and sit back, content to listen to Avery tell Cruise about her morning, their hands clasped together under the table. I don't think I've ever seen my packmate hold hands. With anyone.

"How did you find it, Jonah? Was your visit to the romance bookstore hideous?"

"No, not at all. It was thoroughly enjoyable."

My packmate's mouth twitches. "I'm not surprised. A visit to the city dump would be 'thoroughly enjoyable' if Avery was tagging along."

Avery sticks her tongue out and groans. "Please!"

"I suspect he's correct," I argue.

"Well," she says, "I am not willing to accompany you on a trip to the dump to test out that theory."

"Entirely understandable."

"Avery has agreed to accompany us to the awards ceremony tomorrow evening, though," Cruise says.

"I'm warning you," she leans towards me, placing her free hand on my shoulder, making my heart beat more rapidly, "I am planning to dance with you all. I love dancing."

"I'm afraid I really cannot dance."

"Everybody can dance," she says, so close to me wisps of her hair tickle against my skin, "just some choose not to."

I gaze down at her in wonderment. Everything she says surprises me and maybe, yes maybe, dancing with her is all I want to do.

Chapter Thirty-Three

Avery

I stare at my little black dress, all freshly laundered and pressed. It won't be as glamorous as all the other dresses at the event tonight. In fact, seeing as I picked it up for a bargain at the mall, it'll cost a fraction of the price of all the other dresses there too. But it's my lucky dress, always has been. In fact, it was the dress I was wearing the night I won that money at the roulette table. The night I met Cruise.

I have a funny feeling it's going to be lucky again. Or is that just wishful thinking ...

Jacks taps on the open door and steps inside. She glances at the dress on the hanger.

"Please tell me you are not wearing that dress, Avery?" she says.

"Of course I'm wearing this dress," I say. "Why? What's wrong with it?"

"What's wrong with it? You've owned it for more than five years and – Avery, I love you girl – but your ass is not the size it was when you were twenty-one."

"My ass looks good in this dress."

"Your ass looks like it's bursting to break free of that dress."

"Exactly!" I smooth my hand down the shiny fabric. "What are you wearing?"

"I went out shopping with Miranda yesterday."

I eye my best friend. "Shopping, huh? That's what the kids are calling it these days."

"*That*," she says with a wink, "came after. And I can tell you it was some of the best shopping I've had in my life."

"She seems nice."

"She is." Jacks shakes her head. "Anyway, she took me to this place that sells designer seconds. I bought myself a dress and one for you too. You wanna see it?"

"Nope," I say, "I'm sticking to my lucky dress."

Jacks folds her arms over her chest. "I can't believe those tight bastards didn't buy you a new dress."

"They offered, but I already have one packmate very convinced I'm only here for the money. I don't need to give him actual proof that I am."

"But you're Pack Hamilton's date! I bet they'll be dressed in Armani suits, and you'll be there in your dress from Target."

"Walmart," I correct.

"Jeez," Jacks says, burying her face in her hands. "If I go and tell them to order you to wear the dress I bought you, you'll have to do it, right?"

"No," I say with my hands on my hips.

"But I thought if an alpha–"

"That's not how it works."

She smirks at me, knowing full well that it does. But I'm not backing down on this. It's the lucky dress or nothing.

However, as stubborn as I am on this matter, I don't refuse the hair stylist and makeup artist that arrive at the pool house door a couple of hours before we're due to leave.

"You didn't have to arrange this," I whisper to Cruise, already looking mighty fine in a (God, I hate it when Jack's is right) designer and obviously tailored suit.

"They were already booked for us, so it makes perfect sense they'd do hair and makeup for you and Jacks too."

I stand up on my tiptoes and kiss his cheek. Somehow, I can't believe these tech dudes have ever booked a makeup artist, but I appreciate the thought.

The hair stylist ushers me into a chair while the makeup artist ushers the alpha out of the room, muttering that he can't do his best work with a giant breathing down his neck.

An hour later I emerge looking like an actual princess. My face flawless and my hair in loose Hollywood-style waves over my shoulder.

Jacks steps out of her bedroom a moment later and I have to confess her dress is pretty stunning – a deep purple strapless gown that reaches all the way to the ground.

"Wow, Jacks. You look amazing! Miranda won't want to let you go back to Cardval."

"That is part of the plan," she says. She grins and walks towards me taking both my hands in hers. "You look pretty damn gorgeous yourself, Avery. Those alphas won't know what to do with themselves."

"We don't scrub up too badly, huh?" I say.

"Hmmm," Jacks mutters, "I still think you should wear the dress I got you."

"Nope on a rope."

I pull her along and we step out onto the patio. The sun

is setting behind the distant Rockview mountains and the swimming pool shimmers a deep scarlet.

The five members of the Hamilton Pack are waiting for us, lined up like they're on parade. My eyes scan right along them all and my heart and stomach do a little flip together. How is it possible for five such fine men to wind up in one pack? The odds of that! It seems a little unfair on all the other packs out there.

My gaze lands on Kent last, looking grumpy and stern as always, although the look is broken somewhat by the large dog leaning against his leg, a dog who woofs and trundles over to see me.

"Nope," Jacks says, waving her clutch purse at Barney. "Stay back. I don't want any dog drool on these dresses."

"Oh, don't be silly," I tell her, stepping around to bend down and pat Barney's head. "I'd like to say you all look mighty handsome tonight, but you know Barney beats you hands down. None of you will ever be able to compete with his good looks."

"Jeez," Declan says, "you must not like us as much as I thought. Have you seen the number of wrinkles on that dog?"

"Exactly," I say, landing a kiss on Barney's crown and probably ruining my lipstick. "He's adorable."

"You look pretty adorable yourself, Omega," Cruise says, his voice low.

"Stunning," Max adds.

"Beautiful," Jonah agrees.

"A complete knockout," Declan says.

Kent simply stares at me and says nothing. Eventually, he clicks his fingers. "Come on, Barney. Time to go inside."

"Can't we bring him with us?" I say as the dog trots obediently after his master.

"No," Declan says, "you're our date tonight, not his." He holds out the crook of his elbow and I take a hold and let him lead me to a limo waiting on the drive.

"Sweet," Jacks says, diving straight inside the vehicle. "I've never been in one of these before."

"How about Miranda?" I ask.

"We're picking her up on the way," Declan says, helping me into the car.

"Oh, *Pretty Woman* style."

"*Pretty Woman*?" he says with a crease on his brow.

"Don't worry," I say, patting his arm. "It's another film we can watch together."

"Maybe I'll leave that delight to Jonah."

Jacks discovers the mini-bar and pulls out all the bottles before deciding on champagne and popping the cork before the last alpha is even in the vehicle.

She pours it into crystal glasses and hands them out.

"I thought she was meant to stop you from getting drunk," Cruise whispers in my ear.

"It's a fine line," I confess, "half the time she's the one getting me drunk."

"Terrific," Cruise says, and I giggle, kissing his cheek. "I thought you promised to take care of me, anyway."

"I can think of many ways I'd like to take care of you tonight, Omega. That dress!!"

Is – I hate to admit it – maybe a little tight. I can barely breathe. I definitely won't be able to eat much at the dinner. But it's worth it.

Hopefully, my lucky dress will work its magic on Kent.

I flick my gaze to him and his darts away from mine.

I can't tell if that's a good sign or not.

Probably a bad one. He was probably simply glaring at me like always.

We pick Miranda up from a small house in the suburbs and then the limo weaves itself slowly through the congested streets of the city, pulling up a half hour later outside the grand-looking Crystalheim Hotel, a huge fountain tossing glittering water into the air and tall palm trees lit up with fairy lanterns. A crowd waits either side of an already-busy red carpet which leads straight through the open doorway.

"There are this many tech people in Rockview?" I say with my nose practically pressed up against the window.

"There are an awful lot — on account of our business," Cruise says. "But many have flown in from across the world and then the great and the good from the city are here too."

"I didn't think there would be this many," I mutter.

"Are you nervous?" Jonah asks seriously.

"Here, down another glass of this," Jacks says, thrusting a glass towards me.

"I'm fine," I tell them all, as a man in a crisp uniform opens our limo door.

Cruise climbs out first, followed by Declan who reaches inside the car and offers me his arm. I go to take it, but Kent yanks me back by the elbow. His touch makes me jolt as if I've been struck by a live wire.

"Don't talk to any of the reporters on the red carpet," he growls, snapping away his hand. "In fact, don't talk to anyone."

"Kent," Max says lowly.

"You're a dickhead, man," Jacks says, her voice already sounding slurred. She pushes me out of the limo and as she does, I hear an almighty rip.

"Oh shit," I mumble.

Declan tugs on my arm, but I tug right back, refusing to

move from my position, halfway in and halfway out of the vehicle.

"It's okay, Omega," Jonah whispers by my ear, "no need to feel nervous. We'll be right here."

"I'm not nervous," I say.

"If you're worried about Kent," Max says, scowling at his packmate.

"It's not that," I hiss.

They all stare at me waiting for an explanation. Heat zooms straight up my throat and into my cheeks.

"What is it?" Cruise asks eventually, leaning into the doorway beside Declan.

"My dress!"

"Your dress looks incredible, sweetheart. You're going to be the most stunning woman here tonight."

"You'd look good in a garbage bag," Declan adds.

"A ripped garbage bag?" I ask.

"Ripped?"

"I just felt my dress rip," I mutter.

Cruise and Declan's eyes swim over my body.

"Looks fine to me," Declan says.

"No one will notice," Cruise adds.

"They will," I insist. "The rip's right down my ass." I lean in and add with a whisper: "And I'm not wearing any panties."

The two alphas gape at me. Through the bond I can tell Cruise is more occupied by my lack of panties, than by my current predicament.

Jacks cackles behind me. "I told you not to wear that dress."

"It's my lucky dress!"

"Oh yeah, *so* lucky!"

"Jacks," I say, "what am I going to do?!"

"Do you have another dress, sweetheart?" Jonah asks gently, resting his palm on my shoulder.

"Back at the pool house," Jacks slurs, "we'll head back and catch you up later. Sorry," she says to Miranda.

"No, we'll take her," Cruise says, already attempting to shuffle me back into the car. "If we leave now, we can make it back in an hour."

"But it's starting now!" I shriek.

"Then we'll be fashionably late," Declan says.

"You can't," Kent says from somewhere deep in the car. "Max and Cruise, you're meant to be giving the opening speech. Declan you're meant to be schmoozing with the board. And Jonah you're down to give out the first three awards."

"We'll get Miriam to do it instead."

"No, I'll take her," Kent says, so firmly I don't think anyone will be brave enough to argue with him. "I'm not due to give out an award until the second half. I have time."

Before the others protest, Jacks pipes up. "I'm coming too. I don't want you murdering my best friend," she says with a wag of her finger.

Kent growls at her and my usually stubborn friend actually shies away.

"I'm not going to murder her."

I look around all their faces, landing, once again, on Kent's last. He wears his usually stern look.

"Are you sure?" I ask him.

"Totally."

"Then let's get going. I don't want to miss too much of this party." I shuffle back inside the vehicle, feeling the rip in my skirt widening even further. "The rest of you out."

Jacks makes a grab for my hand. "I'm not leaving you

with that asshole," she says, clinging to me. Jeez, how much champagne did she drink?

"Jacks, I can look after myself." I peel her hands off my wrists. "Do you think you could look after her?" I ask Miranda, surprised to find the woman looks more amused and enamored by Jacks' behavior than disgusted.

"I'd be happy to." She pulls Jacks out of the limo and the others follow, Jonah pausing by the doorway.

"Are you sure about this, Avery?"

I stare Kent right in the eye.

"I've dealt with far more scary monsters than him in my time. I'm not scared."

And is it my imagination or does the corner of Kent's mouth twitch?

Chapter Thirty-Four

Avery

Kent takes a seat by the driver's window and thumps on the darkened partition. It lowers and he leans through to speak with the driver. Then he leans back out, the window zips upwards, and it's just the two of us gazing at each other through the murky gloom of the vehicle.

His eyes are intense. All dark and brooding and there's so much emotion swirling in them it's like staring into a hurricane.

It's too much.

I turn my head and watch the busy Rockview streets instead, examining all the people out on a Saturday night. All dressed up and buzzing with energy.

Soon, I realize we aren't passing down streets I recognize anymore.

"This isn't the way home," I say, with narrowed eyes.

"Where are you taking me? The airport where you can bundle me onto an airplane and send me back to Cardval? Or maybe a back alley where you really do intend to dispose of me?"

Kent keeps staring straight at me, his dark scent swirling ever more thickly in the stuffy limo.

"There's a little boutique around the next corner. I know the owner. It will be quicker than going back home." His mouth twitches again. "Besides, who knows what that friend of yours picked out for you? I'd rather have control over what you're wearing if you're going to be seen out with us."

"That's rather controlling," I huff.

He shrugs his shoulders. "I'm an alpha. I like control."

I cross my legs. "The store won't be open."

"Ibrahim has called ahead. I know the owner. They're opening it for me as a favor."

"Hmmm," I say, turning my head to gaze out the window again and watching as we pull off the main road with its large department stores and office towers and around to a smaller shop with mannequins crowded in the window. A light shines from within and Kent opens the door and climbs out before the vehicle has come to a complete stop.

"Wait here," he instructs, before walking towards the shop. A door opens and a young man greets him in the doorway. They talk for a few minutes and then Kent returns to the limo and gestures for me to follow him.

"Come on, the shop assistant has a few dresses in your size." My size? How does he know my size? "Let's find something quickly. I need to get back."

He holds the door open for me and waits for me to climb out.

I remain exactly where I'm sitting.

He huffs in irritation. "The shop is right there. You can see it. I'm not planning on murdering you in front of—"

"It's not that," I yelp.

"The shop is perfectly reputable. I hear it's even considered ... trendy. I'm not going to try and put you in some horror dress – unlike your friend."

"Hey, Jacks has very good taste," I say. after all she's chosen me as her bestie, hasn't she? "It's not that I don't trust you," although that's not strictly true, "or your intentions. It's just that ..."

"Yes?" he says.

"My ass."

"Your ass?"

"My ass."

"Do you ... have a problem with your ass?"

"Yes! It's hanging out of my dress!!"

He stares at me. For a third time this evening, the corner of his mouth twitches. Almost as if he's thinking about smiling.

He rubs his hand over his face, then shrugs off his dinner jacket.

"Here," he says, "tie this around your waist."

I take the jacket from him gratefully.

"Thank you," I say, lifting my hips and sliding the jacket under me, then tying the arms around my middle. The jacket smells strongly of the alpha and immediately I'm engulfed in his delicious scent.

I swallow and, ignoring his proffered hand, climb out of the limo.

"Good evening, Madam," the shop assistant says, beckoning me inside. "So happy we could help."

"Thank you so much for doing this," I say. "I had a bit of

a costume malfunction." I point to my behind. The shop assistant examines my outfit. I'm sure he must know I'm wearing a Walmart dress, but he maintains an entirely straight face.

"The dress is a terrific shape on you."

"If a little too small," I whisper to him.

"We'll have to find you something similar, don't you agree, Sir?" he asks as Kent follows me into the store.

"Something durable. Something she isn't going to rip."

"Well, with curves like hers ..." the shop assistant mutters, then scurries away when the alpha glares at him.

"Do you like frightening people?" I ask him, tipping my chin back to look at him.

"I don't frighten people."

I scoff. "You just glared at that poor dude with such venom, he nearly shit his pants."

"He should keep his opinions on your ... curves," he says with a curl of his lips, "to himself."

"He's clearly gay."

"Doesn't matter. It's objectifying."

I can't help laughing at that.

"What?" he says, a look of unease replacing the scowl.

"Objectifying is what you alphas do best."

"Sometimes it can't be helped." His gaze flicks down my body and then back to my face. "Why didn't you let Cruise buy you a dress for the event tonight?"

"Who says he offered?"

"This is Cruise. Of course he offered."

"I wanted to wear my lucky dress."

"You can't seriously believe a dress is lucky."

"I can and I do. Well, did. Until it let me down tonight."

"Why do you need luck?"

I hesitate, almost on the verge of telling him the truth. I

decide there is no point. "I have a habit of messing things up," I point to my ass, "I was hoping the dress would help. Seems it did the reverse."

He opens his mouth to reply but then the shop assistant is there beckoning us through to the changing rooms. He's hung a selection of dresses out on the rack ready for me to try. I run my palm along the row. Silk, satin, velvet. Crystals, embroidery, lace. And so many designer labels my eyeballs nearly pop right out of their sockets.

"I can't wear these!" I say, snatching my hand away.

"Is there a problem?" the shop assistant asks, his eyes darting anxiously towards the alpha.

"Don't you have anything less expensive?" I mutter.

Kent scoffs. "You're our date. You're expected to wear designer."

"Yeah, but–"

"I think you should try this one," the assistant says, diverting a coming argument. "It's really a very similar shape to the one you're wearing, only more elegant perhaps." He lays it across his arm so I can take a better look. It's made from a soft scarlet satin with a bodice top, spaghetti straps and a mermaid skirt with a small train.

I take a little step towards it – drawn there like a magpie. I reach out, then snap my hand away when I snatch a glimpse at the price tag.

"I'm not sure," I say.

"Try it on," Kent says in a voice that borders on a bark. "This is taking too long."

The shop assistant grabs my hand and pulls me into the nearest cubicle, hanging the dress up on a hook and yanking back the curtain.

The alpha's scent is swirling round me like some seductive fog now and it makes me a little giddy. I rest my palm against the mirror and take a few minutes to compose myself, before I strip off the jacket and my ruined dress, and step into the gown. It's not quite as tight as my lucky dress but I'm unable to do the zipper up on my own.

I step out from behind the curtain and find Kent slumped in a chair scrolling his phone, the shop assistant nowhere in sight.

"Oh," I say.

He looks up from the screen of his phone and his whole body jerks as his eyes land on me.

We stare at each other like idiots again and then finally I say:

"I need help with the–"

Just as he says, "It looks ... good. Let's–"

"I'm sorry," I say in amusement. "You go first."

"It looks good."

I can't help fishing for a better compliment than that. His scent and the darkness of his eyes suggest he likes this dress a lot.

"You don't think it's a bit ..." I turn to the side, so he gets the full effect of my curves. I'm being a flirt, but I'm also an omega and sometimes those instincts are just too darn hard to suppress. Especially with such a strong alpha scent in my mouth and his eyes looking hungrier by the minute.

"A bit ..." he says gruffly.

"Figure hugging?" I draw my hands down my waist and over my hips, his eyes following the movement.

He opens his mouth, but no words come out. Then he shakes his head. "You wanted help with the zipper?"

"Uh huh," I say, watching as he stands and stalks towards me, my heart starting to thump in my chest.

This man is a grumpy asshole, standing in the way of my potential happiness. I should not find him this hot. But

I've always been a sucker for the moody, broody ones and he has that down to a very, very fine art.

He comes to a halt right in front of me, his large frame towering over my smaller one, the warmth from his body almost palpable.

"Turn around, Omega," he says.

I give him my best disapproving bratty look, making it clear I don't like the order even if I'm already spinning around.

He slides his hand under my loose hair, his fingertips brushing my shoulder and my back and making my skin tingle. He brushes my hair to one side, then there's a pause, before he grips the zipper and yanks me a little backwards towards him, then he glides the zipper achingly slowly up my back, making my heart thump that little bit harder.

When he reaches the top, he pauses again, then brushes my hair back into place.

I almost swoon.

Instead, I peer over my shoulder at him. His eyes are all darkness now.

"Done?" I ask.

"Yes," he growls.

"And is it suitable? Are you happy with it?"

"Fuck, Omega. You know you look like sin and paradise rolled into one in this goddamn dress."

And then he's marching towards the door.

Chapter Thirty-Five

Kent

The award ceremony is in full swing when we arrive back at the hotel. That doesn't stop every creep in the ballroom eyeing the omega as we weave our way through the tables towards our seats, my hand lingering in the small of her back.

Just to guide her. Just so I'm there in case anyone tries to snatch her.

Not because I want to touch her skin again. Not because I want to stroke my palm down her curves. Not because I want her close to me.

There are only two seats remaining at our table, side by side. I curse under my breath.

I'm going to be sitting beside her all night. Drowning in her scent and her dark eyes. Entranced by her pretty smiles. Knowing beneath that sinful dress she's all bare.

As she lowers herself onto her chair, smiling and waving at my packmates, Cruise bending in to kiss her cheek, I consider spinning around and marching right out of this ballroom.

Jonah was right. She's a temptation that is agony to resist.

But fucking resist I will. I'm not a fool. I'm not a young, ignorant alpha anymore. I'm not my goddamn father.

I pull out my chair and gingerly lower myself into it, trying hard to ignore the way Cruise has already hooked his arm over the back of the omega's chair.

Every eye in this place is still on us. There will be no doubt in our pack's interest in this girl. It's probably already all over the internet. I consider pulling my phone out of my pocket and checking but what's the point?

"That definitely wasn't the dress I picked up for Avery," the friend says from the chair next to mine. I groan inwardly. I was so focused on the omega's wiggling ass, I failed to notice Jacks' occupying the place beside me.

"We took a detour," I say, motioning to the nearest waiter to come pour me some wine. I need a drink. I think I'm going to need several.

"You let her pick out that dress?" she chuckles.

"What does that mean?" I ask.

"I assumed if you had your choice, you'd dress the girl in a paper bag. That or a nun's robes and habit. Although," she says, swirling wine around her glass, "Avery has this ability to look good in just about anything. Not that she realizes it of course. She doesn't appreciate how stunning she is."

"Sure," I say flatly, remembering the way she'd shimmied her hands over her hips in a manner that suggested she knew just how goddamn stunning she is.

"You really have the wrong idea about her, don't you?" she says.

I point to the stage, where the host is announcing the next award.

"Do you mind?" I say.

She shrugs and turns away to Miranda on her other side.

I ignore the two women flirting on my left side, and my packmate and the omega on the other, and give all my attention to the awards ceremony. Laughing at the right moments, applauding at the appropriate ones, making mental notes on the up-and-coming stars of the tech world. People we might want to poach or do business with.

I fail to ignore the way the omega's thigh brushes up against mine. Or the way, every so often, her fingers wander to the bite mark hidden beneath her hair. Or the way her scent seems to respond to mine, rising and falling in tandem, becoming sweeter and sweeter as the night draws on.

Then finally, it's my turn to hand out the last award and give the closing remarks. My collar strangles my throat, sweat trickles down my spine, the bright lights blind me, but at least I'm away from her, away from her and staring straight down at her in that scarlet dress surrounded by my packmates.

As soon as the last applause dies away, I march straight off the stage and to the bar. I need something stronger than the wine. Something that will numb all these urges and desires.

At the bar, I'm relieved to find no omegas, only alphas, all also in search of hard liquor.

I find a space, catch the barman's attention, and order a double scotch. I'm waiting for my drink when a large palm slams against my shoulder blade.

I spin around and find Hardy from the Stormgate Pack grinning at me like an idiot.

"Congratulations, man. She's fucking beautiful." He's an old business associate, his pack providing security for ours and ours providing tech support for his. I've known him for coming up five years. He used to be this big, hard man who had grown men trembling in their boots. Tonight, he's wearing a pair of turtle-shell-rimmed glasses balanced on his nose, and is that baby sick on the shoulder of his jacket? Gross. I grimace.

He laughs. "You don't look very happy about it."

"About what?"

"The beautiful omega your pack has landed."

"We haven't landed anything," I say through gritted teeth.

"Sure," Hardy says, tapping the side of his nose and then peering out to the dance floor where Declan already has the omega spinning under his arm.

"She's just a date."

"Well, fuck man, you'd better get on and make her more than that pretty darn quick. There was a pack of unmated alphas sitting on the table behind ours, couldn't stop talking about her."

I peer around the ballroom and he's right. The interest the omega has generated is in no way fading. There's actually one alpha hovering behind Declan like he wants to snatch her from his arms. And there are several more openly gaping at her.

Hardy squeezes my shoulder with a big fuck-off grin. "Take my advice. Build the little thing a nest, bond her, mate her, knock her up. It's the best fucking feeling in the world, man. There's nothing like building your pack family, holding your kid in your arms. All the money in the world can't buy happiness like that!" He leans in and whispers in my ear: "We're expecting another."

I can feel my brow dampening.

Another kid? Is that the third or the fourth now? Jeez!

I'm just about to make my excuses and leave, not sure I can hear any more of this, when River Casspian, Hardy's brother-in-law and champion racing driver, joins us.

"You wielded any information out of him yet?" he asks Hardy.

"Nothing."

River grins. "Come on, where did you find her? I've got unmated alphas chewing off my ear, wanting to know. Like I'd know," he says, resting his palm against his chest. "I'm a happily mated alpha these days. Barely notice an omega in the room if she isn't mine."

"And yet you noticed Avery?" I can't help but growl.

"Avery, huh?" He winks at Hardy, and I consider punching him in the face. "I couldn't help but notice her, the way you paraded her through the ballroom like that. Molly's convinced she isn't from around here."

"She isn't," I say. "And she's not our omega. In fact, she's going home in the next few days."

The two alphas stare at me like I've lost my mind.

And with her scent in my nose and the fresh memory of the way she felt beneath my palms, I'm very, very damn close to losing it all together.

I pick up my drink from the bar top and make my way to the corner of the ballroom. Somewhere dark. Somewhere I can't be seen. Somewhere I can lurk in peace.

I tip a large mouthful of liquor into my mouth. The liquid scorches my tongue and my throat, blasting away the scent of the omega in my nostrils.

I sigh in relief, taking two more gulpfuls as if it's medicine.

My blood cools but it doesn't last for long. Not when my eyes are dragged towards the dance floor. In her vivid red dress, the omega stands out in a sea of black and gray suits, the disco lights falling down on her and illuminating her.

I watch her body move, her hips swaying from side to side, her ass wiggling.

Everyone else falls away, slips into irrelevance, and it's like we're alone in this ballroom, just her and me. My drink remains half drunk in my hand, a hand that trembles, my fingers growing tighter and tighter around the glass.

My feet want to move. My body wants to move. My hands want to reach out and take.

I grind my teeth together, fighting against that want but not strong enough to look away, too entranced, too captivated.

Maybe I'm just like my goddamn father after all.

Chapter Thirty-Six

Avery

One dance with Declan and I'm so dizzy from all the spinning and giggling I have a stitch.

"Mercy," I say as the song fades. "Mercy."

"I thought you were made of sterner stuff than this, Avery," Declan says. "In fact, I thought you were the dancing-all-night kind of girl."

"Depends," I say.

"On what?"

"What I'm wearing. This dress is tight—"

"I noticed," he says darkly.

"—and I need a minute to breathe."

"Come on," he says, wrapping his arm around my waist and leading me to the edge of the dance floor. "Let's grab you a glass of water."

"You grab water. I'm going to powder my nose."

Declan swings his gaze around the ballroom. "I'll come with you," he says.

"To the bathroom?"

"There are a lot of alphas here tonight."

"Are there?" I say. All my attention has been occupied by the Hamilton Pack. I've barely noticed anyone else, let alone spoken to anyone. But now as I peer around, I see that he is right. There are a lot of alphas. In fact, I've never been in a room with quite so many before.

"Yes. All looking at you like you're a piece of meat to be devoured."

"But I'm with you. No one would—"

"This is Rockview, Avery. You're not in Kansas anymore."

"Oh," I say, suddenly feeling mighty vulnerable in my dress. "Well in that case you can escort me as far as the bathroom door, but you're not coming in."

"It would be my pleasure," he says with a little bow.

In the bathroom, I'm not surprised to find a group of omegas crowded around the mirror, clearly gossiping. Their conversation halts as I enter, which means they were obviously talking about me. They all watch as I stride towards a cubicle and then start whispering again as soon as I lock the door.

They talk in hushed tones but if they think they're being subtle, they're deluded. Or perhaps they want me to hear. They criticize my dress, my hair and my makeup and one claims she's heard I'm an escort from Las Vegas.

I'm ready to give the lot of them a piece of my mind, but when I emerge a few minutes later, there's only one left, brushing a comb through her caramel locks.

She smells like caramel too, although her scent is slightly muted, and I spy the necklace of bite marks around the base of her throat. I can't help staring at them from the corner of my eyes. They look so beautiful, making my own lone bite mark look pretty pathetic in comparison.

"Don't mind them," the omega says waving towards the door. "They're just jealous."

"Jealous?" I say, walking towards the sink and washing my hands.

Jealous of me? Most of the time the only emotion I generate from other omegas is pity or disgust.

"Yep, jealous. They'd all give their left arm, left leg and their first-born child for a date with the Hamilton Pack." She tucks her comb away in her purse. "I'm Bea by the way. From the Stormgate pack." She holds out her hand. "I don't think we've met before, have we? Although I don't know many of the omegas in the city that well." Her voice has a slight accent to it and I'm guessing she's not from Rockview originally either.

"Avery," I say, shaking her hand. "I'm only here visiting."

"Visiting?" the woman says, her face perplexed. "I assumed ..." I tilt my head to one side. "Sorry," she says, blushing, "you just seemed really loved up. I guess I thought something serious was going on and you would be a permanent citizen here soon."

"Oh no," I say, feeling as confused as she looks. "It's not serious." Is it? "I guess I'm just having a fling or something. I'll only be here for a few more days."

"A fling, huh?" she says with a kind smile that seems to invite me to indulge more and the words come rushing from my mouth before I can stop them. I've been dying to talk to someone about all this, someone who would understand. Jacks is my bestie for life. But she's a beta. She'll never truly understand what it's like to be an omega with all these uncontrollable emotions and desires.

"I've never been with a pack before. This is my first time. There aren't too many packs where I'm from and the ones we have never showed any interest in me—"

"Never showed any interest!" the woman says, her eyes widening. "But you're so darn cute. I mean, your ass and your scent!"

I smile. It's not often another omega has ever offered me a compliment – apart from my sister and my mom. Over the years it's mostly been snide comments and catty remarks.

"Thank you," I say, "but I'm also flat broke with no family name or connections."

"The alphas back home care about that stuff?"

"Apparently so."

The woman rests her hip against the sink and scissors her fingers through her hair. "I also have no money and no connections," she lowers her voice to a whisper, "and I landed Pack Stormgate – one of the wealthiest packs in the city."

I'm not surprised, the woman is gorgeous and in the three minutes we've been talking, far kinder than any other omega I've met before.

"And," I hesitate, "are you happy?"

"Am I happy?" The woman grins so wide I'm surprised her cheeks don't split. "So happy," she gushes, resting her hands on her stomach. I notice the slight curve of her belly. "We're expecting baby number three."

"Wow, congratulations," I say. I fiddle with the straps of my dress. "And were ... were all your alphas on board from the start?"

"Hmmm," she says. "Y-e-s, but it was sort of complicated at the beginning. We had some work to do before we got there, let's just say that. But you know, I think most relationships have bumps in the road." She strokes her hands over her stomach. "Are some of the alphas being a bit hesitant, then?"

"One is."

"Hence, the fling thing." Bea rolls her eyes and tuts. "Sometimes alphas are like children. They don't know what's best for them."

"I might not be best for them."

Bea steps a little closer and leans in. "How's the sex? You know that's one of the best ways to tell. The chemistry between an omega and alphas when it's right is ..." She fans her hand in front of her face.

"Oh, it's pretty hot," I whisper back. "Way hotter than I even imagined it could be." She nods eagerly. "But ..."

"Uh oh, that doesn't sound good."

"The last alpha, the reluctant one, he will barely look at me, let alone talk to me. Let alone ... you know."

"Is there something wrong with him? I mean, jeez, you're gorgeous."

"Lots of omegas are gorgeous," I mutter.

"And bitches," Bea adds with a knowing look. "Trust me, I ought to know." She reaches out and grabs my hand. "I have a feeling he will come around – but you need to make him work for it, okay? He can't just act like a jerk one minute and expect forgiveness the next."

"You're right."

"So," she steps a little closer, "how did you meet? The Hamilton Pack is notorious for avoiding omegas. They hardly ever come to events like this, and my alphas tell me they haven't dated anyone in years and years."

"Really?"

"Oh yeah. I've heard omegas in bathrooms like these

plot all sorts of complicated ways to throw themselves in front of that pack, but they never succeed. In fact, I hear they won't even hire unmated omegas to their company – that's how keen they are to avoid them. It seems crazy to me."

"I'm having a hard time understanding it too. I thought every pack dreamed of their own omega."

"That's what they say." She smiles at me. "Maybe they've just been holding out for the *right* omega. So come on, how did you meet?"

"How did we meet? Now, that is a story!"

"Oh goodie, I love a good meet-cute."

I open my mouth to spill the tea, but then a loud alpha voice sounds from the other side of the bathroom door.

"Avery!" Declan yells. "I'm coming in!"

Before I can respond, he's crashing through the door.

"Are you okay?" he asks, his face flushed with worry. He rests his hands on my shoulders and examines my face.

"I'm fine," I say, "just talking to Bea, here."

He turns his head and registers the other omega for the first time.

"Declan Hamilton, this one is clearly a keeper," Bea says. "Don't you let her slip through your fingers."

"I have no intention of letting her slip away," he says, his grip tight on my shoulders as if to prove his point.

"Good to hear it," Bea says, winking at me and leaning in to add: "You'll have to tell me the story of how you met another time. We should do lunch." She turns to the alpha. "Give Avery here my pack's number, okay, Declan?"

He gives her a little salute, and she leaves the two of us alone in the bathroom.

"What was that about?" Declan asks when the door slams shut.

"Girl talk," I say, bopping him on the nose. He lifts one eyebrow in a manner that says, 'careful now'.

"Should I be concerned?" he asks.

I shrug my shoulders. His gaze travels all over my body.

"As we're right here," he whispers into my ear, "fancy getting nasty in one of those cubicles?"

I bop him on the nose a second time. "And ruin another dress? No. I think I'd rather tease you and keep you waiting."

The alpha groans. "You're cruel."

"I am. Come on, otherwise people will assume we *are* getting nasty in the bathroom."

"Wouldn't be a bad thing. I want all those alphas out there to know you're mine."

I consider reminding him that I'm not. But I don't want to sour the mood. I want to enjoy the night.

"As I'm likely to be in the gossip columns tomorrow, I'd rather they didn't include details about me fucking an alpha in the bathroom. My mom might read it!"

I take his hand in mine, and we make our way back into the ballroom. In the doorway, we linger, searching the crowd for the others and my gaze is drawn to the far wall. Kent's there, drink in hand, staring right at me.

I recall Bea's words in the bathroom, and dropping Declan's hand, strut towards his grumpy asshole of a packmate.

Chapter Thirty-Seven

Kent

"Hi," she says, taking the drink straight out of my hand and taking a tentative sip. She wrinkles up her nose as the liquid hits her mouth. "Yuck, that is revolting."

I take it from her hand and stare at her.

"Are you going to skulk alone in the shadows all evening?" she asks.

I keep staring. I don't trust myself to speak, but hopefully she'll get the hint and leave me alone.

"How about you ask me to dance, instead of gaping at me all evening?"

"I'm not gaping," I let slip. Then I add quickly, "Don't flatter yourself."

This time it's her turn to stare at me, an I'm-not-convinced-by-that-bullcrap expression written all over her face.

"I'm keeping an eye on you," I add. "Making sure you're taking care of that dress and not pulling any more stunts."

"And? How am I doing so far? Do I pass the Kent Hamilton seal of approval?"

Does she pass the test? Shit! She fucking aces it.

"Well, you haven't flashed your ass at anyone so far …"

She laughs and I have to look away. It's like gazing at the sun. Blinding.

"Just come and dance with me, will you?" she says, her fingers brushing against mine. "Please," she adds in that omega whine, that bedroom whine, the one I've had to block out with loud music and headphones back at the house.

My alpha drive kicks in. He wants to please the omega. He needs to please her.

He's fucking impossible to ignore. He wants her badly, wants to press her up against this wall and rut and knot her in front of everyone in this ballroom. He wants to sink his teeth in her neck right next to Cruise's scar. He wants to rip that dress off her and feast on her slick. He wants–

"Alpha?"

I focus back on her face. My scent's high as a kite and so is hers.

I grab her hand and pull her towards the dance floor. They're playing some fuck-off pop song, all bouncy and cheery, everyone skipping around like this is kindergarten. I don't give a fuck, I yank her right up close, wrapping my arms around her waist and holding her like we're slow dancing.

She looks up at me, clearly taken back.

"You wanted to dance," I huff.

"I'm not complaining," she says, rubbing her soft body ever so slightly against mine and sending that alpha-drive wild. I'm hard in an instance and there's no way she can miss it.

In fact, she whines a little, right at the back of her throat, so quietly only I can hear.

How is she faking this? How is she so fucking convincing? And do I care? Right now, do I care if this is all some clever act? Does it matter if it's real or not? If it seems real, if it's convincing enough, does it matter if her heart is not really in it?

She rests her head against my chest, her hair tickling my chin, reminding me of something.

Something that niggles at the corners of my memory.

My mom. The way her hair used to tickle my face when she'd lean down to kiss me.

A hollow kiss. An act just like this. A show for the audience. No real affection behind it. No real love.

Is this the same?

How did I know back then that it wasn't real? How could I tell?

It was the coldness in her eyes. The disinterest in her expression.

My mom never wanted me. I was just a means to securing the life she did want. A simple plan – a plan women all over the world have been enacting for centuries – beguile the stupid man with your pretty face, have him thinking with his cock, get yourself knocked up with his child and ensure yourself a lifetime of wealth and luxury.

Doesn't matter that you don't really want the child. Or the man. Just the money.

I hold the omega more tightly against me.

If she's here for the money, then she's still here, isn't she? She might stay forever.

My hands grip her tiny waist, her tits press against me through the thin material of her dress.

The other people on the dance floor jerk and bounce around us. They fade away. It's just me. It's just her.

Her heart pounds. Her scent rises. Her breath whistles.

I slide the hair away from her neck, just like I did in that store, and more of her scent perfumes the air. I lower my nose, closer to her warm skin, admiring Cruise's teeth marks in her skin. So raw, so new. I trace my thumb over the scar, and she gasps, her eyelids fluttering.

She's so perfect. So damn omega.

I want to claim her as mine.

"Let's go home," I growl into her ear.

"No," she says.

I blink. Not sure I heard that right.

"No?" I mutter, the alpha inside me roaring in displeasure. This omega is ours to command as we wish. If we want to rut her, then we will.

I shake my head, trying to dislodge those thoughts.

"I'm not ready for that, Kent."

"You're enjoying the party too much?"

"I am but ... we need to be friends before we can be anything else. Heck, acquaintances who actually speak to each other would be a start."

"You weren't friends with Cruise before he bonded you," I hiss in her ear, holding her tight so she can't wiggle away.

"I was blind drunk," she says.

"And Declan? Max?"

"I don't always get things right. I make mistakes – a lot of mistakes. Sometimes – occasionally – I'm smart enough to spot them before I make them. You have treated me like trash, Kent Hamilton."

"So now you're punishing me?"

"Maybe, a little," she confesses. "Although I'm also punishing myself here too," she adds with a mutter.

"Punish me in other ways," I growl.

"No," she says firmly. "I need to do what's right for me. You may be hot and growly and broody – but you're also rude, unkind and arrogant."

"Right," I say, my jaw stiffening against her verbal blows.

"I really like this pack," she says, resting her palms on my chest. "I never dreamed I'd ever have a pack. But I think I owe it to myself not to bond to a pack with a giant asshole in their midst."

"So that's it? You've led us all on – playing a game, making us believe–"

"Kent!" she says, "I'm asking you to prove to me you're not an asshole, not prove to me you are." She smiles at me, and I don't even possess the power to stay angry. Her smiles are so disarming.

"But I am an asshole." I tell her. "I've always been an asshole."

She shakes her head. "I don't believe that. I don't want to believe that."

I think about her words as Jonah steals her away, opting for a slow dance just like I had regardless of the rock track playing next.

Declan meets me at the edge of the dance floor.

"Are you softening towards our girl?" he asks.

"*Our* girl?"

"Kent, I've never seen you look at anyone or anything like that before in my life. Not even Shelly. You're as captivated as the rest of us."

"She thinks I'm an asshole."

"You are an asshole."

"I know that," I snap. "But she doesn't want an asshole. She wants me to prove I can be ... whatever the opposite of rude, unkind and arrogant is."

Declan grins. "You think you can?"

"Ahhh, shit, I'm 32! Probably not–" Declan goes to argue. "But I'm going to try."

"It'll be worth it, Kent. To have an omega. To have Avery. It will be worth it."

"I may need some help," I confess, plunging my hands in my pockets and staring down at my shoes.

"Hey, what are packmates for?" he says, squeezing my shoulder.

Chapter Thirty-Eight

Max

I watch as my usually quiet and reserved packmate occupies the very center of the dance floor, swaying with the omega while others rock out around him. Usually standing out like that would make him uncomfortable but he seems oblivious, totally drawn in by the woman in his arms. Did our plan work? It was only a moment ago she was dancing with Kent. Is this happening then? Really happening?

"Do you see this?" I ask Cruise as he returns from the bar with a drink for me and one for himself.

He takes a sip, peering out onto the dance floor. "He's completely smitten. You should've seen him at lunch."

I try not to smile. Cruise is so fucking smitten himself it's untrue. Jonah, beneath his nicely presented suits and his neat spreadsheets, is a romantic. You don't build a library because you want to read, you build one because you love books. And anyone who loves something that much is a romantic.

Cruise on the other hand, he's far more hard-headed than that. At least, that's what he's had me believe all these years. One little omega – one little omega with dark eyes and a seductive smile – and that hard shell has cracked right open, revealing he's just as soft in the center as the rest of us.

Things have changed. Things are going to change a whole lot more.

"We're going to need to build a nest," I say.

"Yeah," Cruise answers dreamily, watching our omega in our packmate's arms.

I think I could watch this all night. It's the biggest surprise to me – how much I love watching our omega with one of our packmates. It's such a fucking turn on.

However, the pleasant view is rudely interrupted.

Soon Jacks is standing in front of us, swaying in her heels, supported by Miranda.

"I think I may need to take this one home," Miranda says with amusement twinkling in her eyes. "Seems she can't handle her drinks as well as she claimed."

"Im jus fine," Jacks slurs before planting a kiss on Miranda's cheek. "We can 'av anoffa dwink if ya wan."

"Jees, how much did she drink?" I ask.

"And is she speaking with an Irish accent?" Cruise mutters.

"She's been doing that for the last fifteen minutes." Miranda shrugs. "And as for drinks, I've had the same amount."

"How many?" Cruise asks Jacks.

Jacks holds her hand in front of her face and, squinting

hard at her fingers, attempts to count. After losing her count three times, she gives up. "No idea."

"We'd better get her home," I say.

"I don't mind doing it," Miranda says.

"Yes, but if she passes out," Cruise says, "it's going to take two of us to lift her."

"Im weally weally not dwunk," Jacks says, yawning and resting her head on Miranda's shoulder, "jus sweepy."

Avery appears behind her friend, hand clasping Jonah's.

"What's wrong?" she asks.

"Jacks has had one too many," I tell her.

Avery walks around her friend and taps her on the shoulder.

Jacks eyes are closed but she swipes unsuccessfully at Avery's hand.

"We'd better get her out of here," she says. "This is the sleepy stage. The vomiting stage will start in about twenty minutes."

"Does this happen a lot?" Cruise asks with a frown.

"No," Avery says firmly.

"It's irresponsible to drink this much," Cruise mutters.

"Yes, because who knows what might happen," Avery hisses. "You could end up bonded, married and in bed with a stranger."

Cruise shuts his mouth, clearly put in his place.

Yeah, things are going to change a lot and I am here for that.

Between us, Cruise and I half walk, half carry Jacks through a discreet exit at the back of the ballroom; Avery, Jonah, Declan and Kent following after us. Jacks is half-comatose so she makes no complaint about being mishandled and we lay her out on one of the seats of the limo, Avery climbing in to sit beside her.

"I'm sorry about this," she says to us all, rubbing Jacks' back as we pile into the vehicle and it pulls away, Jacks moaning at the sudden movement.

To my surprise, rather than snap out one of his snarky replies, Kent says, "It happens to the best of us."

Declan nudges me in the ribs and whispers in my ear. "He's trying not to be an asshole. Seems he's finally come around."

I settle back in my seat, a grin pulled across my face and catch the omega's gaze when she peers up. I wink at her, letting her know exactly what I plan to do to her when we arrive home. Remove that sinful dress for starters. I suppose it's not that surprising Kent has been won round, not with her looking the way she does tonight.

"But I know this was an important event for you guys and—"

"Avery, all the important engagements and aspects of the evening have already passed," Jonah says.

"And usually we'd have left by now, anyway," Declan adds, taking her hand and pulling her away from the now-snoring Jacks and into his lap.

"Why?" she asks.

"Too many omegas out on the hunt," Declan says.

"Or their mothers," I add.

"Because you're all so fabulously gorgeous and every omega is falling over her own feet to meet you."

"Fabulously gorgeous, huh?"

"Hmmm," she says, attempting to shrug her shoulders nonchalantly. "You're all right."

"But not good enough to tempt you?" Declan asks.

"I could be tempted," she says, eyes scanning all over the five of us in a way that has my cock stirring in my pants.

"And what would tempt you?" I ask, reaching over to ghost my palm up her smooth leg.

"Cruise's tongue? Declan's fingers? Or my cock?"

She flicks her gaze over to Jonah and then back to mine. "Actually ..." she says.

"Yes?" I ask, suddenly intrigued.

"The thing Jonah does with his glasses."

"Me?" Jonah says, clearly surprised. "What thing do I do with my glasses?"

Avery kicks off her heels and sliding off Declan's lap, maneuvers her way over to Jonah's, her body rocking with the sway of the vehicle. She perches on his lap and even in the darkness of the vehicle, I can see his face flush. Then she lifts his glasses from his face and balances them on her own nose.

And how does she do that? How does she manage to make Jonah's glasses look sexy? The least sexual object known to man is suddenly more erotic than most women's pussies.

"This," she explains, mimicking almost exactly the way Jonah adjusts his glasses when he's thinking, or nervous or distracted.

"I do that?" he asks.

"All the time," we say in unison.

"And it's very sexy," Avery adds, placing his glasses back on his nose.

He hesitates for one moment and then pulls her more firmly into his lap.

"I'm not sure whether to believe you or not," he says frankly.

She combs her fingers through his hair. "I also find your freckles very, very sexy." She giggles. "Oh God, maybe Jacks is not the only one who's drunk too much."

"You find freckles and glasses sexy?" Declan says with amusement.

"I find lots of things sexy, Declan Hamilton."

Jonah blinks up at us all, a little shell-shocked, and I wink at him. The omega may have won him over, but it looks like he has also done the same with her.

Chapter Thirty-Nine

Avery

Back at the house, Max lifts Jacks into his arms, carries her out of the car, around the mansion and out to the pool terrace.

"We'll go force her to drink some water and then we'll put her to bed," Declan says, following Max, Cruise by his side. "Are you coming?"

"In a minute. I'm just going to say goodnight," I say, glancing at the other two alphas before I tip my head back to look at the sky shining brightly with a litany of stars. I wasn't lying to Jonah. This city is beautiful, the stars crazy vivid every night I've been here.

"Goodnight, Avery," Kent says from the other side of the pool, recapturing my attention.

"Goodnight," I say, and he hesitates. I bet he's hoping I'll invite him to join us at the pool house. But for once, I'm sticking to my resolve and my word. I won't be issuing any such invitation. Which is damn hard when he gives me puppy-dog eyes to rival Barney's.

He hesitates again and I steel myself against all the omega urges to run and comfort the crestfallen alpha.

"Avery," he says. "Do you think you'll stay?"

I gaze into his eyes, for once devoid of all that brooding, hurt and resentment, and then I glance over at Jonah.

"You know what?" I say, "I think I will."

He hesitates, then nods and slumps away and I honestly can't tell if he's pleased or not about it.

I shake my head.

"I'm pleased you've chosen to stay," Jonah says.

"You are?" I ask, tilting my head to one side. "And why is that, Alpha?"

He swallows, reaching up towards his glasses, then catching himself and halting. His hand hangs in midair. I cock an eyebrow at him and with his light eyes turning darker, he lifts his hand and does that thing with the glasses.

I let out a whimper – maybe a little bit of a theatrical one but his eyes become even darker anyway. Then I sashay up to him, hips swaying, loving the way that makes his ears burn and his pupils widen. In front of him, I stop, rise up on my tiptoes and kiss his mouth. A slow lingering kiss, sucking his lower lip into my mouth.

Immediately he grabs my elbows and tugs me in close, right up against his hard muscular body so I feel his heart thumping against his ribs. Then he's kissing me back in a way I never thought such a quiet, reserved alpha would. With passion, with enthusiasm, with force.

He kisses me until we both lose our breath, breaking apart and panting, his shoulders heaving up and down.

"I'm glad you've chosen to stay because I have developed feelings for you, Avery," he says, his eyes skipping over my face, his hand tight on my arm. "Very strong, overwhelming feelings."

"I can tell." I giggle, giddy from that kiss, knowing I've made the right decision here. "So, are you going to join us in the pool house?"

"If I may," he says, stroking his palms down my bare arms.

"On one condition."

"Name it."

"The glasses must remain on."

"Avery, I can't see without them, and I can assure you I'm very keen to see everything."

I take his hand in mine and lead him to the pool house, meeting the others as we step through the door.

"How's Jacks?" I ask.

"Just fine," Cruise says. "All tucked up with a glass of water and a packet of painkillers ready if she needs them."

"And a bucket?" I ask cautiously.

"I think we're safe on that front."

"Where's Kent?" Declan asks.

"Back at the house ... I'm ... I'm not quite ready to let him join us yet."

"How long are you going to keep him out in the doghouse, sweetheart?" Declan asks.

"For as long as it takes," I say.

"You're a hard taskmaster."

"I'm trying to make sensible choices. You say you want me for this pack, but I need to know that binding my life to yours will work out. I don't want an alpha who will take his bad moods out on me or bark at me every time something goes wrong in his day."

"Kent isn't like that."

"He needs to prove that to me."

"So, are you going to stick around, Omega, to give him that chance to prove himself to you?"

"Urgh," I say, shaking my head with a big grin. "I guess so. I mean my parents are going to freak out about this but ..."

"But?"

"Yes, I'll stay for a bit."

Declan whoops, wraps his arms around my thighs and lifts me high into the air, spinning me around.

When he places me down on the ground, the others gather round me, enveloping me in one huge alpha hug. One huge alpha hug that is, I have to admit, addictive. I want this to work. I really hope Kent can prove to me it can.

"So how are we going to celebrate?" Declan asks.

"I can think of a few ways," Max says darkly. "Most of them involving the removal of this frankly sinful dress."

I wiggle my ass and pout, knowing both those things will drive these alphas wild. "You don't like my dress? You know your packmate chose it."

"Take it off, little omega," Max growls.

"Manners," I tease him.

He growls again, with more menace this time. Jonah edges forward. "Miss Avery Loren, would you be so kind as to remove this unholy dress so your alphas can ..." he adjusts his glasses giving me a dark look, "fuck you?"

"Better?" Declan asks with a smirk.

"Much," I say, swiveling around and motioning to my zipper.

Jonah gets there first, the others muttering curse words at him under their breath, and he glides the zipper down my back, his fingertips following against my bare skin. When it's undone completely, he rests his palms on my shoulders and hooks his fingers under the spaghetti straps. He slips them off my shoulders and the dress crumples to the ground.

"Truly beautiful," he leans in to whisper by my ear.

"But is she a good omega as well as a beautiful one?" Declan says. "Is she wet for us alphas?"

He already knows the answer to that. The aroma of my slick is strong in the air.

"Come on, let's see. Open your legs for us and touch yourself," Max commands. "Show us whether you're all wet. Show Jonah just how beautiful you are."

I twist my head around to look at the other alphas.

"Do as he says, Omega," Cruise orders.

Biting my lip, I dip my right hand inside my thighs, and they watch as my fingers disappear between my pussy lips.

"I need to see," Declan groans, and he takes a hold of my waist and drops me down onto the nearest couch.

And then they can see everything. Me touching myself. My fingers lost between pink, swollen lips, everything glistening with slick.

I inhale sharply. My heart beats like a drum. I've never put on a show like this before. Never done anything so intimate in front of others. But what I'm learning in our short time together is how easily it is to wind these alphas around my little finger. How a look or a word, a movement or a scent, can have them dropping to their knees. It's powerful. My life has been a crazy mess, veering in directions I never wanted. But this is control.

"You like touching yourself?" Declan asks, his voice hoarse.

"I'd prefer if you touched me, Alpha," I purr.

"I'm going to, sweetheart. Don't you worry about that.

But first we all want to watch you touch yourself, want to see how you make yourself come. Can you do that for us?"

Cruise leans down and growls his approval against my throat. My fingers move on command.

I start off slow, gentle, ringing my clit, the movement of my fingers hypnotizing the alphas. But as slick begins to flow down my thighs, and needy little moans escape my throat, my fingers grow faster. I rub at my clit frantically, my legs shaking and my stomach tightening, my gaze flitting from one alpha to the next.

"That's it," Jonah says, his eyes wide with wonder. "Make yourself come for us."

"Hmmm," I murmur.

I grip onto Declan with my free hand, my breath catches in my throat, my body stills and then I let out one long sigh as pleasure ripples through my core.

I thrust my fingers up inside myself, and moan, slick all over my hand and wrist.

In the next breath, Declan and Cruise drag me further back onto the soft cushions of the couch, spreading my legs wide so they can all see my fingers moving inside me.

Then Declan snatches my hand away, and thrusts his own fingers inside me, making me lift my hips and groan with pleasure.

"That feel better, sweet girl? Did you need something thicker?"

He has his forefinger inside me, but I'm so wet, he adds his middle with ease and then he's testing the stretch and adding a third.

"See that, Jonah?" Declan says, his eyes on me not his packmate. "This little one can take two of us at once. Fuck, she could probably take three."

The idea turns me on, and I squeal and come again

around his fingers, dancing on his fingertips like he's a magician.

"And see this, Jonah?" Declan mutters. "Can you see her pussy? See the way it's milking me. Such a good girl, aren't you, Avery?"

"Need a knot," I pant. "Need a knot right now."

"Want more than one?" Cruise asks me, his midnight eyes almost jet.

"Yes," I say. "I want you all." In fact, I feel desperate for it. Like I'm falling into heat.

I'm slung over Max's shoulder and carried up to the bedroom in the next heartbeat, where Max positions me on my hands and knees on the bed and Cruise and Declan kneel behind me. Then they plunge into me together, finding a rhythm where one thrusts as the other slides out. It's intense and tears quickly gather in my eyes, my breath lost in my lungs, the sensations overwhelming. I come in the next breath, clenching and squeezing around both the alphas, begging for a knot.

They don't give it to me though, instead they're moving away, making room for their packmates. Max lies out on the bed and orders me onto his cock, reverse cowboy style, then Jonah is hovering above us both and I experience the intensity of two alpha cocks inside me all over again.

For a moment, Jonah is still, catching his breath, my cunt rippling around them both, desperate for friction, for a knot, for alpha seed.

Then with a deep groan that sounds more animalistic than human, he glides from me, rubbing up against Max's cock, and slams into us both; Max's hands are tight at my waist, holding me in place, making sure I take everything they have to give me.

Jonah stares into my eyes. His are wild like a man who's lost his mind. Like Romeo mad with passion and love.

"It's never felt this good," he mutters as he fucks me. "It's never felt like this before. Avery, you're so special. So perfect for us."

I lift my hands to his body and stroke the contours of his muscular chest, his skin pale and freckled. He takes my hand in his, bringing it to his lips and kissing my palm as he rocks his hips against mine. I cup his cheek and I sense Cruise through the bond, there right with me, feeling it all.

I want that connection with all of them. I want to be theirs.

"Let me knot you, pretty bookworm," Jonah begs, and I smile up into his boyish, beautiful face.

As they knot me together and I'm whipped away to some other plane, I see a vision, a vision of the future, of how it's going to be, the six of us, together. And finally, finally, I let myself believe.

Chapter Forty

Kent

The house is cold and empty as always and I wonder if it'll ever be home now, or whether the poolhouse is now our new home? It's less grand, less fancy, but I can see it's more homely, cozier, somewhere appealing to an omega.

"Barney?" I call out, listening for his footsteps.

The house remains quiet, and I walk down the long hallways, searching first my room and then the office. I find him curled up near my desk, bathed in the blue light from my computer screen.

"Barney?" I say and he lifts his head to look at me. "Didn't you hear me calling?" I guess the old boy's getting deaf now too. I pat his head and he licks my hand, his brows rippling and his nose twitching. He can smell the omega's scent on my skin.

"Yeah, seems like the little minx has finally won me around

as well." I scrub my hand over his face. My body trembles with anticipation. I want that little omega so fucking much.

But as I stand, the computer screen catches my eye. My inbox lies open and there's a new email right at the top marked urgent and confidential.

My heart stops beating and bile swims up into my throat.

I don't have to look. I don't have to know.

But it's there beckoning me almost as strongly as the omega; it's red-flag ominous.

I glance towards the door.

Temptation pulls me in opposite directions. I have a strange feeling one will lead me to happiness, the other misery.

"Leave," I tell myself. "Delete the message and leave."

But my feet don't move. I drop into the chair and click on the message instead.

Barney scoots closer to me, leaning his body against me as I read the words.

A message from the private detective I hired yesterday.

He wants me to call him urgently.

I don't have to. I could still leave.

But I've always been too darn curious for my own good. It's led to success – building this empire of a company – it's also led to pain, learning things I'd rather not have known.

It's like a scab though, one I can't help picking even when I know it will make me bleed.

I press on the private detective's contact details and connect the call.

The video call rings, loud in the silence of the house and Barney huffs, irritated his peace has been disturbed.

It keeps ringing, and, for a brief moment, I'm relieved.

He's not going to answer. The decision has been taken out of my hands.

Then the rings cut short and a voice cuts through the silence.

"Mr. Hamilton?"

My heart sinks and I brace myself.

"Speaking. Apologies for calling so late but you said this was urgent."

"Yes. I thought you'd want to know the outcome of my investigation as soon as possible. At least, that is what you said."

"What have you found?" I say in irritation.

Maybe I'm wrong about this. Maybe he simply wants to report that he's found nothing. That I'm clear to be with this woman. That we all are.

"It seems the lady in question is an actress."

I try to process this. But I can't. Firstly, he's wrong, and secondly, I don't understand the implications.

"She's not," I tell him. "She's a waitress." I figured that much out from my own social media snooping.

"No, Sir. I'm afraid she is an actress. In fact, she studied acting for four years at the school for performing arts in Cardval. Came top of her class. She's been in small scale productions and had a few minor parts in TV shows, commercials, that kind of thing ever since."

I remember that photo, the one with her face lit up as if she'd been standing under a spotlight. Standing on stage. How had I missed that? How had I not seen it for what it was?

Because I was too entranced by her goddamn face.

"There was no evidence of this on her social media."

"Looks like she deleted most posts relating to her acting

career several weeks ago. Most probably in readiness for this sting."

I stare at my computer screen so hard, my vision blurs and a noise in my head buzzes so loudly I wince in pain.

"A sting?" I finally stutter.

"Yes, Sir. My conclusion is that this girl is a very good actress who ensured she placed herself in your packmate's path with the ultimate aim of securing your pack."

"She says she was in Vegas for a bachelorette party."

"One it seems she helped to organize. In fact, I can see she made the bookings herself. Monday night's a strange time to have a bachelorette party, don't you think?" I nod slowly. "I've also looked into her financial record. She's broke. No savings, no assets. Living at home, making very little money from her paying job as a waitress. I'm sorry, Sir, but it's clear she sees you as a sizable meal ticket."

My heart still isn't beating, and a coolness seems to settle over my body. Like snow settling on my skin.

I'm not even angry – not anymore.

Just disappointed. Damn disappointed. Disappointed and – shit – I wanted to believe it. I wanted them to be right.

I didn't want this story to go the way it always does. I wanted this one to be different. I wanted her.

But I should have known. Fuck, I should have known!

There is no way an omega like Avery could ever, ever want an alpha like me.

My mom's words spin around and around in my head like they always do, whispering to me.

"I've tried, Kent, my darling, I really have. But you do make it rather impossible. You were such an unlovable child, and unfortunately, you've grown up to be just like your father too."

My heart splinters, a stabbing pain in my chest, and I have to force my body not to shake.

"This won't be enough to convince my packmates," I tell the man, my voice sounding cold in my own ears. "You're going to need to find me more evidence."

"I'm in the process of doing that, Sir."

"Good," I say.

I hang up.

I want to scream. To tear down the whole fucking world.

But I can't move. I'm frozen to the spot. Buried under all that frigid snow. My blood so icy cold, I shiver.

I rest my hand on the crown of Barney's head and steel myself for what's to come.

It isn't going to be pleasant, but it has to be done.

Chapter Forty-One

Avery

In the morning I wriggle my way out of the sleeping pile of alphas.

"Where are you going?" Max groans.

"I need to go check on Jacks and break the news to her that she's going home alone."

"Tell her later," Max says, tugging me back towards him and attempting to nibble along my shoulder.

"I need to check she's still alive," I squeal, pulling away and scurrying out of the bed before any other alpha can grab me.

I find Jacks sprawled across her own bed dressed only in her underwear.

I give her shoulder a poke.

"Are you okay?" I ask her.

She groans loudly.

"Noooo," she wails, "the ground won't stop spinning."

"Have you drunk any water?" I ask, searching for the glass the alphas left her in the room.

"About ten liters. But I vomited most of it up anyway."

"Oh Jacks," I say, rubbing my palm between her shoulder blades.

"I'm sorry," Jack mumbles into the pillow. "I just ... really like her and that made me nervous and so I got drinking to settle my nerves. And then ... I've blown it with Miranda, haven't I?"

"You don't usually get nervous around women."

"She's special."

"She is, huh?"

"Yes," she sobs, "and now she'll never want to see me again."

"Oh, she will."

"She won't."

"She will, trust me. I have about ten messages on my phone asking if you're all right."

"You do?" Jacks asks, rolling over and then clutching her head, her eyes screwing up in agony. "I need to text her. Apologize," she says, patting the mattress around her in search of her phone. "And then I need to apologize to your alphas." She grimaces.

"Okay, but first I need to tell you something."

Jacks halts her phone search.

"What?" she asks suspiciously.

"I'm ... I'm not coming home with you today."

"You're not?"

I shake my head. "I'm going to stay a little longer."

"A little longer as in 'forever'?"

"We'll see about that. We need more time to see if this can work first."

"Oh my God, Avery," Jacks says, sitting up in bed and seeming to forget all about her hangover. "I'm so happy for you." She wraps her arms around me in one hell of an alcohol-soaked hug. "But also sad. Cardval is going to suck without you. I'm going to miss you so much."

"I know," I say. "I'm going to miss you too." I can't quite bring myself to say it out loud yet, but I don't think I'll be returning to Cardval. My new home is here with the Hamilton Pack.

I cling to her and then yelp as my phone blasts out from my lap.

Jacks pulls away and I lift my phone to my face, squinting at the screen without my contacts.

"It's Isla," I say, hitting accept.

"Avery," my sister says in a loud whisper.

"Hi Isla," I say chirpily. "How are–"

"There's no time for that. She's about to call. I'm giving you a heads up."

"Who?" I ask.

"Mom!" she squeaks. "She's out of her mind."

"Why?" I ask, sitting bolt upright with panic.

"Why?!! Avery, your face is everywhere today."

I glance at Jacks who shrugs.

"Isla," I say. "Calm down." My sister sounds like she's about to hyperventilate. "I don't understand what you're saying."

"You went out with Pack Hamilton somewhere last night and your picture is everywhere this morning."

"Oh sh–" I start but then my cell starts vibrating in my hand. I look at the screen. "It's her. She wants to video call."

Jacks grimaces a second time.

"Good luck!" Isla says, cutting the call and leaving me to stare at my mom's incoming one.

"You could ignore it," Jacks suggests.

I give her a look. We both know that is a bad idea.

I glance down at what I'm wearing. Luckily my own pajamas and not one of the alpha's shirts. I adjust my hair to cover my claiming bite, and then I accept the video call.

"Hi Mom," I say with a wide smile.

My mom scowls at me. "Don't you 'hi mom' me young lady. Ten days! Ten days you've been gone with no more than a couple of pathetic text messages in all that time."

"I'm sorry, Mom, we've been really busy with this job, shooting every day and–"

"Pack Hamilton," she says.

"Erm ..."

"Do you have any idea how many people have called me this morning asking if that's my daughter photographed with Pack Hamilton? *The* Pack Hamilton. They're all saying you're dating Pack Hamilton. And me, your own mother, had no idea!"

"Erm ..."

"Are you dating?" she asks in such a forceful Mom way, there's no chance I can't answer her.

"Well ... yes."

The squeal of excitement my mom emits down the phone is so loud, Jacks ducks her head under the nearest cushion.

"And it is *the* Pack Hamilton? The real Pack Hamilton?"

"Yes, Mom."

"And you're dating dating? It wasn't just a onetime only date?"

"No, we are dating."

My mom squeals again and I consider joining Jacks under the pillow.

"It's early days, Mom. Please don't get too excited."

"Early days, schmearly days," She says, dismissing the idea with a sweep of her hand. "I've seen the photographs, Avery. They're clearly crazy about you. Crazy! This is your opportunity, darling. Your opportunity to grab a pack and a filthy, rich one too." She hiccups with excitement. "You need to make the most of this, Avery. You'll have to stay out there in Rockview for as long as you can – give them plenty of time to fall in love with you! Oh, my darling! You will be sorted for life! You will want for nothing. You'll have everything you could ever dream of!" I try to interrupt her, but she keeps plowing right on. "And once you're settled, you can invite Isla to stay – and maybe Georgia too – and set them up with all Pack Hamilton's rich alpha friends, and you can all quit those awful jobs of yours. And we can visit London and Paris and Rome like we've always wanted to. Maybe even the pack's private island."

"They have a private island?"

"All rich men have a private island, darling. Oh my, this is so exciting!"

I stare at her manic smile on the screen. "One step at a time, Mom."

"This is happening, Avery. You are going to be the Pack Hamilton omega and you are going to live like a princess. Like a queen! We all will!"

I smile at her. It's hard not to. I think she's right. I think I am going to be theirs. That feeling in my stomach that blossomed last night, the one telling me this is the real thing, is stronger than ever.

But I mustn't get carried away. I'm going to be cool-headed and sensible about this. I need to remember that

Kent hasn't proven himself to me yet. Plus, I've had enough failed relationships to know the early days can be amazing and the latter ones not so much.

"This run of luck may peter out eventually," I tell my mom, trying my best to rein both of us in. "It may transpire that we're ill suited. That we don't get on as well as we'd like."

"I don't think you should worry about that," my mom chuckles, "if it means you could fly around the world to luxurious places on a private jet."

"Well, I care. I don't want some dude who is going to treat me poorly. I want love and respect and all those good things."

"Don't be silly, Avery. You realize those things only exist in fairy tales and romcoms."

"How about you and dad?" I cry.

"Oh," my mom says, dismissing the idea with a flick of her hand. "Your father and I are the exception to the rule. Most marriages I know are more about convenience than love." When I stare at her with shock, she quickly adds, "But that won't be the case with you, my darling. You're all going to be very much in love. And you're going to be rich beyond your wildest dreams." She claps her hands in excitement.

"Mom, I've got to go," I say, deciding it would be wise to end this conversation before she becomes even more delusional.

"Why? Are you going to meet them now?"

"Erm ... yes and I don't want to be late."

"No, no, you mustn't be. You must try your utmost not to mess this up, Avery. And wear something low cut. You have a very nice figure. Use it to your advantage. What alpha is going to care about punctuality when there are a nice pair of–"

"Yes, thank you, Mom," I say, rolling my eyes. "I'll speak to you soon, okay?"

"Yes, keep me updated." She blows me a kiss and I hang up, flopping down beside Jacks.

"I feel sorry for your sister," Jacks says, "your mom is going to be out of control."

"I know," I mutter, "I feel both guilty and relieved that Rockview is far, far away from Cardval." Then I groan, remembering that means my bestie will also be far, far away. "I'm going to miss you, Jacks."

"Then we need to make the most of our time together while I am still here. I'm getting dressed and we are going out to celebrate your new, amazing life. We can go to that bar they're always talking about on Instagram. The one only *rich* people are allowed into." She scrambles to the edge of the bed. "I'll invite Miranda. I guess I will be seeing more of her now after all, seeing as you'll be living out here. I know it's far, but you'll let me borrow the private jet, right?" she says, mimicking my mom's voice and winking at me. I toss a pillow her way and she dives back across the bed, hugging me.

"Really, I'm genuinely happy for you," Jacks says. "You deserve this, Avery. You deserve love and happiness and most of all, lots of cock. Now, go put on something glam."

"I don't own something glam."

"That red dress."

I blush. "May not have lasted the night."

Jacks grins. "Then how about the dress I got you? Go on," she says, pushing me towards the door. "Go get dressed. Your cousin's bachelorette party wasn't the only one you skipped. You skipped your own too. We have some making up to do!"

She cackles and staggers off to the bathroom.

I giggle, rolling my eyes and opening the door, coming face to chest with Cruise.

He stares at me, blinking.

"Oh hi," I say, smiling, my stomach warming like it always does when I set eyes on this man. "Jacks wants us to spend a girly day together before she heads back to Cardval. You don't mind, do you? I think the bond has pretty much released now, although we won't go far, I promise."

I stand on my tiptoes and kiss his mouth. His brow furrows.

"Where are you going?" he asks.

"Oh God, who knows!"

"But ... you need money," he says, his voice hoarse.

"Oh ... no..." I blush, "I mean ..."

His brow furrows harder. "You can take my credit card, if you need to."

"Really?" I say. I have negative five dollars in my account. He said he'd cover my wages while I was staying here but then we never actually talked about the practicalities of making that happen. We haven't needed to. I've been here the whole time, living in their house, eating their food. I haven't needed any money all week. But going out ... "Thank you."

I hug him and begin to skip away, when he catches my wrist.

"I'll arrange for Sam to come with you too. I don't like the idea of you out there alone, especially now people know you are connected to this pack."

"Are you sure that's necessary?"

"Absolutely, Omega. Stick with him."

I nod, and then I skip off towards the bathroom.

Jacks' optimism, even my mom's, has rubbed off on me and done nothing for my attempts at sensible and level-headedness. In fact, I feel flushed and dizzy and so freaking happy.

Finally, something in my life is going to work out.

Chapter Forty-Two

Cruise

I watch Avery disappear off beyond the property gates feeling stunned, those words I'd overheard earlier still rattling through my head.

Those words about private jets and expensive vacations.

I didn't think she was interested in our money. I didn't think she was like that. Was I wrong?

An unease I've not felt since I woke up that morning bonded to the omega sloshes through my gut.

I can't shift it as I slump back down towards the house, a heaviness hanging over my head.

I can't tell the others. It would color their opinion of Avery and, despite the conversation I've just witnessed, I believe in her. I believe in us. I believe in this.

Okay, so she's happy about the money and so is her family. I suppose anybody would be until they learn what a millstone it is around your neck. Bringing responsibilities and restrictions entirely at odds to the ones experienced when you don't have a cent to your name.

And don't I want to spoil our omega? Don't I want to buy her everything her heart desires? Don't I want to make her happy? Is it so wrong if she wants that too?

I don't know. I just don't know.

I scratch at the back of my neck, then rub at the old scar on my stomach, those words going round and round in my mind. I'm unaware Declan and Max are waiting for me at the end of the drive until I'm almost upon them.

"You received the sinister sounding text from Kent too, then?" Max says.

"Huh?" I say.

"You got a text from Kent?"

I pull my cell from my pocket. "I don't know," I say, staring at my screen, the words swooping in and out of focus.

"He wants to talk with us in the kitchen. Come on, man, let's see what it is now," Declan says, slapping me on the back.

I jolt like he just struck me, and he eyes me with curiosity.

"Everything okay?" he asks.

"Yeah, fine," I say, my feet feeling heavy, my brain clouded, like they used to before I met that omega ray of sunshine.

Kent is pacing in the kitchen. He looks nervous. Something Kent never looks, and it has me feeling the same way too.

"Damn it, Kent, what the fuck is going on?" Declan asks.

For a moment, I wonder if he overheard that conversation between the omega and her mom as well. But that couldn't have been possible, could it?

If he did, then what the hell must he think?

I fidget on my feet and Declan swings his gaze between the two of us, color draining from his face.

"What's going on? What's happened?"

I go to speak but Kent beats me to it.

"Hear me out, okay?" he says, raising his hand. "Before you all jump in, let me speak, let me get to the end."

"I don't like the sound of this," Jonah mutters.

"What have you done, Kent?" Max asks.

I expect Kent to say nothing. That he's done nothing.

Instead, he stops his pacing and faces us all.

"I hired a private detective to look into the omega."

"You did *what?*" Max says, outraged. An hour ago, I would have felt the same. Right now, I'm too damn stunned. I don't know what the hell to think or feel.

"I asked you not to jump in. Let me finish." Max opens his mouth. "Please," Kent says. Max scowls at him but says nothing. Kent's shoulders rise and fall. "The omega is an actress," he says finally. "In fact, she's a very good actress."

My heart stops beating and rips right down the middle, the pain so intense, I screw up my eyes and grip the corner of the counter. It splinters all over my body, fierce and raw.

I was wrong. Wrong all this time. It wasn't real. None of it was.

It's just like before. Just. Like. Before. It's happened again. I can't believe it. How could I be so stupid?!

It takes me several attempts to start breathing and force my eyes open.

The world swims in and out of focus, my friends' voices muffled like they're underwater.

Declan scoffs and shakes his head. Max glares at Kent

like he's hoping to burn a hole in him. Jonah adjusts his glasses.

My heart hurts so much, I want to sink to my knees and sob into my hands. But I keep standing, somehow I keep standing.

"What are you saying, Kent?" Jonah asks carefully.

"She didn't tell us that, did she? And why do you think that is? Why keep that a secret?"

"I assume you're back to thinking the omega is not genuinely interested in us," Jonah says.

"For fuck's sake." Declan sighs. "Okay, the omega is an actress. Okay, she omitted to tell us that detail. But what does your gut tell you? Because my gut tells me this thing between her and us is real. And truth is, our best business decisions, our most successful ones, the ones that helped shape Hamilton Enterprises into the company it is today, were based almost entirely on our guts. And right now, my gut tells me that Avery is genuine. That this connection between us is genuine. That she'd make the perfect little omega for our pack. I'm absolutely certain of that."

He looks to me to back him up, but my gaze falls to the floor.

I would have been absolutely certain of that too only a couple of hours ago. I believed it wholeheartedly. Until I tuned into that conversation on the other side of that door.

Now I'm not certain at all, my gut churning and nausea burning my throat. The pain hurts so much I can hardly stand it. It takes everything I possess not to fling back my head and howl in agony.

Is that how she views me? Views us? As her ticket to the high life? Was this all make-believe after all? All about our money and our wealth? Not about me, about our pack, about us, at all?

I'm not like Declan. I can't charm women with the flash of my smile. And I'm not like Max either, who has women falling at his feet every time he flexes his muscles. And as for Jonah, it's surprising how many women go for that nerdy thing.

But me? I've never had women fawning over me. Or at least I didn't until we became powerful and wealthy.

Did I learn nothing from before? I should have known. I should have listened to Kent. I should have seen this for what it was. I've been an idiot. I've been an idiot all over again. Only this time it hurts so much more.

I barely listen to any more of the conversation happening around me. Instead, I stare at my shaking hands, wishing there was a hole in the ground to swallow me whole.

"Cruise?" I lift my head at the sound of Declan's voice. He examines my drooping shoulders and down-cast face and frowns. "Oh, come on man. You can't seriously believe she's faking all this?"

"She didn't tell me she was an actress. In fact, she kept it hidden."

"So what? Maybe she thought you would be suspicious of her motives if she did."

"Yeah, well."

"And have you told her your deepest, darkest secret?"

"So, I'm no angel. Doesn't change the fact that she's an actress and according to Kent," I glare at him, "a good one."

Declan frowns harder. "If she was such a good actress, she'd be making millions in Hollywood and would have no cause to honeytrap us!" He lands his hand on my shoulder, making me flinch. "What do your instincts tell you?"

I sigh. "That this is real, but it could be the bond or–"

"I've known bonded folk who hate each other's guts. The bond can't create what isn't there."

"Yeah," I say, "I know." I lower my voice. "And Declan, I was right there with you, buddy, wanting to believe in her. No, not just wanting to believe in her – *believing* in her. One hundred percent. I wanted this to be real. I wanted that more than you'll ever understand." I swallow and the next words seem to leave my mouth without me moving my lips, the words sounding far, far away. "But then, I overheard something."

The room stills around us, the scents of my packmates bristle.

"What did you overhear, Cruise?" Kent asks firmly.

I take an inhale of breath and then I recount the conversation. Every damn painful word of it and by the end even Declan's face has fallen.

We've been had. Fooled. Beguiled. Tricked. Hoodwinked.

The whole damn lot.

Avery Loren is no more interested in us than she is in swimming with sharks or climbing Mount Everest.

The whole thing has been a ruse. All of it.

She never wanted us. All she's ever wanted is our money. Just like Milana. And Cindy. Just like Julia. And Tanya. Just like Kent's mom. Just like every other omega we've ever met.

Just like before.

Chapter Forty-Three

Avery

"Come on," Jacks says. "One more cocktail."

"Your liver must be made from steel," Miranda says, shaking her head at Jacks in an affectionate way.

"Jacks ruined her liver long ago," I tell her.

"Lies! All lies, Avery Loren," my best friend says. "Now come on. Another cocktail. Who knows when we will see each other again? We're making the most of it!"

"The drinks cost more than I make in one shift!" I hiss, feeling uncomfortable in the designer dress Jacks bought me. It's not like the red dress from last night. I felt at ease in that dress, probably because of the Hamilton alphas circling me, drowning me in their wonderful scents. Today all I can think about is wrinkling the damn thing or spilling my drink down it. Plus, it's itchy against my skin and the material too thick for a warm bar like this one.

"So what if they cost the Earth?" Jacks says. "Your men are paying. Just add it to the tab."

"Jacks!" I say.

"They won't mind," Miranda says, bobbing a straw in and out of what remains of her drink. "They're really generous. I've worked the gardens of a lot of the wealthy people in this city and most are tight-fisted assholes." Jacks nods. "The Hamilton Pack, they're different. They look after their staff. You know last Christmas, they paid for all of us to travel home to our families. And Freddricho's family lives in France!"

"See," Jacks says. "They aren't going to begrudge you a few drinks with your friends. With your best friend! Your best friend who you are going to be separated from for the first time in your life." She pouts at me. "Don't worry, Avery. They're crazy about you."

"They are, you know," Miranda adds. "I've been working for them for three years and I've never – not once – seen them bring a girl home with them."

"They were probably hooking up outside the house," I mutter.

"No, I don't think so. That kind of behavior ends up all over social media. You're the exception."

"She is, right?" Jacks says with affection. "Let me get you another drink, what would you like?"

I look at her sheepishly. "Honestly? What would I like?"

"Yes. Do you want champagne? To celebrate in style?"

"I think you're best laying off the champagne, Jacks," Miranda chuckles.

"What I'd honestly like," I say, gathering up my purse and standing to my feet, wobbling slightly in my heels, "is to head home to my alphas. I miss them."

"Awww," Miranda says, "that is so sweet."

"It's vomit-inducing, but I am so damn happy for you, girlie," Jacks says, smiling at me with affection. "Home it is then." She reaches for her own purse.

"No, you stay here," I say, raising my eyebrows and motioning towards Miranda with my eyes. "Enjoy yourselves. I'll come see you off at the aeroplane later, okay?"

"Are you sure?"

"Most definitely. But," I add, tapping my hand against my purse, "you are going to have to pay for your own drinks. It still doesn't feel quite right."

"It's okay," Miranda says, "I know a cute place round the corner. The drinks there are a quarter the price and the atmosphere is a million times better."

"Have fun," I tell them, blowing them kisses and hurrying out.

It's stupid and ridiculously giddy but I really can't wait to get home to my alphas. In fact, I'm positively needy for them. Maybe I can convince them to snuggle up with me in the soft bed, gathering all the cushions and covers around us. Maybe I'll let Kent join us. And then afterwards ...

I sigh. I don't think I'll ever be able to get enough of these men and the way they make me feel.

Sam drives me back to the pack's house and I grow more and more giddy and needy the closer we get. I've only been away from the alphas a few hours but I'm already excited to see them again, to breathe in their scents and soak up their warmth.

I can't help grinning to myself like a cheshire cat.

I don't deserve to be this happy. I've never *been* this happy before.

My bond shimmers in my stomach and I never appreciated how good that would feel, what a comfort it would be –

a constant reminder of my mate right in the core of my being. I can't wait to add more.

My heart leaps when their property comes into view and the gate draws open for us, the car climbing the long, manicured drive.

Cruise stands at the end, aware through our bond that I was coming home, and my heart leaps again, ten times higher, to see him standing there waiting for me.

I race out of the car before it's even stopped and run towards him, ready to wrap my arms around his neck and smother him in kisses.

But then I halt, my feet nearly tripping over one another, my body folding in half.

My bond, searing so high, tumbles, crashes, plummets right back down to earth. The impact makes me gasp.

Something isn't right. Something doesn't feel right.

I peer up at my mate as tears swim through my eyes. Cruise stares at me with pain written in his features, although his posture is rigid and his jaw set.

Something is wrong.

I shiver involuntarily as if the air has turned frigid and reach for him automatically through the bond. All I meet is a solid stone wall. Impenetrable. I can't break through to his thoughts or his emotions.

What the hell?

I stumble forward.

"Cruise?" I say, clutching my stomach, the bond icy cold, making me tremble. "Cruise, what's wrong? What happened?"

Something bad happened. Something really bad. Is someone hurt? Someone in trouble. Is someone ....

"You're an actress, Avery," he says, his voice cracking as he speaks. "You never told me you were an actress."

"What?" I say, his words making no sense to me.

"You're an actress. Have you been acting all along? Are you acting now?"

He watches my face closely as if he's searching for the truth.

Why is he asking me this? Why does it matter?

"I was an actress," I say, my brow crunching in confusion, the bond so icy it hurts in my stomach. "A failed actress. I haven't worked in six months."

"Why did you fail?"

"Because ..." I hesitate. The barrier he's erected between us is already causing me enough pain in my heart as it is. I don't want to rake over my failed dreams now too. Dig up even more pain. I can't ... I can't tell him. I can't force those memories to the surface. They are too raw. Too awful. It's why I've buried them away.

"Because you decided there were easier ways to make money," he whispers.

"Because," I repeat, "I was no good." I look away from him.

I tried so hard. Learning lines into the early hours of the morning. Endless, endless auditions. Rejection after rejection until I couldn't take it anymore. And then ...

"Good or not," he says, "are you acting now?"

I screw up my brow and shake my head. Cold sweat trickles down my spine and the pain in my stomach makes me pant. Why is he asking me this? He knows how I feel about him. He's been inside my head constantly. Why is he doubting me now?

"You kept it hidden from me," he says and even over the distance, I can see the pain in his eyes. A pain I don't understand.

"Because it hurts, Cruise!" I sob, my words catching in my throat.

He shakes his head.

I take a hobbling step towards him. It's painful to move. So painful – in my chest as well as my stomach.

He doesn't believe me. I can see it in his eyes.

"The bonding was never a mistake," he says, his shoulders sagging as if he's being crushed by a great weight. "It was all an act."

"But it was a mistake!" I say. "I don't even remember how it happened!"

"Me neither," Cruise agrees. "Which is funny because I've never blanked out in my life before."

"What the hell are you accusing me of here, Cruise?" I whisper, my skin suddenly unbearably hot, my legs unsteady, my world spinning and spinning.

"I heard you talking. I heard you talking to your mom. I know this has all been about the money. Fuck, I was a fool to believe it wasn't."

He closes his eyes and pulls his body rigid once more. When he opens his eyes, the pain has gone and his features hardened. I don't see affection there anymore, just a hard-hearted man, and everything inside my heart screams with agony. My body shakes, nausea swims through my stomach, heavy tears begin to roll from my eyes.

This can't be happening. This can't be real. This isn't Cruise. This isn't the man I've been falling in love with. The one who convinced me he was falling in return.

This is some kind of mistake. A terrible, terrible mistake.

"Congratulations, Avery," he says. "You're a much better actress than you've given yourself credit for."

"Fuck you, Cruise!" I choke out, the tears streaming

down my burning-hot cheeks. "The only one who's been fooled here is me!" I thump my fist against my aching chest. "Because I thought you were a nice guy, one of the good ones. But *you've* been the one acting, you're the one who's fooled me. Because now I see you're just like all the other alpha assholes out there!"

He flinches as if my words have wounded him.

Well good because his have cut me deeper than any knife could. Sliced deep, deep into my heart. I trusted him. I trusted them all. I opened up my heart to them and started to believe.

"It looks like we've both had a lucky escape then," he says, his voice shaking. "Saved from a far greater mistake than we've already made."

I wrap my arms around my trembling body and glare at him. I'm not going to beg. I'm not going to plead. Even if the omega inside me wants me down on my knees, clinging to his ankles. I don't want a pack who doesn't believe in me, even if every bone in my body aches to be near him, to make him see sense, to fix this stupid mess.

"I've had the housekeeper pack up your things," he says in that voice devoid of all emotion, so cold I shiver even harder. "Your bags are already loaded onto the jet along with Jacks'. There's no need for us to make this any more painful than it already is." He looks at me and that rigid persona falters again, for just a moment.. He buries his face in his hands. "Shit, I thought this was real, Avery. I really thought it was real."

"It was," I whisper, but he doesn't seem to hear me.

Instead, he jerks his hands away from his face and once again that stony figure returns. "My lawyers will be in touch about annulling the marriage and reversing the bond."

I stare at him in disbelief. Now I see it – the cold-hearted, ruthless business mogul the papers all talk about. Right before my eyes. Was he always there and I was just too blinded by stupid omega emotions to see it? There's no compassion, no empathy.

I take another step towards him. The bond in my stomach hums with the hope of reconnection, but all it meets is more of that stony wall.

He stands his ground and I no longer feel any ounce of comfort from his presence, only intimidation, fear. He's so much bigger than me, so much more powerful. He could crush me so easily. He's doing it right now, crushing everything I had begun to believe in.

Stupid, stupid, stupid.

I should have known this couldn't be real. Like every other promise. Every man who ever made me believe in him. Every director, agent, scout who ever said this was it – my big break. All those promises, drifting away like smoke on the wind. None of it real, none of it lasting.

I thought this time was different. But it was the biggest deception of them all.

"Make sure it is the lawyers, Alpha, and not yourself or one of your packmates," I say, swiping away the tears from my face, my own heart and my own features hardening too. "Because I never ever want to hear from any of you ever again."

I glance into his face one more time. How did I ever find kindness in those eyes, companionship, love? I take one final look at the steely demeanor of my mate – the last time I will ever lay eyes on him – and then I spin away, staggering back to the car, every part of my body crying out in agony.

"Avery," he whispers, so quietly I'm not sure if I really hear it.

But I keep walking and he doesn't call out to me again,

doesn't plead for me to stay, doesn't renege those words and say this was all a big mistake, a stupid misunderstanding.

Instead, he stands there cold as winter and watches as I drive away, back to Cardval, back home, far, far away from him.

Gone forever.

Gone.

Chapter Forty-Four

Kent

I know I shouldn't, but I track the omega's flight all the way back to Cardval anyway. Every mile she moves further away from us is a painful one. Even if it's for the best. Even if it was inevitable.

Barney lies by my feet, whining to himself. Something he started as soon as the omega left. Seems he was no keener than the rest of us to see her go.

I watched from the shadows when Cruise confronted her earlier. A large part of me hoped she'd have some reasonable explanation. Something that would turn this situation around. Fuck, I'd prayed for it. I wanted this to be real just as much as the others.

But she hadn't given us anything. And she hadn't even put up a fight. No pleading or begging. No screaming and shouting. Just a cold recognition that she was beat, that the game was up, that the truth had been discovered.

Shit, I still can't believe it.

We must have gotten sloppy over the years. Complacent. Convinced that no money-grabbing omega would fool us again. But she was so convincing, so different from any of the rest. It felt so real when I held her in my arms.

And yet, not so different after all.

I'd started to believe. I'd felt my heart opening up, pumping again, a warmth returning there I haven't felt in years.

But now all that's gone, and I just feel an ache, sharp and painful and constant.

Max slumps down beside me on the sofa, damp and sweaty from taking his frustration out at the gym.

Cruise has locked himself in his room refusing to talk to anyone, Declan is out drinking somewhere, and Jonah has buried himself in his work.

"What are you doing?" Max asks as he wipes the towel hanging around his neck over his brow.

"Tracking her flight," I confess. "I wanted to make sure she got home safely."

Max is quiet for a moment. Then he says, "She's not ours to worry about anymore."

"It's going to take some time for my brain," and my heart, "to compute that," I say, eyes locked on the little image of the plane soaring over the map.

"Isn't this what you wanted?" he says with some bitterness.

"For your fucking hearts to be broken?" For mine, so carefully protected, to be broken too. "No man, that isn't what I wanted."

"Don't pretend you hadn't fallen for her too, Kent. I saw it. It was obvious."

"You don't know what you're talking about."

"I've known you a long time. And I do."

I frown. "It doesn't matter now, though, does it? She's gone."

"And yet you're here watching her flight."

I slam my thumb against the side of my phone, plunging it into darkness and shoving it into my pocket.

"We need to get back to work. Get back to normal. I'll call someone about fumigating the pool house. We don't need her scent lingering in the air, taunting us."

"It won't be that simple. She was different. This was different." Max shakes his head. "I've never seen Cruise this way before, man."

"What way?" I ask.

"Just lying on his bed, staring at the ceiling."

I huff and jump to my feet, Barney lumbers after me and we enter Cruise's bedroom together.

It's as Max described. Cruise lying out like he's comatose, or dead.

"Cruise," I say, "get the fuck up."

He doesn't move, doesn't even acknowledge me, just keeps on staring, his eyes unblinking.

I lean down and jab his shoulder. His body moves with the nudge, then flops back into place.

"Cruise, man, stop dicking about. Come on, let's get out. We can go take Barney for a walk." I nudge him again, harder this time. "Come on. She was just a girl."

"Leave ... me ... the ... fuck ... alone!" he growls with such menace, Barney whimpers and scurries from the room.

I stare at my packmate in disbelief, then shake my head and leave.

Time. He just needs time. Time to mend his heart and then he'll be back to his normal assholey self.

It's what we all need.

We were perfectly happy before she came along. We'll be perfectly happy now she's gone.

I'm halfway down the hallway, determined to get out of the house whether Cruise is coming with me or not, when the housekeeper scurries towards me.

"There's a man here to see you, Sir."

"A man?" I say, continuing to pace down the hallway as she follows after me. I'm not expecting anyone and any meetings I did have planned I'd arrange for the Hamilton Building, not here at the house. "Did he give a name?"

"A Mr. Crane."

I halt. "Where is he?"

"Waiting at the gate, Sir. I didn't know whether to let him in."

"For God's sake, let him in," I say, already walking that way.

I meet him at the top of the drive, the exact spot where Cruise confronted Avery only hours before. He's smaller than he appeared on the video screen and scrawnier. In fact, his jacket does little to hide his bony frame.

"What is it?" I say.

I thought we were done. He gave me what we needed. He discovered the truth. There's no more to be done here.

"You asked me to uncover more proof, Sir, about the situation. I've spoken to some of the members of staff who were working that evening and I have the footage from the casino," he says, patting his jacket pocket. "I think you need to see it."

"I don't. We've already dealt with the situation," I snap, the man grimacing.

"You'll want to see it."

"Can't you just tell me what it shows?"

"I think it would be better if you watch it yourself."

I argue with him some more, but the man is so damn insistent, I finally relent.

I lead him back inside the overly quiet house. The housekeeper's turned the AC down too low, and a cold breeze sweeps through the building, frisking all the blinds.

In my office, the man plugs a memory stick into my computer and loads up the file. It's CCTV footage of the casino floor, trained in on one of the roulette tables. The video is good quality, crisp and clear. But there's nothing on screen to capture my attention.

"What is it?" I say with irritation.

We already know the girl is a con-artist. We've already dealt with the problem. I don't need my nose rubbed in it.

"Wait," the man says, speeding up the video so the wheel spins at triple speed and people fly around like they're walking on air. And then he hits pause.

It's the omega. Her dark hair gathered up and pinned, showing off the graceful sweep of her neck and her slender shoulders. Her curves captured in the little black dress she destroyed before the awards ceremony.

Even on screen, she has the ability to stop my heart from beating. She's so beautiful, lighting up the screen like some kind of siren. Like the movie star she dreamed of being.

I watch as she climbs onto a stool, setting one lone chip down on the table in front of her. At first, she sits and observes, tapping her finger against the chip. Then finally she plucks up the courage to place a bet. Just one chip. The wheel spins, the ball bounces, one, two, three times, then lands on a number. Her number. She smiles in astonishment, flopping back in her chair. Her chip grows into a pile.

She places some more bets. Someone brings her a drink. She loses some spins; she wins some more. She's given another drink and another. By now her pile of chips is considerable and growing. One or two people stop to watch.

"I don't see what this has—" I begin.

"Here," Crane says, pointing to the very edge of the screen. Cruise, dressed in a suit, his jacket hooked in one hand, a drink in the other. "It's Mr. Hamilton; straight after he left the conference dinner."

Cruise walks across the top of the screen, then halts suddenly. He twists his head. His gaze is drawn to Avery as if she's a magnet. For a moment he just stares, as if she's the most captivating thing he's ever seen, then he makes his way over to the table.

She hasn't seen him. She's too engrossed in her gambling, laughing and clapping her hands in joy every time the wheel spins. Her pile of chips has more than quadrupled. She's on a roll.

Cruise hangs around the edge of the table, eyes locked on the omega, ignoring everything around him. When the chair next to hers is vacated, he grabs it immediately.

He leans in and asks her a question. She turns her head and registers him for the first time.

Except, there's not the usual jolt of recognition. Just a polite smile and a return to her chips.

"She didn't recognize him," I say.

"No," Crane answers. "I spoke to the croupier and the waitress. Both stated their belief that Miss Loren seemed unaware of who Mr. Hamilton was."

I watch some more. Gradually, the pair start to talk. A waiter brings more drinks and then more. Cruise picks a number for Avery. Places a bet himself. They're laughing together now, his arm slung over the back of her chair, her body leaning ever so slightly towards his.

"He approached her, and he made the move," I say, staring at the screen, an icy coldness penetrating through my veins. "He made the move on her."

"Yes," Crane says, pausing the video. "I've spoken to several people there that night to confirm the footage. Your packmate approached the omega. He engaged her in conversation. She was unaware of who he was. I can show you more, although I'm sure you can guess how it went down. The casino was plying them with drinks, hoping to make back the money the girl had won."

The ice in my veins takes a hold of my heart, the air in my lungs won't move. I collapse forward on my chair, burying my face in my hands.

I try to suck in air, but I can't breathe. I can't breathe! My lungs stutter. My chest burns. My throat screams. My vision blurs. My head blares.

He made the first move. Cruise. Not Avery.

It was no honey trap. No con job. No master plan.

It was real all along. Oh, so real.

"Fuck!" I cry out.

What have I done? What the hell have I done?

And how the hell am I going to fix it!

****Pack Gamble Part Two* coming soon**

Thank you so much for reading. If you enjoyed this book, please consider leaving a review or rating — it's a great help to indie authors like me!

Also by Hannah Haze

All available on Amazon and Kindle Unlimited.

Contemporary RH omegaverse

In With The Pack

In Deep - Rosie's story

In Trouble - Connie's story

In Knots - Alexa's story

In Doubt - Giorgie's story

In Control - Sophia's story

The Rockview Omegaverse

Pack Rivals Part I

Pack Rivals Part II

Pack Choice

Pack Gamble Part I

Pack Gamble Part II

Paranormal RH romance

The Arrow Hart Academy

Fractured Fates

Twisted Ties

Shattered Stars

Contemporary MF omegaverse series

The Alpha Rock Stars

The Rockstar's Omega

Rocked by the Alpha

Fourth Base with the Alpha

Contemporary MF omegaverse standalones

Oxford Heat

The Alpha Escort Agency

Omega's Forbidden Heat

Contemporary MF omegaverse novellas

The Omega Chase

Online Heat

Christmas Heat

Alien omegaverse MF romance series

The Alpha Prince of Astia

Alien Desire

Alien Passion

About the Author

I'm a British romance author who loves writing soft and steamy omegaverse romances, sure to get your pulse racing and your heart fluttering. My couples are destined to find each other - and when they do, oh boy!

My other loves include long romantic walks in the countryside, undisturbed soaks in a hot bath and even hotter stories. I have one husband, three children and a very naughty cat. When I'm not writing stories, I'm thinking about stories, listening to stories, reading stories or dreaming about them. Come follow me!

Sign up to my newsletter:
www.hannahhaze.com/about
Join my readers' group:
www.facebook.com/groups/375024943829423/
Visit my website:
www.hannahhaze.com
Catch me on TikTok:
www.tiktok.com/@hannahhaze_author

Acknowledgments

Lots of big thank yous as always and there's always so many people to thank!

Firstly, and as always, a massive thank you to all my lovely readers. Please forgive me for this cliff hanger — you know I will make it up to you in book two. Lots of groveling to come ...

A thank you to my incredible beta readers for their time and feedback — Lili, Melissa, and Sara. You are the best.

A special mention to the amazing L.V. Lane for providing the inspiration for that stickman scene. Check out her brilliant omegaverse books as well as her hilarious stickman artwork.

Thank you to Eve from Eve Graphic Designs for another gorgeous cover and to James from Buckley's Books for editing another of my steamy books.

Finally, all my love and gratitude to Mr. D, Stephy and my gorgeous children for their continued support, encouragement and all round fabulousness. Big kisses to you all!

About Hannah's Omegaverse

I write soft and steamy omegaverse romances — stories that are on the sweeter side — mixing the sauciness of omegaverse dynamics with contemporary plots.

My omegaverse stories are set in a modern world just like ours, except people can be one of three kinds — Alphas, Betas and Omegas. Betas are just like you and I, but Alphas and Omegas are slightly different biologically. In my stories, the characters are often battling with their biological urges, needs and instincts, and trying to fit into a modern world which can be judgemental and sometimes prejudiced.

ALPHAS

Alphas are generally larger, stronger and more aggressive. Their instincts can make them domineering and controlling. Alpha males are also a little anatomically different where it counts the most. Yep, I'm talking the peen — at the base there is a knot which expands when an Alpha comes, locking him into his partner where they remain stuck together for a period of time. Biologically, this increases the chance of pregnancy. Some Alphas can control the expansion of their knot, others can't.

OMEGAS

Omegas are smaller and their instincts can make them more submissive — especially towards an Alpha. Only an Omega can 'take' an Alpha's knot. An Omega has regular heat cycles where they are especially fertile. During this period they become hot and horny and very uncomfortable unless they are fucked and knotted frequently by an Alpha.

HEATS, RUTS AND BITES

Similarly to menstrual cycles, the Omegas in my world have differing heat cycles. Some have very regular heats, some have them less often, and others control or suppress them with medication. A heat typically lasts three or four days. When an Omega falls into a heat, their scent alters and they become especially alluring to any Alpha close by.

An Omega in heat can drive an Alpha into rut. An Alpha in rut isn't hindered by the usual biological restraints that your average guy is. I'm talking about permanent erections, no recovery, and the ability to come multiple times! (Sounds like fun, huh?)

Both Omegas and Alphas have glands at the back of their necks, the source of their scents. These glands are especially sensitive when the Omega or Alpha is turned on. Biting this gland is known as claiming and binds the pair together, often irreversibly. It also leaves a scar and changes the Alpha or Omega's scent which signals to others that they are 'taken'. During a heat, when an Omega is at the mercy of their biological urges, an Omega can often beg for an Alpha to 'claim' or bite them.

About Hannah's Omegaverse

SCENTS, BLOCKERS AND SUPPRESSANTS

Both Omegas and Alphas have heightened senses of smells and distinctive scents. An Alpha and Omega can recognise another Alpha or Omega by their scent alone, often over great distances. Their scents can also signal how they're feeling — especially when they are aroused or aggravated. Omegas and Alphas can mask their scents using blockers. They can also try to quell their Alpha and Omega instincts with the use of suppressants — for example an Alpha might take an emergency suppressant to stop themselves responding to an Omega in heat.

SOFT AND STEAMY OMEGAVERSE

In my world, Alphas and Omegas are rare and viewed as a source of fascination by Betas. Alphas are often struggling to fit into a society where aggression and violence isn't tolerated, and Omegas are torn between their desire to be independent and their instinct to be controlled. It is often true love and the perfect partner that allows them to find the balance, acceptance and happiness they need and deserve. Happily ever afters guaranteed!

Printed in Great Britain
by Amazon